W9-CUK-004

The Ghost of Llano Estacado

Abridged Translation of the
Original Karl May Manuscript Published under the Title

Der Geist des Llano estakado

A Travel Narrative
by
Karl May

Translated by
Herbert Windolf

Original German text by Karl May [1842 – 1912]
First published 1888
in 'Der Gute Kamerad', in serial format

English translation by Herbert Windolf

Copyright © 2005 by Herbert Windolf
Cover design by Michael M. Michalak
All rights reserved.
No part of this book may be reproduced, restored in a retrieval
system, or transmitted by means, electronic, mechanical,
photocopying, recording, or otherwise, without written consent
from the author.

ISBN: 0-9766400-5-8

This book is printed on acid free paper.

Nemsi Books - rev. 09/13/2005

Acknowledgements

My thanks go to Michael M. Michalak, publisher of this narrative, to Felipe Morales for checking Karl May's and my Spanish, and to Dieter Schüring, for making sure that the musical terms were sound.

This narrative is based on a download from the Karl-May-Gesellschaft website.

Karl May – translated by Herbert Windolf

Foreword

The Spanish name Llano Estacado, meaning Staked Plain, is part of the high plains of the United States, located west of today's Lubbock, Texas. It covers an area of about 30,000 square miles, extending to the state of New Mexico. It is a strikingly flat and monotonous area at an elevation of between 3,000-4,000 feet. Local water-retaining depressions and washes that, due to the meager rainfall, rarely hold water occasionally break this semiarid plain. Sandstorms can cut down vision in the midst of day and scour the unwary with tiny bullets of sand. It is said that even Indians hesitated to cross this wasteland. Myth holds that the Coronado expedition planted stakes as guideposts for the return trip when it first crossed the plain westward, giving the area its name.

Karl May has used the myth of the stakes as a backdrop for his story of 'The Ghost of Llano Estacado'. Again, he assembles many of his Western heroes for new adventures and the performance of good deeds, in the process adding a few new characters.

One of his recurring characters, Hobble-Frank owner of the Villa "Bear Fat" in Saxony, know-it-all, mangler of half-knowledge, with his persistent and extensive elaboration's, may have been funny a hundred years ago when read in German. However, his argumentative discourses, when translated into English, become rather tedious. They often have no meaning for the English-only reader, since they deal with local events and characters of his (and Karl May's) home state, and mangle geography and ancient history in an attempt to be funny. At worst, they make no sense when translated. Hence, I have taken the liberty to severely edit his profuseness to make the story line flow more smoothly.

Rest assured, that I have otherwise stayed as close as possible to Karl May's writings and left even his many, many compass directions unaltered.

Herb Windolf, Prescott, August 10, 2005

Karl May – translated by Herbert Windolf

Contents:

Karl May – translated by Herbert Windolf

The Ghost of Llano Estacado

Karl May – translated by Herbert Windolf

1. Bloody Fox

Two men came riding along the creek, a White and a Negro. The White was dressed oddly, wearing Indian moccasins and leather pants in addition to a tailcoat that had once been dark blue but was now faded and raggedy. High shoulder pads, pocket flaps, and polished brass buttons enhanced this already peculiar appearance. The long tails hung like wings down either side of his horse. His head was adorned with a gigantic black straw hat that was decorated with a faux yellow ostrich feather. The slim little man was armed with a double-barreled rifle slung over his shoulder. A knife and two revolvers stuck from his belt. Attached to the latter were several bags, that held ammunition and other odds and ends, but the bags appeared rather empty now.

The Black was a broad-shouldered giant. He too wore moccasins and Indian leggings consisting of two separate leg coverings. But that is most advantageous if one rides bareback. The dress of his lower body didn't quite match that of his upper, it consisted of the dress-coat of a French dragoon officer. This piece of clothing must have entered Mexico during the French invasion and eventually ended up on the body of the Black. The coat was much too short and tight for the herculean Negro and since it could not be buttoned, it was open and exposed the rider's broad, bare chest. He did not wear a shirt, as women who laundered and pressed such were scarce in the West. He therefore compensated the lack with a large red and white checkered bandanna, which he had tied around his neck and fashioned into a huge bow. He wore no hat, so that one could see and admire the many small, shiny curls, which he had lovingly fashioned. He too was armed with a double-barreled rifle, a knife, a bayonet that he must have found somewhere, and an aged rider's pistol that had once seen better times.

Both rode good mounts. One could surmise from the appearance of the horses, that they must have traveled a long distance this day, yet they still trotted along vigorously, as if they had not already carried their riders for many hours.

Rich grasses sprouted along the creek's banks, but only for a certain distance. Beyond it grew only spindly yucca, fleshy agave, and dried-up bear grasses with their wilted, almost fifteen foot high blossom stems.

"This is poor soil," the White remarked, "Up north we had it better. Isn't that so, Bob?"

"Yes," replied the other. "Massa Frank is right. Here, Massa Bob don't like it either. I hope we soon get to Helmers Home, because Massa Bob is hungry like whale. Could swallow house."

"A whale couldn't swallow a house. It's gullet is too narrow," Frank explained to the Black.

"May open gullet like Massa Bob when eating. How far is to Helmers Home?"

1

"That I do not know exactly. As the way was described this morning, we should be there soon. Look, isn't that a horseman approaching over there?"

He pointed to the right across the creek. Bob reined in his horse and put his hand up to shade his eyes against the sun, which was low in the western sky. In a manner peculiar only to him, he opened his mouth wide so that he might see even better and, after a while, answered, "Yes, it is horseman, little man on big horse. He come here to Massa Bob and Massa Frank."

The horseman in question approached at a rapid trot, but did not head for the two, rather he seemed intent on crossing their path obliquely. He gave no sign of seeing them.

"Odd character," mumbled Frank. "Here in the Wild West one is usually glad to meet someone else, but this one doesn't seem to be interested in making our acquaintance. He's either a misanthrope or doesn't have a clear conscience."

"Massa Bob call him?"

"Yes, call him. He'll likely hear your elephant trumpet better than my zephyr whisper."

Bob cupped both hands to either side of his mouth and screamed at the top of his lungs, "Hello, hello, stop, wait! Why run away from Massa Bob?"

The Negro certainly had a voice that could raise the dead, it caused the stranger to rein in his horse. The two hurried towards him.

Coming closer they realized, that they were not facing a man of small stature, but a youngster, barely out of his boyhood. He was clad like a cowboy, in buffalo skin pants and jacket, both adorned with tassels. On his head he wore a broad-brimmed sombrero. A red woolen sash served him as a belt with one end dangling down his left hip. The sash held a Bowie knife and two pistols. Across his knees he held a heavy double-barreled Kentucky rifle and in the Mexican custom, attached to both sides of the saddle, hung leather shields to protect the legs from arrows and lance stabs.

Despite his youth his face was deeply tanned by sun, wind, and weather. A two finger wide blood-red scar marred his forehead extending from his left temple to above his right eye, giving him a rather fearsome appearance. He did not give the impression of being a young, immature and inexperienced fellow at all. He held the heavy rifle in his hand as if it were a feather, his dark eyes intently focused upon the two whilst he sat proudly and confidently astride his horse in a manner of someone much older. His horse stood stock-still, awaiting his command.

"Good day, my boy," Frank greeted him. "Are you familiar with this area?"

"Very much so," the stranger responded with a slightly ironic smile forming on his lips, probably because Frank had addressed him with 'boy'.

"Do you know Helmers Home?"

"Aye."

"How far is the ride from here?"

"The slower, the longer."

"Gosh! You seem to be very sparing with words, my boy."

"Well, because I'm no Mormon priest."

"Oh, then excuse me. You are probably peeved at me because I addressed you with 'boy'?"

"Wouldn't think of it. Everyone can choose how to address another. But then they must also be prepared to accept my response."

"Okay. Then we are agreed. I do like you. Here's my hand. Just address me as you wish, but answer me properly now. I'm not familiar here and need to get to Helmers Home. I hope you aren't going to show me the wrong way."

He reached over offering the youth his hand. The youth shook it as his eyes glanced smilingly at the tailcoat and straw hat. He then answered, "He be a rascal who leads others astray. I experienced it myself. I'm on my way to Helmers Home. Come along, if you care to follow me."

He set his horse to a trot with the two now following, turning away from the creek to head southward.

"We would have followed the creek," said Frank.

"It would also have taken you to old Helmers, but in a wide arc. Instead of three quarters of an hour, it would have taken you two."

"Then it was fortuitous that we met you. Do you know the owner of the settlement?"

"Very well in fact."

"What kind of a man is he?"

The two horsemen had taken their young guide between them. He now mustered them with a searching look before responding, "Don't go there if you don't have a clear conscience. Rather turn around."

"Why?"

"He has a sharp eye for any skullduggery and keeps a clean house."

"I like that about a man. We have nothing to worry about."

"If you are good guys, no. Just the opposite, he will help you any way he can."

"I've heard that he runs a store?"

"Yes, but not for gain, only to help the frontiersmen who come to his place. He carries everything a hunter needs and sells it for the lowest possible price. But someone he doesn't like can't get anything from him, even for good money."

"He must be quite a character?"

"Oh no. He just tries to keep away the riffraff that's making the West unsafe. I don't need to describe him to you. You will get to know him. Only one other thing I'd like to yet tell you which you'll likely not understand, maybe even laugh about: He's a German, a man of sterling qualities. That says it all."

3

Frank rose in his stirrups and called out, "What? I wouldn't understand it? Even laugh about it? What do you think! I'm delighted to find a fellow-countryman here at the edge of the Llano Estacado."

Their guide's demeanor had been serious. Even though he had smiled twice, it seemed as if he did not quite know how. He now looked at Frank in a manner that could be construed as pleasing and asked, "What? You, a German! Is it true?"

"Yes. Obviously! Don't you recognize it immediately?"

"No. You speak English unlike a German would and look more like a Yankee's uncle who's been thrown out the window by his nephews."

"Heavens! What are you thinking? I'm German through and through. And whoever doesn't believe me I'll run my rifle through his belly."

"A knife's enough for that. But if that's so, then old Helmers will be delighted since he's also from over there."

"From Germany?"

"Yes. And he's very fond of his fatherland and his language."

"That I believe! A German can never forget either. Now I'm doubly pleased and look forward to reach Helmers Home. I should actually have guessed that he's German. A Yankee would have called his place Helmers Ranch or something like that, but only a German would come up with Helmers Home. Do you live nearby?"

"No. I neither have a ranch nor a home. I'm like a bird in the air or an animal in the forest."

"A poor devil then?"

"Yes."

"In spite of your youth! Don't you have parents?"

"Not a single relative."

"But you've got a name?"

"Sure. I'm called Bloody-Fox."

"Bloody-Fox? That tells of a bloody event."

"Yes. My parents and all my relatives were murdered in the Llano Estacado along with our entire group. Only I remained alive. I was found with a gaping skull, I was about eight years old then."

"God forbid! Then you truly are what I called you earlier: A poor devil! You were attacked by robbers and killers."

"That's what happened."

"Then you saved nothing but your life, your name, and the terrible memory."

"Not even that. Helmers found me lying among the cacti, put me on his horse and took me to his home. For months I lay in a fever and when I came to, I didn't recall anything, nothing at all. I had forgotten my name, even today I cannot recall it. Only the moment of the attack has been burned into my memory.

4

I would be happier if I had forgotten that too, for then I would not have this raging desire for revenge, which persistently drives me through this parched and terrible land."

"And why were you given the name Bloody-Fox?"

"Because when I was found I was covered with blood. Then, during my fever fantasies, I repeatedly called out the name 'Fuchs' (German for fox). It was assumed, that it was my name."

"Then your parents must have been German?"

"Sure. After I recovered, I couldn't recall a single word of English or German. I was unable to speak at all. But while I learned English slowly, German came to me quickly and I became fluent at it, as if I had spoken it before. Helmers was like a father to me. At the time he didn't yet live at his present home. But I couldn't stay there. I had to get away, out into the wilderness like a falcon whose parents had been torn apart by vultures, and who must now circle the bloody place until he succeeds in finding the murderers. His sharp eye must and will discover them. May they be a hundred times stronger than he and may he have to give his life, he will lose it gladly, for his death will also be that of the murderers'."

He ground his teeth audibly and reined in his horse so hard that it rose up.

"Then you've got the scar on your forehead from the attack?" Frank asked.

"Yes," he answered with a scowl, "but let's not talk about it any more. It troubles me too much and you might see me rush away and desert you. Then you'd have to find Helmers Home by yourselves."

"Yes, let's rather talk about Helmers. What did he do in the Old Country?"

"He was a forestry official. I believe Head Forester."

"What? Really!" Frank called out. "I was too!"

Bloody-Fox displayed surprise, scrutinized Frank once again and said, "You too! That will turn out to be a most pleasant meeting!"

"Yes, I followed the same career. But if he had this fine employment as a Head Forester, why did he give it up?"

"He became annoyed. I believe the forest he was in charge of was privately owned and his patron a proud, inconsiderate and frequently angry man. The two of them often disagreed, resulting in Helmers receiving a poor report and subsequently no further employment. This is why he went far away. Do you see the red and black oak woods over there?"

"Yes," Frank replied, looking in the direction indicated.

"That's where we meet the creek again and beyond the woods are Helmers' fields. Until now you have asked me questions. May I now also ask some of you? Isn't this stout, upstanding Negro here called 'Sliding-Bob'?"

This caused Bob to rise up in his saddle as if he wanted to dismount.

"Ah, oh," he called out, "why Massa Bloody Fox insult good Massa Bob?"

5

"Oh, no. I don't want to call you names or insult you," the youth responded, "I'd rather consider myself to be your friend."

"But why then call Massa Bob how Indians call him, because Massa Bob always slid from horse long ago? But now Massa Bob ride like the devil!"

To demonstrate that he was telling the truth, he gave his horse the spurs and galloped away towards the woods. Frank, too, was surprised about the young man's question.

"You know Bob? That's almost impossible!"

"No, no. I also know you."

"That would be ... What's my name then?"

"Hobble-Frank."

"By golly. That's correct. But, boy, who told you? I have never in my life been in this area."

"Ah," the youngster smiled, "who wouldn't recognize a famous frontiersman like you."

Frank now blustered so that his tailcoat threatened to become too tight and said, "Me, famous? You know that too?"

"Yes."

"Who told you?"

"An earlier acquaintance of mine, Jakob Pfefferkorn, who's usually just called 'Fat Jemmy'."

"Thunder and lightning! A friend of mine! Where did you meet him?"

"A few days ago at Washita Fork. He told me that you arranged to meet at Helmers Home."

"That's true. Is he coming?"

"Yes. I left earlier and headed here directly. He'll follow soon."

"That's good, that's wonderful. Then he told you about us?"

"Yes, he told me about your trip out to Yellowstone. When you earlier told me, that you had been a forester, I knew at once who I was talking to."

"Will you then believe that I'm a good German?"

"Not only that, but a good and very kind fellow in general," the young man said with a smile.

"Then the fat one didn't malign me?"

"He wouldn't think of doing it! How could he malign his good friend Frank?"

"Well, you know, at times we have quarreled extensively about things, which someone without a higher education would have difficulty comprehending. Fortunately, since he's now aware of my quality, there's no better friend in the whole world. – But there's Bob and we have reached the woods. Where do we go from here?"

"Across the creek and through the trees. That's the way. Riders like Bob have no need for a trail."

"Yep, right," the Negro agreed proudly. "Massa Bloody Fox has seen Massa Bob ride like Indian. Massa Bob go through thick and thin."

They crossed the creek and the little woods unhindered by any brush, then passed along fenced corn, oat and potato fields. In places the black fertile soil of the Texan hill country, which produced rich harvests, could be found. The creek's water increased the settlement's value. It ran close by the living quarters, behind which were the stables and sheds.

The stone house was built wide and deep to compensate for its lack of a second story. However under each of the two gables there was a small attic room. In the yard in front of the entrance stood four giant post oaks, their trunks rose straight as arrows to the very top. Many sturdy branches provided shade for several simple tables and benches. One could immediately see that the living room lay to the right of the entrance and the store, mentioned by Bloody-Fox, to the left.

At one of the tables sat an older man with a pipe in his mouth who critically inspected the three new arrivals. He was of a tall, robust build and had a weathered face and a full, dense beard; a true frontiersman whose hands, one could see, had rested little and worked hard.

When he recognized who was guiding the strangers he rose and called out from afar, "Welcome, Bloody-Fox. You come again at last. There's news."

"From where?" asked the youngster.

"From over there," Helmers indicated, pointing westward with his hand.

"What kind? Good?"

"Regrettably, no. Apparently the hyenas have been on the plains again."

Americans call the Llano Estacado the Staked Plain, the Spanish and English terms have the same meaning.

This news seemed to literally electrify the young fellow. Jumping from his saddle, he quickly approached Helmers to ask, "Tell me about it right away."

"It is little enough and can be summed up in few words. But first, will you not introduce me to these two gentlemen?"

"That's also quickly said. You are Mister Helmers, the owner of this farm, and these two gents are good friends of mine, Mister Hobble-Frank and Mister Sliding-Bob, who have come to visit and will perhaps purchase something from you."

Helmers looked the two over and remarked, "I first want to know them before I trade with them. I've never laid eyes upon them before."

"It's quite all right. You can accept them. Have I not called them my friends."

"Seriously or courteously?"

"Quite seriously."

"Well, then they are welcome."

He offered Frank and the Negro his hand and invited them to sit down.

7

"The horses first, Sir," said Frank, "you know a frontiersman's first duty."

"Very well. From your concern for the animals I see that you are good fellows. When do you plan to travel on?"

"We may have to stay for a few days, since we expect to meet some good friends here."

"Then take the horses behind the house and call for Hercules, the Negro. He will be glad to help you."

The two followed his advice. Shaking his head, Helmer's gaze followed them. He then said to Bloody Fox, "Peculiar fellows you've brought. A French cavalry captain with black skin and a gentleman with a straw hat sporting an ostrich feather that was fashionable some fifty years ago. That's remarkable even here in the Far West."

"Don't be mistaken, old man. I'll name but one and you will trust them. They are good friends of Old Shatterhand whom they expect to meet here."

"What? Really?"

"From whom did you learn that? From those two?"

"No, from Fat Jemmy Pfefferkorn."

"You've seen him too? I've met him only once, but would love to see him again."

"You soon will. He's also coming. He's part of the group the two are expecting."

Helmers quickly took a few puffs from his pipe, which was ready to go out. Then with a joyous face, he called out, "What news! Old Shatterhand and Fat Jemmy! That's a great pleasure and a joyous occasion. I'm honored, must run to my little old Barb to tell her about ---"

"Hold it!" Bloody-Fox interrupted the farmer, holding him back by his sleeve. "First I want to hear what happened on the plains."

"A crime, of course!" replied Helmers, turning back to him. "How long since you were here?"

"Almost two weeks."

"Then you haven't seen the four families who wanted to cross the Llano. They left more than a week ago, but never arrived on the other side. Barton, the trader, came from over there, but he never met them."

"Were the Stakes in order?"

"No, that was the problem. If he hadn't traveled across the desert for twenty years he too would have been lost."

"Where is he?"

"He's up in the little room resting. When he arrived he was very weak, but didn't want to eat anything, just sleep."

"I must see him, must wake him despite his tiredness. He must tell me!"

Excitedly, the young man hurried off and disappeared into the house. The farmer sat down once more to smoke his pipe. He dealt with the youth's haste by shaking his head, but then his face took on an expression of pleasant satisfaction. One could deduce the reason for it from the words he mumbled, "Fat Jemmy, hmm! --- Even Old Shatterhand, hmm! --- And such men only bring other good men along, hmm! --- A whole company is coming, hmm! --- But I wanted to tell my Barb about it."

He jumped up to tell his wife about the pleasant news when Frank returned around the corner of the building.

"Well, Mister. Did you find Hercules?" Helmers asked.

"Yes," Frank replied. "Bob is with him. I could leave the horses in their hands. I had to get back to you to tell you how happy I am to have found a colleague."

He spoke English, the same language that was used during the earlier conversation.

"A colleague?" asked the farmer. "Where and who?"

"Right here, and you, obviously."

"Me? How so?"

"Well, Bloody-Fox told me that you had been a head forester."

"That's correct."

"Then we are colleagues, because I too have been a disciple of the forest sciences."

"Ah! But where, my dear fellow?"

"In Germany, or more exactly, in Saxony."

"What? In Saxony? Then you are German? Why then do you speak English and not use your beautiful mother tongue?"

Helmers had spoken the last sentence in German to which Hobble-Frank immediately responded likewise, "With the greatest pleasure, Herr Oberförster (Mister Head Forester)!" and Frank rapidly rattled on in his Saxon dialect, "When it's about my hereditary mother tongue I don't play around, but go for it at once. You'll recognize immediately by the purity of my syntactic expressions that I hale from that German region where, as all know, the most flexible and most highly evolved German is spoken. That is in Moritzburg, near the residential city of Dresden. That is the place with the chateau where the statue of August the Strong stands in front, along with the famous carp pond. I greet you therefore in the name of the noble forestry sciences and hope you realize, that you are dealing here with a respected *ingenium magnam sine mixtura Clementius!*"

It was weird. As long as Frank spoke English he remained a reasonable and modest little fellow. But as soon as he fell into German there arose within him a conviction of his greatness.

At first Helmers wasn't sure what to make of it. He pressed the proffered hand and didn't respond directly to the effusive vocabulary. He asked this 'colleague' to sit down and tried to gain some time by going into the house to get

9

some refreshments. Returning, he carried two bottles and two beer steins in his hands.

"Grand! That I like!" Frank exclaimed. "Beer! A true pleasure! The noble juices of barley open the sluices of manly discourse best. Is beer already brewed in Texas?"

"Quite a lot. You must know, that perhaps some forty thousand Germans have already settled in Texas, and where there are Germans, beer will be brewed."

"Yes. Hops and malt, God behold! Are you brewing this heavenly juice yourself?"

"No. But I have a supply brought in from Coleman City as often as possible. 'Prosit', Mister Frank!"

He had filled the steins and toasted Frank, who responded, "Please, Mister Head Forester, you need not address me as Mister Frank. I'm an easygoing fellow, just call me 'colleague'. That's best. I've never gone for highfalutin' etiquette. And your beer isn't bad at all. So, why should we waste our time with honorifics."

"That's right!" Helmers agreed laughing. "You are a man to my liking."

"But where, actually, have you studied?" Frank asked.

"In Tharandt."

"I thought so right away. Isn't Tharandt the *alba vater* of all forest students of the world."

"Did you mean to say *alma mater*?"

"Nah, not in the least. Now, don't you try to correct my classic Hebrew Latin as Fat Jemmy tried earlier, much to his detriment. If you do that, our beautiful, newfound relationship could quickly take a turn for the worse. As an eminent authority, I cannot tolerate it. And by the way, where is that good Bloody-Fox hiding?"

He went to see a guest of mine to get some information. Where did you meet him?"

"Out there, by the creek. About an hour from here."

"I thought you had been together somewhat longer."

"That's not at all necessary. I have such a sympathetic character that everybody makes friends with it quite quickly. The young fellow has told me already all about himself. I truly feel for him and wish that our relationship would flower. Do you know some more details about him?"

"Not if he has already told you everything, no."

"How does he make a living?"

"Hmm. From time to time he brings me a few nuggets from which I conclude, that he has made a small find."

The two conversationalists, with Frank being the most profuse prattler, continued their discourse touching on Goethe, Schiller, Gallileo, Spartans, and

Tchercessians, with Frank continuing to argue in his superior vein. But when Frank exclaimed that Gallileo once declared in Hebrew: *Sancta complicius*, meaning: And it moves nevertheless (Und sie bewegt sich doch), Helmers could no longer restrain himself. Jumping up he broke into a roaring laughter. For Hobble-Frank to declaim this in his tailcoat and feathered straw hat, and at that in his corrupt Latin, was just too much to take.

"What are you laughing about?" Frank asked insulted. "Just because I am your colleague you can ---"

Luckily Bloody-Fox's egress from the house interrupted him, otherwise a thunderous *philippica* would have erupted. He peered at Frank's red face and asked, "What's the matter? What are you arguing about?"

He spoke German, since he'd heard Frank using that language. This caused Frank to once more enter into a rambling and unintelligible discourse, which was only stemmed when Bloody-Fox said, "I will think about all that, but right now I haven't got the time. I can only think about the poor folks who have been murdered in the Llano Estacado."

He must have been forewarned by Fat Jemmy on how to deal with Hobble-Frank. He took care not to disagree with him, rather he changed the subject to one that would intrigue and also steer Frank from his wrath. It worked since Frank asked, "People have been killed? In the Llano? When?"

"That is not known. They left here more than eight days ago, but didn't arrive on the other side of the desert. They must have perished."

"Maybe not. Perhaps they took another route than originally intended."

"That's what I am afraid of," Bloody-Fox responded, "the crossing of these dangerous plains can only be made in one direction from here. It's just as dangerous as crossing the Sahara or the Gobi deserts. There are no wells in the Llano Estacado, no oases, and no camels, which can survive for many days without water. This makes the Llano so terrible, although it is smaller than the great African and Asian deserts. There is no obvious pathway. This is why stakes have been planted to indicate the right path that needs to be taken. This is what gave the desert its name. Whosoever ventures from the designated path, indicated by these stakes, is lost and will die of thirst. Heat and lack of water corrupts his brain, preventing clear thought. One rides in a circle until the horse collapses beneath the rider, then both are doomed."

"You are saying that no one should venture from the staked path," Helmers summed up, when he saw Frank shaking his head.

"Yes," Bloody-Fox asserted, "that's what I meant to say. Everyone follows this rule. There are few people who know the Llano well enough to find their way across without relying on the stakes. But what happens when criminals pull stakes to set them up in a different direction?"

"That would be devilish!" Frank exclaimed.

"Certainly. But it's being done! There are criminal gangs whose members set the stakes in a different direction. Who follows these will be lost. The stakes will suddenly stop. By that time the traveler is so far from safety that he cannot return."

"But he or they could just return along the staked path," Frank argued.

"By that time it's most likely too late, for he or they will be so far into the desert that the grasslands can no longer be reached, and he's done for. The brigands need not even kill their victims, no, they just need to wait for them to perish from thirst and then rob the corpses. That's happened many times before."

"But can they not be caught?" was Frank's response.

Just when Helmers intended to answer this question, a man slowly approached from around the corner of the house, his arrival was thus only noticed then. The man was dressed entirely in black and carried a small parcel in his hand. He was of a tall and slim build, his face narrow and pointy. He wore a chapeau claque, resting low on his neck, which, together with spectacles and his black dress, gave him the appearance of a clergyman. He approached the three in a peculiar slinking gait, lightly tipped the brim of his hat and greeted them

"Good day, gentlemen. Have I arrived at the residence of Esquire John Helmers?"

Helmers mustered the man with a look that clearly stated his instant dislike for the fellow and then responded, "Helmers is my name, but the esquire you can leave off. I'm neither a justice of the peace nor do I care for any such titles. These are just foul apples a gentleman doesn't care to be pelted with. Since you know my name, may I also ask for yours?"

"Why no, Sir. My name is Tobias Praisegod Burton and I am a missionary of the Latter Day Saints."

He said this with a self-confident and unctuous mien, which, however, in no way had the intended effect on the farmer for he answered shrugging his shoulders, "You are a Mormon then? That's no recommendation. You call yourselves Latter Day Saints. That's pretentious and presumptuous, and since I am a very modest fellow and don't have the least mind for your self-righteousness, it will be best if you quickly slink away again in your pious mission boots. I do not tolerate any proselytizer at my settlement."

This had been spoken in a very direct, even insulting tone. But Burton maintained his obliging mien, once more politely touched his hat and responded, "You are mistaken Mister, If you think I intend to convert the residents of this blessed farm. I have come here only to rest and quench my thirst and hunger."

"Well. If that's all you're looking for you may have what you need, provided you can pay for it. I hope you have money on you?"

Again Helmers examined the stranger, then made a face as if he had seen something less than pleasant. The Mormon raised his face to the sky, cleared his throat several times, and declared:

"Although I am not excessively blessed with the treasures of this sinful world, I can still pay for food, drink, and a bed. I had actually not expected such an expense, since I had been told that John Helmers' Home is a very hospitable one."

"Ah. And from whom did you learn that?"

"I was told that in Taylorville, from whence I came."

"Then you have only been told a partial truth, for whoever told you forgot to add, that I extend free hospitality only to such people who are welcome to me."

"Then this is not the case with me?"

"No, not at all!"

"But I have done nothing to you."

"Maybe. But when I look at you closely I get the impression that only bad things will follow you. Don't take it badly, Sir! I'm a straightforward fellow and tell everyone what I think of him. You have a face --- a face --- hmm, once one sees it, the hands begin to itch. This is what's called a --- a --- a --- box-your-ears-face."

Even now the Mormon acted as if he had not been insulted. Once more his hand tipped his hat and he said mildly, "In this life it is the fate of the just to be misjudged. It's not my fault to have such a face. If you don't like it, it is not my problem but yours."

"That's so? But you need not let someone tell you that. If a fellow would tell me plainly that he doesn't like my face, the very next moment he would feel my fist in his own. It takes a great lack of honor or even greater cunning to take this quietly. But let me tell you: I actually don't mind your face at all. It's just that I don't care for the way you carry it around. I've the feeling that it isn't your real face at all. I think you put on a very different face when you are by yourself. And then there's something else I don't like about you."

"May I ask what you mean?"

"I'll tell you even without you asking. I very much question your story of having come from Taylorville."

"Why? Do you have enemies there?"

"Not a single one. But tell me where you are headed?"

"Up to Preston, on the Red River."

"Hmm! Coming through here is not the most direct way."

"No, that is true, but I heard so much good about you, that my heart demanded to meet you."

"Don't wish for it, Mister Burton. It may not do you any good. Are you then on foot?"

"Yes."

"You don't own a horse?"

"A horse? No, I do not."

13

"Oh, don't try to tell me that. You hid the animal somewhere around here and my guess is that it wasn't for very honorable reasons. Here, every man, every woman and child rides a horse. Without one there's no getting around. A stranger who hides his horse and then denies that he owns one cannot have anything good on his mind."

The Mormon clapped his hands together and exclaimed, "But Mister Helmers, I swear that I truly do not have a horse. I walk on feet of humility across these lands and have never sat in a saddle."

That's when Helmers rose from the bench, stepped up to the man, put his hand heavily on his shoulder and said, "What are you telling me, me, who has lived for so many years right here on the border. Do you think I'm blind? I do see that riding has shaved off the wool from the inside of your trousers. I see the spur holes in your boots, and ---"

"That is no proof, Sir!" the Mormon interrupted him, "These boots were used when I bought them. The holes were already there."

"Oh! You've been wearing them for how long?"

"For two months."

"Then the holes would have long filled up with dirt. Or do you delight in cleaning them out every day? It rained last night. A long hike like yours would have dirtied your boots very much. Since they are so clean its positive proof that you rode here. Then you smell of horse, and look, next time you put your spurs into your trouser pocket make sure no wheel gets stuck on the seam," Helmers pointed to the man's trousers.

"I found these spurs only yesterday," the Mormon defended himself.

"Then you should have left them since you have no use for them. Anyway, it shouldn't concern me whether you are riding or walking. For all I care you could ice-skate around the world. If you can pay, you can have food and drink, but then head out again. I won't have you here over night. I only accept people I can trust."

Helmers stepped to one of the open windows, said a few words, then returned to his place on the bench and didn't seem to pay attention to the stranger any longer.

Burton sat down at the next table, putting his bundle beside him. Whilst shaking his head, he folded his hands and bowed forward in devotion, patiently awaiting whatever would be provided. He certainly gave the impression of a man who had been done a great injustice.

Hobble-Frank had followed the conversation with great interest. Since it was finished, he no longer paid attention to the Mormon. Not so, Bloody-Fox. Upon the appearance of the stranger his eyes had opened wide and he had kept him in his sight the entire time. He had left his horse close by and had not taken a seat since he had intended to leave again. He now touched his forehead as if trying to remember something. Then he dropped his hand and took a seat

The Ghost of Llano Estacado

opposite the farmer, so he could keep a close watch on the Mormon. He made every attempt not to show his interest, but a sharp observer would have noticed that something unusual occupied his mind.

Then a stout, older woman came through the door to bring bread and a huge cut of roasted beef loin.

"That's my wife," said Helmers, introducing her to Frank in German, while he had spoken English with the Mormon. "She speaks German as well as myself."

"I am mighty pleased," Frank said, offering her his hand. "It has been quite a while since I used my German mother tongue with a lady. You are most welcome and blessed my charming Mrs. Helmers. Might your crib also have swung in Father Rhine or Sister Elbe?"

"Even if my crib did not swing in any of these rivers, but on land instead, I was nevertheless born in Germany," she replied with a smile.

"Well, naturally, that with the Rhine and Elbe wasn't meant literally," and once more Hobble-Frank entered in one of his profusely confusing declamations.

The good woman was at a loss how to answer the peculiar little fellow. She looked at her husband imploringly, who quickly came to her aid, explaining, "This gentleman is a dear colleague of mine, a well-schooled forester, who surely would have had a splendid career back home."

"Most certainly," Frank injected, "with arms and legs I would have climbed the forestry's ladder of success, had not fate called me to America."

And once more he was on a roll, ending it with, "I sincerely hope we will get to know each other well, my dear Mrs. Helmers!"

"I'm sure of that," she nodded to him.

"Most certainly, for all well educated people are drawn to each other. What's below the clouds is of no concern to us. And, by the way, my beer's all gone. Could I have another?"

She took his stein to fill it again. Using that opportunity, she also brought the Mormon some bread, cheese, water and a small glass of brandy. He started his frugal meal without complaining that he had not received any meat.

It was now that Bob joined them.

"Massa Bob done with horses," he reported. "Massa Bob join in eating and drinking!"

At that moment his look fell on the Latter Day Saint. He stood still, looked at the man briefly and then shouted, "What sees Massa Bob! Who sit there! This be Massa Weller, the thief, who stole Massa Baumann much money!"

The Mormon jumped from his seat shooting a terrified look at the Black.

"What are you saying?" Frank cried, jumping up too. "This man is supposed to be this Weller fellow?"

"Yes, that be him. Massa Bob know him very well. Massa Bob looked at him very closely back then."

15

"What luck!" exclaimed Helmers. "Wouldn't that be a most wonderful meeting! What have you got to say to that, Mister Tobias Praisegod Burton?"

The Mormon had overcome his initial shock. With a contemptuous arm movement towards the Negro he responded, "This Black is out of his mind. I don't understand what he is saying nor what he wants."

"But his words were clear enough, weren't they? He called you Weller and says that you stole from his former master Baumann."

"My name is not Weller."

"But maybe that once was your name."

"My name has always been Burton, like it is now. The nigger seems to mistake me for someone else."

At that Bob approached him threateningly telling him, "What you say is Massa Bob? Massa Bob is Negro, no damn nigger! Massa Bob is colored gentleman. If Massa Weller again say nigger, Massa Bob will thump him with fist like Massa Old Shatterhand has taught him."

Helmers now got up to step between the two antagonists, "Bob, no violence! You accuse this man of theft. Can you offer proof?"

"Yes. Bob bring proof. Massa Frank also knows that Massa Baumann be stolen money. He can witness."

"Is that correct, Mister Frank?

"Yes, I can confirm it," he answered.

"How did the theft take place?"

"It happened like this: My comrade Baumann, also known as 'The Bear Hunter' by those who know him, had started a store up by the Platte River. I was his friend and partner. Business went very well at first, the place was often visited by gold prospectors who came from the Black Hills. We took in lots of money and nuggets and kept quite a stash. One day I had to do a circuit to collect outstanding debt from the diggers. When I returned three days later I learned that Baumann had been robbed in the meantime. He had been by himself except for Bob. He had taken in a stranger by the name of Weller for the night. The next morning the fellow had disappeared along with all the valuables. The pursuit was unsuccessful since a thunderstorm had wiped out the thief's trail. Since then there hasn't been a trace of the man, although we inquired about this Weller all the time. Now, Bob claims to recognize him in this Latter-Day-Saint, and I'm sure he isn't mistaken. Bob has good eyes and an even better memory of people's faces. Back then he assured us that he had looked at the man so well, that he would recognize him even in disguise. That, Mister Helmers, is all I can say in this matter."

"Then you didn't see the thief yourself at that time?"

"No."

"You are therefore not in a position to confirm the Negro's assertion that we are facing this thief. Bob stands alone with his claim. You, as well as I, know what to do in this case."

"Massa Bob know exactly what to do!" the Negro exclaimed. "Massa Bob kill the thief. Massa Bob not mistaken, but recognize very well."

He wanted to push Helmers aside to get to the Mormon, but Helmers held him back and said, "Hold it! That would be violence and I can not tolerate such on my property."

"Okay. Then Massa Bob wait until thief gone from property, then hang him from next tree. Massa Bob sit here and watch well. When thief leave, he will not let him from eyes."

He sat down but in such a way that he could keep a close watch of the Mormon.

One could see that he was deadly serious with his threat. Burton looked at the giant Negro and turned to Helmers.

"Sir, I am truly innocent. This black man totally misjudges me and I hope I can rely on your protection."

"Don't rely on me too much," he got as a response, "insufficient evidence has been presented, and the theft is of no concern of mine, since I have no legal authority. Consequently, you can feel safe as long as you are here. But I've already told you to be on your way as soon as possible. What happens then is no concern of mine. I cannot dispute Mister Bob's right to settle this matter among four eyes. If it is any consolation, I can assure you that I shall not faint from fright on discovering you under some tree with one of its strongest limbs twixt your neck and collar."

For the time being that settled the matter. The Mormon sat down again for his meal, but proceeded very slowly and paused often so he might extend the time of his assured safety. Bob rolled his eyes about but never lost his intense focus and Bloody-Fox, who outwardly appeared quite passive, also kept his gaze firmly fixed on the fellow. The young man seemed to have a very peculiar interest in the alleged Mormon.

Everyone was now so occupied with eating, that all conversation ceased. And later, when Frank wanted to resurrect the interrupted conversation about the Llano Estacado he was prevented from doing so by the appearance of another stranger.

"Your home seems to be very popular, Mister Helmers," was his comment, "there's another horseman arriving with intentions on you."

The host turned around to look for the rider. When he recognized him he suggested vividly, "That's one who's always welcome. He is a clever fellow and one who can always be trusted."

"He looks like a trader. Does he want to replace wares you've sold for him?"

17

"You think so because he has those big saddle bags hanging on either side of his horse?"

"Yes."

"Well. You are mistaken. He's no trader, but one of the best scouts you'd ever know."

"Maybe I know him by name."

"I actually don't know his real name. Everyone knows him as 'Juggle-Fred', and he's never minded this name."

"That's a peculiar name. How did he get it?"

"Because he can perform hundreds of tricks which can really make you wonder. He carries the necessary equipment in those two saddle bags."

"Then he is a traveling juggler who occasionally acts as scout and guide?"

"Just the reverse. He's an excellent scout who occasionally entertains his company with tricks. Whoever offers him payment for his entertainment would very much insult him. He seems to have traveled with the famous Prestidigitators and speaks German very well. Why he has come to the West and stays here, when he could have become very wealthy by his excellent juggling, I do not know. It's also none of my business. But I'm convinced that you'll like him."

"That's already very likely, because he speaks German. Tell him right away, that we can use this language."

"Sure. I will tell him immediately. But look at him closely, especially at his eyes, which have different colors. He's two-eyed."

By then the rider they had talked about had come closer. A little distance from the house he halted his horse to call, "Hello, you old 'Lodge Broker'. Do you still have room for a poor needy wretch who can't pay his bill?"

"There's always a room for you," Helmers replied, "just come over here, get off that goat you call a horse and make yourself comfortable. You'll find yourself in pleasant company."

The juggling scout examined those present with a critical eye and offered, "I sure hope so. I do know our Bloody-Fox. I'm not worried about the Black. The other little gentleman in the tail coat and lady's hat doesn't seem to be a bad fellow either. And the third over there, who bites into his cheese like he's chewing a hedgehog's skin, well, hmm, I suppose I'll get to know him yet."

It was interesting, that this man, too, immediately voiced his suspicion of the Mormon. He drove his horse closer and jumped from the saddle. While he greeted their host heartily with both hands like an old friend, Frank was able to look him over.

Even here in the Far West this Juggle-Fred was of a conspicuous appearance. The first thing one noticed was the hunchback disfiguring his otherwise well-formed stature. He was of medium height and stout build but not short-bodied, narrow-chested and long in the arms, as is often the case with hunchbacks. His full round face was shaved and deeply tanned, yet much scarred on one side, as if a terrible wound had once been artlessly mended. Oddly, too, were his eyes, each a different color, the left one sky-blue while the right was deep black.

He wore brown buffalo-calf leather boots with large-wheeled Mexican spurs, black leather pants and a like vest and over it a blouse-like jacket made of a strong blue cloth. His broad leather belt held not just bullets, a knife, and a revolver of substantial caliber, but numerous other supplies a frontiersman is in need of. Drawn low onto his forehead was a rather new-looking beaver hat, from which the animal's tail hung down past his neck. Had the man not had a hunchback, his appearance would have been a strong and pleasant, perhaps even an imposing one. Helmers had jokingly called his horse a goat, a comparison not too far from the truth. The animal was extremely long-legged and appeared somewhat emaciated. Its bare tail stump sported but a few remaining hairs, which must have been very attached to the tail to have held fast for so long. Whether the horse had once been black, brown or red could no longer be determined, since its body was mostly bald. Yet wherever some hair still remained, it was of such indeterminate gray that one could have thought that this old stallion might have already been ridden during the Great Migration. There wasn't even a trace of a mane left. The stallion's relatively large head hung so low that its muzzle almost touched the ground. The long, thick and bare donkey ears hung down like giant leather casings, almost caressing the lower jaw. In addition, the animal kept its eyes closed as if asleep and as it stood there, it presented the unsurpassable image of stupidity and helplessness.

Once the owner of this horse had shaken hands with the host he asked, "Then you have a room for me. But how about some food?"

"Of course! Just sit down. There's still enough meat for you."

"No, thanks. I messed up my stomach yesterday. Beef's too much for me today. I would much rather tackle a young chicken. Can you procure one?"

"Why not. Look, there are enough chickens running about over there."

He pointed to two flocks of young chickens scurrying about under the protection of their mother hens, picking up whatever crumbs might fall down from the tables.

"Thanks," Fred nodded, "will your wife prepare it for me?"

"She has no time to pluck one, nor has she a taste for doing so. And the maids have gone to the corn fields."

"Who's talking about plucking? I don't expect that of anyone."

"Is the chicken by chance to be fried or baked with its feathers still on?"

"Man, what do you think of me? Do you think so little of me that I come across as a man who doesn't know how to relieve a chicken of its feathers? Should you doubt me, I'll show you."

Taking his double-barreled rifle from the saddle-horn he aimed at one of the chickens and fired. When the shot rang out the horse didn't even twitch its

19

eyelids. It seemed to be stone deaf and unable to hear a shot fired in such close proximity.

The chicken collapsed. Fred lifted the corpse to show it around. To everyone's surprise not a single feather remained and it could be immediately eviscerated and baked.

"By the devil!" Helmers laughed. "You got me this time. I should have known you would play one of your tricks. But how did you do it?"

"With my telescope."

"Nonsense. You shot with your rifle."

"That's true. But earlier I observed you from a distance through my pocket telescope and noticed also the young chickens. Of course I immediately prepared to introduce myself to your guests as an accomplished juggler."

"May we get to know these preparations?"

"Why not? It's only a game anyway. I loaded a good quantity of iron filings instead of a bullet or small shot, then aimed so that the shot would hit the bird from the back. That's how the feathers were completely razed and singed off, provided they have not become too strong yet. You see, one needn't have studied black or white magic to become a so-called magician. By the way, the trick served only to introduce myself effectively to these gentlemen. I don't really care for the chicken but would rather partake of your loin roast. I hope you will permit me to join you?"

"Of course. These two gentlemen are friends of mine, good friends also with Old Shatterhand, whom they are expecting here."

"Old Shatterhand?" Juggle-Fred flew up. "Is that true?"

"Yes. Also Fat Jemmy is coming."

"Yippee! That's news that couldn't be any better. For some time I have wanted to get to know this Old Shatterhand, even if only from a distance, because someone like me had better not come too close. I'm more pleased to see this wish come true, than I would be if I had struck gold. I'm real glad to have arrived here at the right time."

"You'll also be pleased to learn, that this gentleman here is German. His name is Frank and he's a colleague of ---"

"Frank?" the magician interrupted. "You mean Hobble-Frank?"

"By the devil! You know my name!" the little Saxon shouted. "How's that possible?"

He had spoken German, which is why Juggle-Fred responded in the same language.

"You need not be surprised about that. In earlier times many good and bad deeds were committed here in the Far West and due to poor communications, the knowledge of them spread very slowly. But today, when something exceptional happens, the news travels quickly from the Great Lakes to Mexico and from old Frisco to New York. Your daring trip to Yellowstone is well known along with all the names of the participants. In every fort, every settlement and beside every campfire, when at least two people get together, there's talk about your ride and the various people who went along. So, you shouldn't be surprised if I know your name. A trapper, who had been way up at the Spotted Tail Water and had met there with Moh-aw, Tokvitey's son, and who had then come down to Fort Arbukle, told the story to everyone he met, myself included, in the exact manner he heard up north."

"Listen," Hobble-Frank suggested, "who knows what's been added to the story between the Spotted Tail Water and Fort Arbukle. That's when a mouse becomes a polar bear, a rain worm a giant anaconda and a modest beaver-trapper the famous Hobble-Frank. I happily admit to us having been real Herculuses and Minotauruses, but what's more true, I don't really like to be talked about. The hero is graced with the virtue of unreserved modesty. That's why I must reject most seriously all additions and live with only the mantle of my personal honor and excellence."

And so Frank rambled on...

Finally, Fred made a rather perplexed face and looked questioningly at Helmers, who whispered to him, "He's a 'charming character'," after which the juggler knew how to take the little man.

Fred responded in a guileless and most unaffected mien, "There's no need for you to explain. I've already learned from my mentioned contact what a paragon of modesty you are. This, of course, puts your merits into a threefold bright light and multiplies my pleasure of getting to know you. I wish to become your friend from the bottom of my heart. Please, shake my hand."

He proffered Frank his hand; however, the other quickly pulled his back.

"Wait, good man. Not so fast! I take friendship very seriously, and must get to know you better. Only after I have checked the other out to ensure that he's not just half-educated and our chemistry is compatible and our beings harmonious, then I can enter into such a momentous agreement."

"Well, so be it, Mister Frank. I do agree with you in general, but don't doubt for a moment, that we will soon be the best of friends."

"That I believe too, as I have already learned from Mister Helmers, that you are a widely traveled and artistic man. You must truly be like Bosco."

"Bosco. Have you heard about him?"

"Heard? I have seen him with my own eyes, even talked with him."

"Ah! Where?"

"Well, you might know that he lived near Dresden, where he also died. Everybody knew him there. Occasionally, he also came to Moritzburg to view the leather wallpaper and red deer antlers at the hunting castle there. You know there are antlers with twenty-four to fifty points. There's even a monstrous one with sixty-six. Afterwards he used to dine at the La Quarte restaurant, where I also often came in the company of the teacher and the factotum to hold our

21

phenomenal academically linguistics meetings. That's where I met the famous Bosco. And so it happened that, when I departed earlier than he, I picked his umbrella instead of my own. He caught it in time and called after me: 'Hey Stupid! Can't you open your eyes! Do you think I want to carry your fire-red rain protector to Dresden?' Of course, I swapped the umbrellas immediately, apologized and said a few witty words, make a deep bow and expedited myself out the door. So, you will understand, that I am quite proud to have had the opportunity for a spirited exchange with this great artist."

"Oh, yes, I do understand. And you can be proud of it too," Juggle-Fred confirmed.

Hobble-Frank entered into one of his idiosyncratic discourses with Juggle-Fred into which Helmers joined in occasionally. When Frank advised him to pick up on some further education abroad, Juggle-Fred responded, "That won't be possible for the time being. I have to complete a task which will keep me here in the West for a while."

"May I ask what task that is?"

"I never talk about it and can tell you only that I want to – nay, must find a person I've so far searched for in vain."

"It might be useful, if you'd tell me, who you are looking for."

"That's my secret."

"Too bad, too bad! I will soon meet people here who know every corner of the West. You might find help and advice from them. I think here of Old Shatterhand, Fat Jemmy, Long Davy, and Winnetou, who ---"

"Winnetou?" Fred interrupted. "You mean the famous Apache Chief?"

"Yes."

"Sure, certainly, you must know him too, since he was along on the dangerous trips you took. Then you will also meet with him?"

"Of course!"

"Where?"

"That he discussed only with Old Shatterhand. Most likely it will be on the other side of the Llano Estacado."

"Hmm. Then I hope to meet him too. I also mean to cross the Staked Plain."

"All by yourself?"

"No. I have been hired by a group of people who want to cross it and then continue on to El Paso."

"Then they are no frontiers-people since they need a guide?" Helmers broke in.

"No, they are Yankees who want to cross over to do some good business in Arizona."

"I don't suppose in diamonds?"

"Yes, precisely. They seem to carry lots of cash to purchase the stones cheaply right on the spot."

Helmers shook his head and asked, "Do you believe in these diamond finds?"

"Why not."

"Hmm. I think the whole story is humbug."

He was quite right. At the time there had been rumors of big diamond finds in Arizona. Names of people circulated whom, due to some lucky find, had allegedly become rich overnight. A number of very precious diamonds, which reputedly came from there, had been shown around. Within a few days, this rumor traveled across the entire continent. Even the gold diggers in California left their profitable claims for Arizona. Speculation was rife. Quickly, organizations were formed with millions at their disposal to purchase the diamond fields and commence large-scale mining. No claim was to be lost. Agents traveled back and forth carrying diamond samples they claimed to have just been picked up off the ground. They fomented and prodded, and quickly the diamond fever had become greater than the gold fever had ever been.

But cautious people kept their wallets closed and soon the crash they had predicted occurred. Some very smart Yankees had however perpetrated the biggest swindle. They had appeared on the scene without making their true identity known and had disappeared again without anyone really having gotten to know them. And, of course, together with them the millions of investment dollars had disappeared too. The shareholders cursed in vain, most of them denied ever having owned any shares in the venture, so as not to be laughed at. The diamond fields so quickly risen to fame lay barren once more and the cheated and disappointed gold diggers returned to their claims, only to find that others, who were smarter, had taken them over. That was the end of the story and no one talked about it any more.

It was shortly after the diamond fever had arisen, that the conversation in front of Helmers Home took place. The farmer was one of those who didn't place much stock into the rumors. Juggle-Fred, on the other hand, responded by saying, "I don't yet want to question the truth of the proposition. If diamonds have been found somewhere else, why not also in Arizona? But it's not my concern. I've other things to do. What do you say, Mister Frank? The opinion of a man of your shrewdness, experience and knowledge would be helpful."

Although Frank's rambling response was not much help in the analysis of the subject, he presented his case in such a guileless manner, claiming that the hearts of Germans were like diamonds, that Helmers commented, "Well spoken!" and shook Frank's hand vigorously. "It's unlikely, that I will ever return to our fatherland, but my heart returns to it every day. You are quite right about the diamonds, which means we ought not to care about the stories that tell of them being found in Arizona. The group Fred is going to guide across the Llano is unlikely to do good business over there. It would have been better if these people had stayed home with their wealth of cash. They could easily lose it without finding a single diamond. They don't seem to be very smart people."

"Why not?"

"Because they let it be known that they carry large amounts of cash. Its never wise to do so, but out here its downright stupid."

"So these people intend to come here? When do you expect them?"

"Tomorrow, in the early afternoon, I guess. They wanted to buy two additional packhorses, which will take them half a day for sure. This was the reason why I rode ahead as I'd rather spend the time with you."

"That was thoughtful of you. How many people are in your party?"

"There's six of them, with some looking and acting a bit green, which isn't my concern. They seem to come from New Orleans and they imagine returning with millions. They act somewhat exuberantly, but again, that's none of my business. They pay me and all else may be as it is."

"Will they find the way here?"

"Sure. I have described the trail so well, that they can't go astray. Yes, Bob, what's the matter?"

That question was directed at the Negro.

The day had progressed and dusk, quite brief at this latitude, had fallen. It was already dark enough that one could no longer see very far. Despite the lively conversation, Bob and Bloody-Fox had kept their eyes on the Mormon, who had made an effort to convey the impression of total disinterest in the conversation. And since the talkers had been of the opinion that a Mormon, who appeared to them to be a true Yankee, would know little or nothing of German, they had spoken so loudly that he had been able to understand every word. His face had remained quite blank during Frank's effusive discourse, which had reinforced the others' belief, that he didn't understand a thing. But as soon as the talk had centered on the diamond fields, he had slid closer on his bench. And when Juggle-Fred talked about the six men he was going to guide through the Llano Estacado, his face had taken on an expression of great interest. Then, when it was mentioned, that the six were carrying large amounts of money, his lips contorted into a satisfied smile which, however, due to the increasing dusk could no longer be noticed.

At times he had lifted his head as if to listen. He also looked into the direction from which he had come. He knew, that with the Negro's eyes keeping him in constant sight, and Bloody Fox keeping him under surveillance, he had to consider himself very much a captive. Despite his attention to the ongoing conversation the air felt increasingly sinister to him. Contemplating the Black's threat, he figured Bob quite capable of executing it. Now, that it had become almost dark, he thought the time had come to make his getaway since it might become much more difficult later, when Bob would take some measures to prevent it. He reached for his small parcel and casually pulled it closer. His intention was to suddenly jump up and, with a few leaps, run off around the corner of the building. Once he had made it into the bushes behind the house, he thought he would no longer have to fear his pursuers.

But he had figured wrong about Bob. Like most Negroes, once having made a decision, they pursued it with the greatest persistence. The Black had observed the Mormon quite well and had noticed how the small parcel had been pulled ever closer and just when the Mormon prepared to make his leap, Bob rose so quickly from his seat, that he almost toppled Helmers from his.

Helmers therefore asked, "What's the matter, Bob?"

"Massa Bob seen that thief want to leave. He reached for parcel. Want to leap away. But Massa Bob knock him down some place else, that's why go with him and not leave out of eyes."

He once more sat down on the outer edge of the bench so that he was close to the Mormon, although the latter sat at the next table.

"You better let the fellow go," Helmers cautioned, "he's probably not worth the attention you give him."

"Massa Helmers right. He's not worth, but money he has stolen is. He not get away, for sure not without Massa Bob!"

"Who's that chap actually?" Juggle-Fred asked quietly, "I didn't care for his looks the moment I saw him. He seems to me like a wolf running around in sheep's clothing. When I saw him, I had the feeling, as if I had seen his pointy physiognomy once before, and that under circumstances not favorable to him."

Helmers explained Bob's persistent attention to the suspect, adding, "Bloody-Fox too seems to be occupied with the fellow, although he does not show it too much. Is it not so?"

"Well," the young man responded, "this Latter Day Saint has done something to me, something very bad!"

"Truly? What was it? Why don't you call him to account?"

"I can't, because I don't know what it was."

"That's weird. If you are so sure that he has wronged you, you must also know what it was."

"But that's precisely it! I have tortured my brain, yet it will not come. It is as if I had dreamed the atrocity but then forgotten the details of the dream. And because of this ill defined, nebulous hunch I cannot go after the man."

"I don't understand this. What I know I know! I just don't have nebulous hunches. And, by the way, it is dark now. Let's go inside."

"No. The fellow hasn't been allowed to enter the house and I must keep him in my sight. I need to stay here. Maybe what I need to settle with him will yet come to me."

"Let me get some light then, so he cannot sneak off."

25

Helmers went into the house and returned with two lamps made of petroleum tins with wicks protruding from the openings. There was no chimney or shade.

Nevertheless, the two flaring and very smoky lights illuminated the yard in front of the door quite well.

Just when the host had hung the lamps to a couple of tree branches, steps approaching from the cornfields could be heard.

"My helpers are turning in," Helmers said.

But he was mistaken. A single stranger stepped into the arc of light. He was a tall, strong fellow with a full beard and dressed entirely in Mexican garb. But he wore no spurs, which was unusual. From his belt protruded the handles of two knives and two pistols. In his hand he carried a heavy silver-inlaid rifle. His dark eyes flew over the gathered individuals with a sharp, penetrating look. To those sitting he gave the impression of a physically strong, yet coarse individual of whom one could not expect any sensitive emotions. When his look passed the Mormon's face one of his eyelids twitched oddly. No one except the Mormon noticed this. It must have been a signal intended only for the latter.

"Buenos tardes, Señores," he greeted. "An evening of Bengal lighting? The owner of this hacienda appears to be poetically inclined. Permit me to rest for a quarter of an hour and to be offered a drink, if something is to be had here."

He had spoken this in a Spanish-English mish mash often used near the Mexican border.

"Sit down, Señor," Helmers replied in the same jargon, "what do you care to drink? Beer or schnapps?"

"Keep off with your beer. I don't care for these German suds. Give me a strong schnapps and not too little. Understand!"

His demeanor and tone were those of a man who was not used to being trifled with. He acted as if he had the right to give orders here. Helmers got up to fetch the desired drink and pointed to the bench, where he had been sitting. However, the stranger shook his head and said, "Thanks, Señor, four are already seated there. I'd rather join that caballero who's sitting by himself. I'm used to the open prairie and don't care to be stuck so closely together."

He leaned his rifle against a tree trunk and sat down next to the Mormon whom he greeted by slightly tipping the broad brim of his sombrero. The Latter Day Saint did so as well and the two behaved as if they were strangers.

Helmers had entered the house. From natural courtesy the others avoided looking at the newcomer directly. This offered the man the welcome opportunity to whisper to the Mormon in the cleanest English, "Why didn't you come back? You know we need information."

"They didn't allow me to leave," the Mormon responded.

"Who didn't?"

"That damned nigger there."

"The one who has his eyes on you? What's he about?"

"He claims that I stole money from his former master and wants to lynch me."

"Well. About the former he's probably right; but the latter he should get off his mind, if not then he risks his black hide being colored red with the help of our whips. Any news?"

"Yes. Six diamond boys with lots of cash want to cross the Llano."

"By the devil. They are welcome! We'll look into their pockets. There wasn't much in those of the last poor suckers. Quiet now. Helmers is returning."

Helmers put a stein full of schnapps in front of the stranger and said, "There it is. To your health! Señor. You must have a tough ride behind you?"

"A ride?" guffawed the man, while he downed almost half the stein's contents, "Don't you have eyes? Or rather do you have too many, that you see what doesn't exist? He who rides must have a horse!"

"Certainly."

"Well. Then where is mine?"

"Must be where you left it."

"Válgame dios! I wouldn't leave my horse thirty miles behind to have a brandy here which, by the way, isn't worth a damn."

"Leave it in the stein then if you don't like it. And I don't recall having talked about thirty miles. From the manner in which you sit in front of me, you look like a man who owns a horse. Where it's been left isn't my business but yours."

"I think so too. It's none of your business at all. Understood!"

"Are you questioning my right to check on those who enter my remote farmstead?"

"Does it mean you are afraid of me?"

"Pah! I would like to see the fellow John Helmers is afraid of."

"I like that, since I meant to ask whether I can stay the night at your place."

These words were spoken to Helmers with a veiled look.

"Sorry, there's no room for you."

"Caracho! Why not?"

"Because you said yourself, that I shouldn't concern myself with you."

"But I can't walk through the night to your next neighbor. I wouldn't get there until noon tomorrow."

"Then sleep in the open. The night's mild, the ground soft, and the sky is the best blanket one can have."

"Then you are truly sending me away?"

"Yes, Señor. Whoever wishes to be my guest must display greater courtesy than you have shown."

"Do you expect me to sing and play the guitar just to be allowed to sleep in some corner? Well, as you wish. I don't need your hospitality. I'll find a spot somewhere. Then I can ponder how I shall talk with you, should we ever meet again."

"Just in case this opportunity arises, you might also ponder on what I might answer you."

"Is that meant to be a threat, Señor?"

With these words the stranger had risen and imperiously faced the host with his bulky figure.

"Oh, no," Helmers responded fearlessly, "as long as I'm not forced to assert myself, I am a very peaceful man."

"I would advise that. Here you live close to the Llano of Death, that requires you live in peace with people, or the Ghost of Llano Estacado may unexpectedly find his way to you."

"Might you know him?"

"Haven't seen him yet. But it's quite well known that he loves to appear before big-talking people so he can take them to hell."

"I don't dispute that," Helmers responded, "but it seems to me that those who have been found with the Ghost's trademark though the head have not been big-talkers but robbers and murderers."

"You think so?" the stranger asked sneeringly. "Can you prove that?"

"Indeed! Without exception these people have been found in possession of items that formerly belonged to those who had been murdered and robbed in the Llano Estacado. That's plenty of proof!"

"If that's so, let me warn you in all friendship: Don't you kill a man on your remote farm or you could also be found some day with a hole in your head."

"Señor!" Helmers flew out. "Say another word like that and I will knock you down. I'm no murderer, but an honest man. I think it more likely, someone who hides his horse so as to give the appearance that one is dealing with a poor, harmless fellow and not with a Bravo, is far more capable of such a deed."

"Am I supposed to be that?"

"If the shoe fits, I don't mind at all. You are the second one today who's made the false claim of having come here without a horse. The first one is the Latter Day Saint next to you. Maybe the two horses of yours are standing side by side. Who knows, maybe there are other horses and riders with them waiting for your return. Let me tell you, that I will guard my house very well tonight and shall clear out the neighborhood tomorrow morning. Its very likely that it will then be proven that you've been quite well mounted."

The stranger clenched his fist, lifted his right ready to strike, stepped quite close to Helmers and screamed, "Man, are you telling me I am a Bravo? Tell it to my face loud and clear if you've got the courage, that I can knock you down ---"

He was interrupted.

Bloody-Fox had given this man less attention than his rifle. When the stranger had risen and had turned his back to the tree, the youngster got up and stepped to the tree trunk to examine the firearm. His face, which until that moment had been almost expressionless, now changed entirely. His eyes lit up and his face shaped into one of utter ruthlessness and determination.

Turning to the stranger, he put his hand onto the man's shoulder, interrupting the tirade.

"What do you want, boy?"

"I want to respond in Helmers place," Bloody-Fox told him calmly. "Yes, you are a Bravo, a robber and a murderer. Watch out for the Ghost of the Llano whom we call the Avenging Ghost, since he avenges every murder with a bullet through the head of the killer."

The giant took several steps back, looked with some surprise at the youngster, laughed derisively and said, "Lad, kid, boy, are you crazy? I can make mush of you with a single squeeze of my hand."

"You aren't going to do that! Bloody-Fox doesn't crush that easily. You thought you could be impertinent to the men here, but now a boy shall prove to you that you are not to be feared, since you are already doomed. From this moment forth consider yourself a corpse. The Avenging Ghost punishes the murderers of the Llano with death. You are a murderer, but since the Ghost isn't present, I shall take his place. Go ahead, say your last three Lord's prayers and Ave Marias; you are going to face your final judge."

The words of the young man, still half a boy, made an extraordinary impression on those present. He now appeared totally different from before. His bearing exceeded even that of a grown man. There he stood, proud, erect, his arms raised threateningly, his eyes flashing like lightning. His expression projected unshakable determination as if he were the harbinger of justice and the executioner of absolute punishment.

Despite being a head taller than the young man, the stranger had turned pale. But then he caught himself, broke into a loud laughter and said, "Truly, he's crazy. A flea wants to devour a lion. That hasn't been heard before. Fellow, why don't you first prove that I am a murderer."

"Don't mock me. What I've said will happen, you can rest assured. Whose rifle is that leaning there on the tree trunk?"

"It's mine, of course!"

"Since when?"

"For more than twenty years."

Despite his previous laughter and his disparaging words the now so obviously changed bearing of the youngster made such an impression on the big man, that he did not deny him answers.

"Can you prove it?"

"Fellow, how am I to prove that? Can you prove the opposite?"

"Yes, this rifle belonged to Señor Rodriguez Pinto from the Estancia del Meriso near Cedar Grove. Two years ago he traveled with his wife, his daughter and three vaqueros to the Caddo farm. He said his good-byes there, but never returned home. Soon afterwards six corpses were found in the Llano Estacado. Traces and tracks indicated that the stakes had been changed, that is, they had been planted in a wrong direction. This rifle was his; he carried it at the time. Had you claimed you purchased it from someone within that time span, your claim could be verified. But since you claim to have already owned it for twenty years, you did not buy it from the guilty one, but are yourself the murderer and as such subject to the law of the Llano Estacado."

"Dog!" the stranger grated. "You want me to crush you? This rifle is mine. Prove that it belonged to this Hacendero. Now!"

Bloody-Fox took the rifle from the trunk and pressed a small silver plate inlay at the lower part of the butt. It clicked open and below it was a second silver plate with the Hacendero's name engraved upon it.

"Look here!" he said showing the rifle to the others. "Here is irrefutable proof that the rifle was the property of the Hacendero. He lent it to me a few times, which is why I know it so well. It is very dangerous for a murderer to carry an item, whose properties he is unfamiliar with. I am not going to ask you, whether you think this man to be a murderer. I think him to be one, which suffices. His time is now limited."

"Yours too!" the stranger screamed, leaping at Bloody-Fox to tear the rifle from him. But Bloody-Fox stepped back a few paces with lightning speed and aimed the rifle at him.

"Stop, or you'll get the bullet! I know very well how to deal with people like you. Hobble-Frank, Juggle-Fred, cover him with your rifles. If he makes a move, shoot him down!"

The two immediately raised their rifles and aimed them at the stranger. This was the law of the prairies, which has but a single yet entirely adequate paragraph. A good frontiersman does not hesitate to abide by it.

The stranger realized the seriousness of his situation. His life was at stake and so he stood absolutely still.

Bloody-Fox now lowered the rifle he was holding, since the other two kept the stranger in check and said, "I have spoken judgment on you and it will be executed right away."

"By what right?" the stranger asked, his voice quivering with anger. "I am innocent. And even if I were guilty, I need not put up with being lynched by such vagabond folks like you, least of all by a child."

"I shall show you, that I am no child. I will not simply kill you as an executioner would. You shall face me eye to eye, each with his rifle in his hand. Your bullet may hit me just as mine will strike you. It shall not be murder, but an honest exchange of bullets. We will put life against life, although I could simply gun you down, since I hold your life in my hands."

The young man faced the stranger proudly and with great self-confidence. His voice was serious and determined and yet his words sounded so calm as if such a duel were a commonplace thing. He impressed all those present, except the one his words were directed at. But, perhaps he did not want to let on what impact his opponent's conduct had made. He once more fell into a loud, derisive laughter and responded, "Since when do immature boys make such boasts here at the border? Don't think that I'm in your hands because of your courage and foresight. Had these men not been here to point their rifles at me, I would have already choked you to death, like I would wring the neck of a brazen sparrow. Are you truly crazy enough to want to take my measure? Then I don't mind. Just be prepared to have spoken your last words today. My bullet has never yet failed. You can bet that it will show you the path to hell. But I hold you and the others to what your big mouth has spouted. I demand an honest fight and then a free and open field for the victor."

"You will get both," Bloody-Fox answered.

"Did you hear me right? When my bullet has dropped you, I can go where I want and no one has the right to hold me back."

It was now that Helmers objected, "That's not how we are betting. Even should you have a lucky shot, there are still other gentlemen who would then like to have a word with you. You will have to answer them too."

"Not so!" Bloody-Fox objected. "This man is mine. You have no right on him. I alone challenged him and have given him my word, that the fight will be honest. You must keep this promise should I fall. After my death it is not to be said that my promise had no value."

"But, boy, think about ---"

"There's nothing to think about!"

"Should a notorious rascal be permitted to gun you down unpunished?"

"If he succeeds, yes, because it is my will to duel with him. Yes, it is true, that he is one of the Llano vultures and should, without much ado, be flayed with cudgels. But such justice is not to my liking, and if I am honoring him with a better death, then this privilege should also be respected when I am dead. Promise then by word and handshake that he may leave unhindered, should he kill me."

"If that's your wish, we must obey. But you will depart this earth with the reproach that your unjustified mildness will enable this rascal to continue his evil deeds."

"Well, as far as that goes, I'm at ease. He has claimed that his bullet never misses. Let's see, whether the bullet in my barrel just punches a hole in the air. Tell me then, fellow, over what distance we shall fire?"

"Fifty paces," the stranger answered.

"Fifty?" Bloody-Fox laughed. "That's not very close. You seem to cherish your skin very much. But it will not matter. You know, I advise you in the

31

friendliest manner that I will aim for the forehead, just like the Avenging Ghost. Watch out for yours. I'm afraid that today you will get a few ounces of lead through your brain. Whether you can cope with that is your business, not mine."

"Quit bragging, lad," grated his opponent. "I got what I asked for: The promise to leave here unhindered. Let's finish this. Give me my rifle."

"Once we are done with the preparations you shall have it, but not earlier, for we cannot trust you. Our host shall step out the distance of fifty paces. When we have taken our positions, Bob can stand near you with a lamp, Hobble-Frank with the other, beside me, so that we can see each other properly for good aim. Then Juggle-Fred will hand you your rifle and Helmers hand me mine. From that moment on, each of us can shoot as he pleases. We each have two bullets in our double-barreled rifles.

"Shall we advance upon shooting?" the stranger asked.

"No. You've determined the distance that we shall maintain. The respective lamp bearer shall shoot down whoever leaves his position before the shots have been fired. To carry this out, Bob and Frank will have their revolvers cocked. The one who attempts to leave before his opponent has fired two shots will be gunned down too."

"Wonderful! Very good!" Bob shouted. "Massa Bob give rascal bullet immediately when run away."

He pulled the weapon from his belt to show it to the stranger with a broad grin. The others expressed their agreement with Bloody-Fox's conditions and began the preparations. All were so occupied with it, that none watched the pious Tobias Praisegod Burton, who seemed to be quite pleased with the development. He slid slowly to the edge of the bench and pulled his feet from under the table, so he could leap away when the time was right.

The two opponents now faced each other over a distance of fifty paces. Next to the stranger stood the Negro, in his left hand he held the lamp, in his right the pistol, ready to shoot.

Next to Bloody-Fox stood Hobble-Frank with his lamp and revolver, not expecting to have to use the latter against the young, honest man.

Helmers and Juggle-Fred held the two loaded rifles at the ready. Even for these two experienced fighters it was a moment of extreme tension. The flickering glow of the two lamps threw a blood-red light on the two groups. The two opponents stood very still, yet in the unsteady light it appeared as if they were constantly moving. Under these conditions it was very difficult to aim properly. With the poor illumination it was also almost impossible to properly see the notch of the rifle's sight and even less the more distant bead.

Bloody-Fox stood there openly, almost harmlessly, as if he were getting ready for a cricket match. His opponent, however, displayed a different mood. Juggle-Fred, who was to hand him the rifle and stood close to him, could see the malicious gleam in his eyes and the impatient twitching of his hands.

32

"Are you ready?" Helmers now asked.

"Yes," both opponents answered, whereby the stranger already reached for his rifle. His intention was to beat Bloody-Fox to the shot if only by half a second.

"Do either of you two still have anything to arrange in case of your death?" Helmers inquired.

"The devil may get you for your prying," the excited stranger grated.

"No," the youngster responded quietly. "I see that this fellow would only hit me by accident, the way he's shaking. But should it be necessary, you'll find all you need to know in my saddlebag. Now, let's get on with it!"

"Well, then hand them the rifles. Fire!"

Frank handed Bloody-Fox the rifle, who took it, weighing it casually in his right hand. He didn't behave at all as if his life hung in the balance.

The other had almost torn the rifle from Juggle-Fred's hand. He turned sideways to offer a smaller target and aimed. His shot rang out.

"Hello! Great!" the Negro hollered. "Massa Bloody-Fox not hit! What luck! What delight."

At the same time he jumped with both legs into the air, twirled around his own axis, and from joy behaved as if obsessed.

"Keep quiet, man!" Helmers thundered. "Who's to aim properly, if you swing the lamp like that."

Bob immediately realized, that his antics hurt exactly the one he wished to win. He immediately stood very still and shouted, "Massa Bob now hold still. Massa Bob not even twitch. Massa Bloody-Fox now shoot quickly."

But the stranger hadn't taken his rifle from his cheek. He fired again– but this shot missed too, even though Bloody Fox had remained as still as before and had presented his entire body.

"Thousand devils!" the stranger shouted.

For a moment he stood as if frozen. Then he bellowed a curse, which can not be presented here, and prepared to escape to the side.

"Stop, I shoot," the Negro had shouted.

The deed occurred simultaneously with the words, but it had not been his shot that had rung out first.

The brief moment his opponent had stood frozen in terror, had sufficed for Bloody-Fox to raise his rifle. He squeezed his shot off quickly without seemingly having taken aim, turned on his heel, reached into his bag of munitions to quickly reload the empty barrel as is customary in the West, and said, "He's done for. Go to him, Frank. You'll find the hole in the middle of his forehead."

He turned his back to where his opponent had stood. His voice had sounded so calm, as if he had done an everyday thing.

Frank and Helmers stepped to the place where the stranger had fallen. Bloody-Fox followed them when he had finished reloading.

The triumphant voice of the Negro already bellowed from there, "What wonder, what bravery, what courage! Massa Bob has shot dead rascal completely. Here lies man not moving from spot. Look Massa Helmers and Massa Frank, that Bob has hit him right in forehead. Is hole in front and come out in back. Oh, Massa Bob is brave frontiersman. He easily overcome thousand enemies."

"Yes, you are an exceptional shot," nodded Helmers, who had knelt down by the dead man to check him out. "But where did you aim?"

"Massa Bob aim exactly for forehead and that's where hit. Oh. Massa Bob is giant, is hero. Massa Bob be invincible, unconquerable, and impregnable."

"Be quiet, black man. You are neither a giant, nor a hero, nor invincible. You haven't done a thing to prove your courage. You shot at an escapee, which doesn't take much. And then, you never thought to aim at the forehead of this man. Here, look at his pants. What do you see there?"

Bob shone his light down there and inspected the spot Helmers indicated.

"There is hole, a tear," he confirmed.

"Yes, a tear your bullet caused. You shot at the pant leg and claim to have aimed for the forehead. You ought to be ashamed! And that across a distance of only six feet!"

"Oh, no. Not Massa Bob must be ashamed. Massa Bob hit forehead. But Massa Blood-Fox shoot too, but in pants. Massa Bob shoot very good, much better than Massa Bloody-Fox."

"Yeah, we know! What a shot, Bloody-Fox! No one can do better! I didn't even see you aim."

"I know my rifle," the young man responded modestly, "and knew it would happen this way, since the fellow was far too excited. He was shaking. That's always stupid, particularly if one's life depends on only two shots."

The man was dead. The round, sharp-edged hole sat in the middle of his forehead and had exited behind.

"Exactly how the Ghost of Llano Estacado would shoot," Juggle-Fred opined admiringly. "Truly, this was an expert shot. The fellow got what he deserved. What are we going to do with the body?"

"My people can bury him," Helmers answered, "the sight of a corpse is not pleasing, yet the worst scoundrel is still a human being. But justice must be served, and where the law has no power, one is forced to take matters into one's own hands. There can be no talk of lynch-justice here, because Bloody-Fox gave him the same chance. He was proven to be a murderer. May God have mercy on his soul! And now let's --- What? What's the matter?"

Bob had called out loudly. He had been the only one not looking at the dead man.

"Well," he said, "Massa Helmers look over there."

He pointed to where the tables and benches stood. It was dark there now, since the two lamp bearers where standing with the group.

"Why? What's there?"

"Nothing. Nothing there at all! When Massa Helmers and other Massas look, there be nothing, because he gone."

"Egad, the Mormon is gone!" Helmers exclaimed while he jumped up from next to the stranger's body. "Quickly, after him! Let's see if we can catch him."

The group dissolved at once. Everyone took off in the direction to where coincidence or momentary guesswork drove him. Only one stayed back --- Bloody-Fox. He stood motionless listening into the darkness of the night. This is how he remained until the men returned, as was to be expected they reported that they had not found any trace or sign of the absconder.

"Well, I thought so," he nodded. "We have been stupid. This pious Mormon may be a much more dangerous man than the dead one over there ever was. I have seen him before, but cannot recall where. Yet I will arrange to meet with him again and quite soon. Good night, gentlemen."

He picked up the rifle the stranger had dropped and walked to his horse.

"You leaving?" Helmers asked.

"Yes, I had wanted to leave a while ago and have wasted precious time on this stranger. I will take the rifle along to hand it to the legitimate heirs."

"When will I see you again?"

"When it's necessary. No sooner and no later."

He mounted his horse and trotted off without shaking anybody's hand.

"A peculiar young fellow," Juggle-Fred said, shaking his head.

"Let him be," Helmers responded. "He always knows, what he's doing. Yes, he's young, but he can be a match for most older ones, and I am convinced, that he will soon have this Mister Tobias Praisegod Burton by the scruff of his neck and maybe a few more of his ilk."

2. The two Snuffles

Two hours before Hobble-Frank and Sliding-Bob met Bloody-Fox, two other men came riding from the direction of Coleman City. But they could hardly have paid this place a visit, for they looked like men who had avoided all habitats for some time.

Although the two mules these men were riding showed signs of tiredness, they also appeared to have been well cared for. However, the two riders provided quite the opposite impression. They were extremely thin, so much so that one could almost believe that they had endured long weeks of starvation. In contrast to that, their glowing skin color and sturdy posture, with which they held themselves in the saddle, spoke of good health. The West's strong, dry air doesn't tolerate superfluous flesh on the bones, yet it strengthens the body's sinews and bestows that particular staying power without which a person would otherwise soon perish.

The exceptional similarity of the two was surprising. Anyone looking at them would think them to be brothers, if not twins. And since both were dressed and armed alike, one could distinguish the two only by a scar, which crossed the left cheek of one of them.

They wore comfortable dark gray woolen over-shirts and pants, solid laced shoes, broad-brimmed beaver hats, and had their heavy, wide blankets suspended from their backs like coats. Their leather belts were covered with rattlesnake skin and carried the usual small weaponry and other utensils indispensable to a frontiersman. Rifles they had too, yet they did not look as if they had recently come from a gunsmith's shop, rather one could say that they looked outright ludicrous. However, someone familiar with what an experienced frontiersman can accomplish with such old flintlock muzzleloaders would never think of turning up his nose at them. The frontiersman by needs values his weapon, but he is not coquettish about it. The plainer it becomes from long use, the greater the reverence he lavishes on it.

Unfortunately, one could not describe these two riders in terms of manly beauty, the reason being that their most prominent feature had developed in a most exceptional manner. It was their noses – and what noses they were! One could have sworn that in this land no other such olfactory organs existed. It wasn't just their size, no; it was their exceptional shape and color. To imagine these noses, one would have to see them. Think of the sap of a birch tree that has hardened into the shape of a grape, shimmering in all possible colors that ever existed on a painter's palette, only then can one begin to form a rough concept of these sensory organs. And yet even these two were surprisingly similar. There were no two brothers more alike and since they had already survived into their mid-fifties they must have experienced many a tempest.

One should by no means think that their facial expression was repulsive, oh no, not at all. Their faces were carefully shaven so that no beard hid their kind expressions. A happy, carefree smile seemed to have nestled into the corners of their mouths and their bright, sharp eyes faced the world so kindly and pleasantly that only a poor judge of men would have insisted to be wary of them.

The area they were traversing looked quite sterile. Its growth consisted mainly of scrubby bushes, some yucca and cacti. It seemed that no watercourse could be found in the vicinity. The rider's examining looks indicated that they were not too familiar with the land they were crossing. From time to time one of them rose in his stirrups to gain a wider view, only to drop back into the saddle with an expression that signaled disappointment.

"A darn poor area," said the one with the scar on his cheek. "Who knows, whether we will still find a sip of fresh water today. Don't you think so too, Jim?"

"Quite so," grumbled the other. "We are getting close to the Llano Estacado. You can't expect more. Or do you, Jim, anticipate finding springs spouting eggnog or buttermilk in the desert?"

"Oh, be quiet, dear brother! Don't get me salivating. Eggnog would be best and buttermilk would do just as well. But neither one we'll find here, I'm afraid we'll have to make do with cactus juice."

"It shouldn't get that bad. We haven't reached the plains yet. Tomorrow we'll reach Helmers Home, which is supposed to lie by a stream. That means we haven't yet left the fertile land behind us. I hope we'll still get to the old silver mine today, which is supposedly located at or near a knoll of bushes and trees as are sometimes found even in the most desolate areas. And you know that my hopes are rarely disappointed, since they usually tend to meander close to reality."

"You might want to keep quiet about that. Haven't our hopes led to nothing so far?"

"Don't say that, Jim. We may not have had a luxurious life, that's true, but we carry a tidy little sum in our pockets, and if we have some luck on the other side of the Llano and the Guadeloupe, we will have made it."

"Yeah, if! To become a millionaire, that's a wonderful feeling, but for the moment, we don't even have anything to eat. We were so intent to get ahead and didn't even take the time to be on the lookout for a roast. I don't even ask for a turkey, but wouldn't mind coming across an old prairie chicken. Wouldn't it be nice to say hello to her with my gun?"

"Your thoughts are much too delicious. I would be quite happy if a complaisant jackrabbit would cross my sights, then we --- watch out! There's one! Molly, stand still for once."

This request, backed up by a jerk of his reins, had been directed to his mule. It now stood still, as if it had understood his words. Exactly in front of the two, a lone jackrabbit had jumped from a clump of grass. Quickly, Tim had his gun to his cheek and fired. The rabbit somersaulted and dropped dead to the ground. The bullet had penetrated its head – a masterful shot with a gun of that type.

This Texan rabbit is of a similar size to the German hare. It is quite abundant and its meat is very tasty. Its ears are very long, similar to those of a mule.

Tim rode to where the critter had dropped, picked it up, then said as he continued his ride, "The roast's here, and I think we'll find a little water hole to quench our thirst. You see, my hopes come true. Two chaps like us always find what they need."

"And diamonds too? That we have yet to see."

"Diamonds too, I tell you," Tim answered with certainty. "Obviously, only if diamonds are truly to be found over there. If the whole story is a swindle, we will be just as badly off as all the others who won't find a thing. I, at least, will not worry my head off, should I learn that we've circled luck in vain. Listen! Wasn't that a shot?"

"Yes, it was. Polly heard it too."

He had referred to his mule, which now sucked air through her nostrils and wagged her long ears energetically. It is usual for a frontiersman to give his mount a name. These two mules were named Molly and Polly, as was apparent from the talk of their masters, two names sounding just as alike as those of their masters, Jim and Tim.

The brothers rose from their saddles and looked into the direction from which the shot had come. The sound had carried farther than they could see since they were in a depression. Then Tim pointed to the sky where a large bird spiraled lazily.

"A turkey vulture," he said. "Isn't it, Jim?"

"No, it's a royal vulture, as you can see from its coloration. It has a pale yellow plumage and must have been feeding on some carrion. It is so stuffed, that it can barely fly. The shot disturbed it in its feeding and we must see what kind of people did so. Out here it's very important to learn who's about. It's not supposed to be very safe this close to the Llano. Such a vulture may easily eat those who disregard that, a thought I do not relish much. So, let's get going, Tim!"

They gave their animals the spurs. However, it is all too well known, that mules can be very stubborn creatures, particularly, when the greatest hurry is called for, they may decide not to move at all. To make up for this behavior a mule may decide to fall into a gallop when the rider would like it to stand still. Unfortunately, Molly wasn't an exception. Barely had Tim let her feel the spurs, when she planted her four legs firmly and stood rigid like a wooden horse. He pressed the spurs harder, which only caused her to put her head between her legs and buck to dislodge her rider. Tim, however, knew his female friend of many years too well and could not be expelled from the saddle.

"Hey, what do you think, you old joker!" he laughed. "I'll straighten you out in a hurry."

He reached back, grabbed the animal's tail, and pulled it sharply forward. All four of Molly's legs left the ground at once then she shot ahead at such a speed that Jim could barely keep up on his Polly. This delicate, yet energetic pull of the tail was the secret means by which the stubbornness of this otherwise very amicable Molly could be quickly broken. Whoever was unaware of this was forced, even when using spurs and whip, to submit to her caprices. So it is, that every animal has its peculiarities, sometimes not just applicable to the individual, but to its entire species. Another species, *Equus asinus*, the donkey or ass has the lovely tendency to fall into its two-tone singsong even in the middle of the night when everyone wants to sleep. The solution to this problem lies in tying a rock or other heavy weight to the tail of this creature, causing it to drop its head and ears and to cease its braying.

When the two riders had come out of the depression they saw, to their surprise, a peculiarly fissured rise at a distance of about six miles, something they had not expected to see so close to the plains. Simultaneously, they noticed a group of horsemen stopped by an object lying on the ground. They were so close, that less than a minute would be required to reach them. Immediately, they reined in their animals. They had to establish, whether the six horsemen might be hostile.

The six had noticed them too and the circle they had formed opened up, yet no hostile action was displayed.

"What do you think?" asked Jim. "Shall we ride over there?"

"I think so. They have seen us and should they be bush runners, there will be a fight anyway. So, let's move up on them, but in such a way, that they can't encircle us. And let's be ready to shoot."

"Well, it's unlikely they are bush runners. They look more like gentlemen out on a pleasant excursion. Their suits look as if they were still hanging in a tailor's shop barely a week ago. They seem to carry a whole arsenal of weapons, but they still shine and shimmer, so that it's unlikely they have seen much use yet. And their horses look so fresh and well fed, that I guess we are facing some innocuous folk here. While it's not the height of pleasure to meet up with such moneybags, I prefer it to folks whose pockets serve only to put other people's property in. So, let's get over to them."

They wouldn't have had another choice anyway, for the six had set their horses into motion to approach them.

"Come closer, come closer!" they were hailed. "You'll get to see something."

"What is it?" Jim hollered back.

"Just come. Hurry up!"

Then they met. Whilst the faces of the six had so far been serious and thoughtful, they now assumed a totally different expression. Twelve wide-open eyes faced the two brothers with obvious surprise. Then the lips of the six men began to twitch until they all broke into hearty laughter.

"By the devil," one of them shouted. "Who've we got here? Two bulb-noses!"

"Two bulb-noses!" the other five fell in.

"Two snouted baboons!"

"Really, really! Wonderful! Beautiful! Two snouted baboons," the six laughed and hollered in unison.

"I beg you, gentlemen, let us examine you more closely," their speaker requested. "We've never seen anything like this before. Permit me to touch these noses just once. I must convince myself they are real and not leftovers from the last carnival."

Until now the brothers had not changed their demeanor. But when the man dared to reach out to touch Jim's nose, the latter pulled his animal back a few paces and said, "Wouldn't you care to introduce yourself first, Sir?"

"Why not? My name's Gibson."

"Thank you. Well, then, Mister Gibson, I will gladly be of service to anyone. I'm also willing to be so to you. But I must also tell you that my rifle will discharge the moment someone touches my nose. I don't mind if you still wish to touch it, but I ask your honorable comrades not to hold me responsible for the consequences."

This was said in such a serious tone that, despite the two peculiar noses, the six ceased their laughter at once. Yet Gibson made one more attempt to jest by saying, "But, Mister, how can you take it crosswise if we laugh about such rhinoceros horns?"

"The fact is, and I'm firmly convinced of this, that a real rhinoceros is insufficiently cultivated to be insulted by your laughter about its horn. But take care and avoid a blunder. You seem to be green and ignorant in both anthropology and zoology and would mistake a baby for a grown hippopotamus. Where I would classify this as inexperience, someone else might more accurately call it stupidity or foolishness, so I consider it my duty to give you fair warning. No creature can be other than how the Lord has created it, and if He has blessed me with a large nose and you with a small, imperfect brain, then we must accept these deficits humbly since, unfortunately, we cannot change them."

"To hell with you!" Gibson exploded. "Is this a rub?"

"Not at all. You just rub it off yourself should you feel dirty and make sure to use enough soap and water. I'm no maid to serve you."

That's when Gibson reached for his revolver threatening, "Ease off, Sir! My bullets are not as tight in the barrel as you may take them to be."

41

"Pah!" Jim laughed. "Don't be ridiculous. Your threat sounds childish."

"Shut up! Or do you want us to teach you manners? We are six against you two."

"That's just it! Six of your ilk doesn't worry us. Hang a zero to the six and we shall give it some thought, whether it's worthwhile to put our fingers on the triggers."

"You seem to keep your mouth in good shape!"

"Our rifles too. Remember that!"

"Well, then, be so gracious as to tell us your names, so that we can learn what famous heroes we have before us."

"Our name's Hofmann, and we are brothers."

"Your noses prove that you are brothers. You can't pride yourself the least on your name, because only a German can be called that. And haven't you learned that people of your extraction don't mean a thing in this country."

"I don't wish to deny you this point of view. He who enjoys such screwed up ideas may keep them. I'm no psychiatrist. Let's go, Tim."

He put his mule into motion, his brother following him. They did not give the six another glance but rode toward the spot where the others had previously stopped. A terrible view presented itself there. The ground was covered by many foot and hoof prints as if a fight had taken place here. A dead horse without saddle and reins lay there too, its body torn wide open, with bits and pieces of the intestines strewn about. The ugly work of the vulture Jim and Tim had seen earlier. But this was not what shocked the two. Nearby lay a human corpse; a white man, scalped, his face crisscrossed by multiple knife cuts making him unrecognizable. His threadbare woolen outfit made one guess him to have been a frontiersman. A bullet through his heart had delivered his death.

"Dear God! What has happened here?" Jim called out, jumping off his horse and stepping towards the corpse. Tim, too, dismounted to kneel by the body.

"He's already dead for several hours," he said, after he had felt the dead man's hand and chest. "He's cold. No blood's flowing any longer."

"Search his pockets. Maybe there is something which will tell us who he was."

Tim followed this request, just when the six horsemen arrived.

"Stop it!" shouted Gibson. "Quit searching the man's pockets! We can not allow the body to be robbed."

Gibson and his companions dismounted and approached. He grabbed Tim by the arm to pull him up, which the latter allowed to happen without resistance. The brothers then exchanged a look of agreement, after which Jim asked, "How did you arrive at the ingenious idea that we intended to rob the corpse?"

"Well, didn't you reach into his pocket!"

"Could that not have been for a different reason?"

"Not with you. One can see at first glance what kind of people you are."

42

"With that you are truly demonstrating an enormous shrewdness, Mister Gibson. It must be a wonderful feeling to be in possession of such an imposing knowledge of men."

"Don't get carried away with your mouth again, or we shall give you short shrift. We have caught you in flagrante delicto. Your brother had his hands in the pocket of the murdered man. That's entirely sufficient. You were in the vicinity. That's suspicious. So, who's the murderer? Be careful, or it could cost you your neck."

Angrily, Jim reached for his knife, but this time Tim was the more circumspect. Giving him a calming look he said, "By gosh, you are a stern task master. You truly act as if we should pay honor to one of the highest officials of the land."

"I'm a lawyer," Gibson responded proudly.

"Ah, a jurist then. So you are one of those highly learned individuals who snake around paragraphs. Let me express my respect, Sir."

And with ironic subservience he drew his hat.

"Mister Hofmann. Quit fooling around!" Gibson thundered. "I am truly a lawyer, and if this is more comprehensible to you being a German, an attorney at law, and know quite well how to get respect. These honorable gentlemen here elected me the leader of our expedition, which makes my word valid."

"All right, all right," Tim nodded. "We don't mind at all. And since you are a lawyer it won't be difficult for you to properly resolve this criminal event that has been perpetrated here."

"That is self-evident and I must insist that you do not leave until I have investigated everything and given my verdict. This case here screams to the heavens and can get you into the most unpleasant entanglements."

"Oh, that doesn't concern us, because we are convinced that your acumen will unravel this entanglement."

Gibson decided not to respond to this renewed disrespect but issued a command to his companions.

"Get a hold of the two mules so that the suspects don't decide to ride off after all."

This too the brothers let happen quietly. They obviously enjoyed observing how these people, lacking in the knowledge of the Far West, would deal with the issues at hand.

To find a scalped corpse was, of course, not an enjoyable event for the brothers. And although the frontiersman is rather hardened when it comes to such incidents, it was, nevertheless, horrible to see the scalped and mutilated face of the dead man. They also needed to consider their own safety since it was obvious that the man had been scalped by a Redskin, and since one could assume that a solitary Indian had not ventured this far east, an entire troop of them had to be in the vicinity. Caution was thus called for, should the ongoing investigation not result in a different explanation. But of Gibson and his companions the two brothers were not at all afraid.

Now the attorney himself checked the pockets of the dead man. They were empty just like his belt.

"He has been cleaned out already," he remarked. "That means, this was not only a murder but also a robbery, and it is our duty to find the perpetrators. The tracks indicate that it was not a single man who committed the deed. There were several. And isn't it said that a guilty conscience calls the killers back to the place of their crime? I believe that we need not go afar to find the murderers. You two Hofmanns, you are my prisoners and shall come with us to the next settlement, to Helmers Home. There, we will examine the case more closely."

With a posture to impress, Gibson had stepped in front of the brothers.

"Hand over your weapons," he declared imperiously.

"I'm happy to comply," answered Jim. "Here's my rifle. Take it!"

He aimed it at Gibson, with the cock cracking. Afraid, Gibson jumped sideways.

"Scoundrel, do you mean to resist?"

"Oh, no," Jim laughed. "There's no intention of resistance. I just beg you to take the rifle very carefully from my hands. It could discharge, which would mean the end of your lawyer's practice. Therefore be very careful."

"Mocking me too! Scoundrel, I'll have you tied up so tight, that you will cry in pain."

"It will be a pleasure. Good bondage is supposed to be the ultimate experience. And so that these other gentlemen get their hands free for this job, we shall relieve them from having to hold our mules. Polly, come here!"

"Molly, come to me," Tim called too.

Until that moment the two mules, which had been held by the reins, had remained quiet. But as soon as they heard their masters' commands, they tore themselves free to join the brothers.

"Hold on to them! Hold them!" Gibson shouted, but it was too late.

"Don't keep trying," Jim laughed. "You will not be able to hold the beasts. They will only trample you under their hooves. It isn't that easy to capture two real frontiersmen."

"If you do not obey, we will shoot you."

"Oh, no you won't! How little we fear you, you can gather from my no longer aiming at you. But I tell you too that anyone approaching us closer than three paces will get a bullet through the head. People of your kind mean nothing here! One only laughs about them. What are six lawyers here at the edge of the Llano Estacado against a single real frontiersman! Here we don't deal in words, but with powder and lead, and in that respect you are like children to us. Believe me, against our rifles you haven't got a chance with your hummingbird firearms. We don't need any lawyers from the East here. We have studied the laws of the prairie and know how to apply them effectively. We are honest people and you have been very much mistaken about us. But we will not hold that against you, because your investigative attempts have delighted us very much. You stood in front of this corpse like a bunch of schoolboys and to listen to your wisdom was highly entertaining. To solve a case like the one here is not learned at a college or university. Remember that! One acquires the necessary knowledge only at the higher school of the prairie, and in this respect every one of you must still be considered an infant. Now the two of us will tackle this case in our way and you will learn of a quite different result. Unfortunately, you are ignorant of what undisturbed tracks mean. You allowed your horses to trample around as they pleased, making it impossible to read the real tracks close by. But we will try to accomplish the task nevertheless. Let's check in a circle, Tim you go to the right, I to the left. Over there we'll meet again."

The tone in which Jim had spoken didn't fail to impress, as it was intended to do. No one said a word. Even Gibson kept quiet. Despite their scowling faces, they made no effort to prevent the brothers from leaving in opposite directions and to retrieve their animals.

Each of the two carefully studied the ground as they walked in a semicircle around the corpse. When they met, they discussed their results and returned to the group. Now they investigated the horse, the man's body, and the trampled ground. The attention they focussed on even individual pebbles seemed almost ridiculous to the others. Finally, they conversed again in soft voices. When they seemed to have come to a conclusion, Tim once more turned to the attorney

"Mister Gibson, you wanted to arrest us, simply because we happened to be around, and because I checked the dead man's pockets. With the same right we could seize you, since you too were sneaking around here and then went through the man's pockets as well. But we know you are innocent and you need not be concerned. We also know that we need not be afraid of you six. What could happen to us? Nothing really! You, however, have no idea of a frontiersman's capabilities. If we wanted to, we would bring all six cf you to Helmers Home, all tied up despite of your weapons. Your only choices would be compliance or death. Good for you, that it is not so! When we arrived, we saw you close by the corpse and had every reason to be suspicious of you, while the distrust you displayed against us was totally nonsensical. That the man had been scalped should have already told you that an Indian had killed him. This had been our first impression, which we confirmed. By the way: his death may have been just. We initially took pity on him, but we have now established that there was no reason for that. He was a bad fellow, a member of a bunch of bush runners, who make the land around here unsafe. Watch out for them!"

Tim's words were received with much surprise.

"What?" asked Gibson. "All that you deduced from the tracks?"

"That and much more."

45

"That's totally impossible."

"You can say so only because you are a greenhorn. One can read tracks as surely as one can read the lines and pages of a book. Obviously, it takes a few years of moving about in the Wild West to learn the script. That's not the case for you, but for us. The man hasn't been killed at the spot where he's lying now. Did you notice that the bullet penetrated his body and exited from his back?"

"Yes."

"Then come along to this side."

The others followed him for a few paces when he stopped and pointed to the ground, which was bare and hard as rock. There was a large spot of blood.

"What is it you see here?" Tim asked.

"This is blood," Gibson answered.

"You notice anything else?"

"No."

"Then you don't have the eyes of an investigator, although you dared to arrest us. Look at this small object here. What do you think it is?"

He picked up the object from the blood spot. It was small, almost flattened like a coin, and despite the blood adhering to it, had a pale metallic shine. Everyone looked at it until Gibson said, "That is a flattened lead bullet."

"Yes. And it is the one that brought death to this man over there. It went exactly through his heart, which means that he was killed in the blink of an eye and was incapable to drag himself over there. Therefore someone must have moved him, perhaps more than one. Wouldn't you agree?"

"The way you explain it, it appears to have been so, at least it was likely so."

"Now look at this dried up clump of grass beside this rocky and bloody area. What do you see there?"

"The grass is pressed down."

"By what and by whom?"

"Who's to know that?"

"We do! A person lay here, and since there's not the least spot of blood, one must assume, that he was not wounded. He wasn't sleeping there, for even the poorest frontiersman has a blanket that he will spread on the ground to rest. Considering also the briefness of time that has elapsed since the murder took place, this track is so indistinct that one can assume this man to have lain here only a short time. Right next to it you see a stroke in the soft sand, broad at the top and narrowing to the end. What was this stroke made with?"

"Maybe with the heel of a boot?"

"Oh, no. I shall show you right away that the man who lay here did not wear boots but moccasins. This stroke would have a very different shape had it been made by a boot. It would be more trough-like. I would swear a thousand oaths that it has been made with the butt of a rifle. And since it isn't even, but begins deep ending in a flattened sideways hook, it is certain, that it wasn't made slowly but in haste. Finally, look at the impression at the lower end of this track. What may have caused it?"

Only after Gibson had scrutinized the respective area closely he ventured to reply, "It appears as if someone had turned on his heel."

"This time you are correct. But the impression is also so clear, that one cannot imagine anything else. If you check the spot closely you must admit that this cannot have been made by a boot heel, but by footwear with a blunt end, in other words, a moccasin. You'll notice there's only one impression, not two, although the ground is soft here. What to you conclude from it?"

"I've no idea."

"Because of the haste I mentioned earlier. The person in question threw himself to the ground so quickly that the other foot remained in the air and could therefore not leave an impression in the sand. Had the man had the time to stretch out comfortably one would surely have found the impression of both feet. We can thus assume he had good reason to throw himself to the ground quickly. And what may have been the reason?"

The lawyer scratched his ear thoughtfully.

"Sir. I must admit, it to be impossible to follow your assumptions so quickly."

"That just proves you to be a greenhorn. In such situations a single minute may determine life or death. There's no time to ponder and reflect. What counts is to have a clear, quick and confident perspective. I will tell you the reason. Look around and tell me whether you notice anything conspicuous."

The six looked around, then shook their heads.

"Well, then. Have a look at this yucca here. You must notice something on it."

This particular plant, a *Yucca gloriosa*, was somewhat stunted due to the poor sandy grounds, yet it still bloomed. Several of its narrow, rigid, lance-like leaves lay on the ground. They had not dropped by themselves, but had been torn off.

"Somebody did something to this plant," Gibson said cleverly.

"All right. And who was that somebody."

"That, one cannot know."

"One can, one even must know! No one has touched this plant, rather a bullet hit it from a distance, which dropped and shredded some of the leaves and left this bullet hole in its central stalk. Don't you see that?"

Only now did the others see it.

Tim continued, "No man shoots at a yucca simply because he's bored. The bullet was meant for the one who dove to the ground behind us. If we now imagine a line extending from where the moccasin-wearing man stood to the yucca and beyond, we know from which direction the bullet was fired. Since it

47

penetrated the lower part of the stalk the muzzle of the rifle from which it was fired, must have been at some higher elevation and you ought to be able to tell me what can be concluded from this."

All looked at him embarrassed, but no one answered, causing him to continue.

"Whoever shot did not stand on the ground but sat in a saddle. That's as certain to me as a horse neighs. From all we have seen here, we must conclude, that an Indian armed with a rifle stood over there, where we looked at the spoor. A horseman coming from northwest took a shot at him, after which the Indian dropped to the ground not having been hit by the bullet. He did it in such a way, that he fell face upward. Why did he do that? Why would an unharmed man drop down in such a way after someone took a shot at him? There's only a single explanation: He wants the aspiring assassin to come closer, wants him to believe he is dead. And the horseman did approach ---"

"How do you know?" Gibson asked surprised.

"I'll show you. Come back to the place where the dead man lies. I can picture the entire event as clearly as if I had witnessed it. Whoever has a sharp mind and the ability to observe approaches such a mysterious event with ease and will soon know what transpired. But you with your legal know-how won't get very far."

He led Gibson past the corpse to a sandy place where some poorly developed bushes grew. There he pointed to a larger impression in the sand and asked how it might have come to be.

"Someone may also have lain here," was Gibson's reply.

"Your guess is correct. But who might it have been?"

"By chance, the dead man before he was killed?"

"No. He was shot right through the heart and couldn't move any more. It was impossible for him to get here. Besides, had it been him, there would have to be a puddle of blood here."

"Then it must have been the Indian again who dropped to the ground over there."

"Not that one either. He had no reason to repeat his maneuver of deception. Also we have already learned that he was not hurt, while the man who lay here was seriously wounded. We are therefore dealing with a third person."

"Goodness," Gibson said, "to you this sand is truly like an open book. I couldn't read a single line."

His companions' expressions also displayed the greatest astonishment. Until now Jim had left the explanations to his brother. Now he continued the lecture.

"There's no need to open eyes and mouths widely, gentlemen. What's such wonderment to you, any good frontiersman can do. Whoever cannot swiftly learn how to read tracks, is best advised to quickly leave the West, for he won't stay alive for long. All famous hunters and frontiersmen owe their success not only to their boldness, cunning and endurance, but also to their ability to read every footprint like a letter that the originator had left for them, either on purpose or inadvertently. Whoever has no comprehension of such letters will soon get a bullet through his head or a knife stab into his heart and rot at a place where it's unlikely a memorial will be erected for him. My brother told you that there's no blood pooled here, which is correct. Sure, there's no big puddle, but some blood is here nevertheless. Drops of blood have caused these tiny dark spots in the sand. Whoever lay here was wounded, even seriously, for one can see from these traces that he writhed in pain. Just look at the lower twigs of the bush and the sand beside the impression. The poor devil tore off these branches and clawed the sand with his fingers. Can you possibly tell me where on his body he had been wounded?"

"To tell this, one would have to be almost all-knowing."

"Oh, no. A wound at the head or the upper torso causes more blood to flow than is visible here. The injury was at his belly, which also explains the pain he experienced. Now have a look how the branches have been torn and trampled from here all the way over to there where the unhurt Indian lay. And have a look at this inconspicuous item lying here on the ground, which hasn't yet been noticed by you. Can you possibly tell me what it is?"

He picked up a bit of leather. Once it must have been tanned more brightly, but time had darkened it. Numerous cuts hat separated it into narrow strips hanging together. The six looked at it closely, but then shook their heads.

"This is," Jim explained, "a torn-off piece of fringed leggings, Indian work. Whoever lay here was also an Indian. His leggings had been tanned with the brains of an elk. He clawed his leggings and in the process tore off this small piece. A shot in the belly isn't the height of pleasure, rest assured. If you get a bullet in your intestines, you'll twist like a worm. I wouldn't be surprised if this Indian has already gone to the Eternal Hunting Grounds. It's unlikely that he could endure the continuation of his ride for long, particularly, since the two of them had to share a horse."

"He rode off?' Gibson asked. "And two sharing a horse?"

"Yes, Mister. It's certain. Now, come along in the direction from which these people came."

He started walking towards the northwest. The others followed, curious about what he was still going to tell them. He came to the circle he had walked off earlier. There he stopped to say, "You are presently getting a lesson in the reading of tracks. Should you be able to apply some of these lessons in the future, you won't be called greenhorns for long, provided, of course, that you have the talent to become frontiersmen. To really explain to you all the tracks here in greater detail I could go on at length, but for that I haven't got the time. I'll have to hurry, because we are faced with a very dangerous gang of murderers and robbers. At the same time we must save the two Indians who are being pursued by the murderers. I will make this as quick as possible. The two Indians, the unhurt and the wounded one, passed by where we stand here. The latter hadn't been injured where he lay, but had already been shot earlier. From the hoof prints I conclude that the two Indians rode their horses side by side, so close that the unhurt Indian could lead the reins of the injured man's horse. The hurt man needed his hands to hold himself in the saddle or to hold them against his belly."

Stepping back a few paces and pointing to the ground, he continued.

"That we are truly dealing with Indians is shown by the hoof prints which show their horses' hooves to be unshod. And here you can see that the horse carrying the hurt man did make a sideways leap. That's where it was hit in the flank by a bullet from behind. It was able to walk on for a little, only to collapse at the spot where we found it. At that time the injured Indian was tossed sideways into the bushes at the spot we just investigated."

He now walked to the right, pointed again to the ground, and continued his explanation.

"Here is the spoor of a single horseman, the one who shot the horse and then at the uninjured Indian. His horse was shod. He was a White. He shot at the horse before arriving here which I could prove to you if I had the time. But he did shoot at the uninjured Indian from exactly this spot where we now stand ..."

"But you can't say that with such certainty," Gibson interrupted.

"Oh, I could swear on it. Look ahead and you will notice that our present position, the place where the Indian threw himself to the ground, and the yucca that was hit by a bullet are all in a straight line. There's no doubt whatsoever. Let's continue. Only eight or ten paces from here you see other tracks. These were five Whites who stopped at the place that has been trampled. Now, please, follow me back and we shall soon be finished."

He led them for a short distance past the place of carnage to draw their attention to three tracks, one of which led sideways. Of the latter he said, "This track was produced by a single horse belonging to a White. The hoof prints are deep; the horse was in a gallop. But a galloping horse, which was at rest only twenty paces away, has surely shied. Something spooked it and caused it to break out. Would we follow its tracks, we would soon find it rider-less and munching on some grasses. Here, to the left, you see the other track. It shows soft imprints and was caused by an unshod animal. But since its imprints are deeper than the previously mentioned Indian horse tracks, despite its slow pace, we can assume that this horse is now carrying a heavier load. The unhurt Indian sat in the saddle with his injured companion sitting in front of him. Then you can see beside this single spoor the tracks of the five Whites. They are paralleling it, so as not to obscure it. Now I'm done. I could have been much more explicit and could have pointed out other things but, as I said, there's no more time for that. Now summarize what you've heard and tell me the sequence of events here."

"I think we better leave that to you, Mister," Gibson responded, now much subdued.

"Well then," Jim said, "I've been clear enough that you ought to understand now what transpired. But I hope you'll admit that it's quite important to be able to read tracks properly. Our investigation has shown that six Whites met two Indians somewhere northeast from here and started a quarrel in which one of the Indians was shot in the belly. The Indians fled with the Whites in hot pursuit. The Indians' horses were superior to the Whites' and gained a substantial lead. Look at the horse over there. It is of best Mexican parentage and may even have Andalusian ancestry. The owner's totem has been incised on the left side of its neck. The wounded Indian wasn't an ordinary warrior, for only chiefs and respected members of a war council have totems. Recall also that the enemy's bullet hit this animal in its front flank. Only a single horse of the Whites was fast enough to catch up with the Indians. This lone White man rode ahead of the group and dared this, because the unhurt Indian had to hold onto his wounded comrade and could therefore do little if anything against him. The two poor devils could find only salvation by getting away. Of course, had I been in the position of the uninjured Indian, I would have jumped off my mount and waited to shoot the White from his horse. There may have been a reason why he did not do that, but it is unknown to me. One can therefore guess that he was still young and inexperienced. His concern for the other may have confused him. Yet he was nevertheless cunning and daring, as I'll tell you momentarily. The White carried a double-barreled rifle. He caught up with the Indians and was able to shoot one bullet at one of the horses. It leaped, ran on a bit, somersaulted, catapulting its rider into the bushes, then dropped where we found it. The other Indian stopped at once and jumped off to protect his companion. The White then shot at him too, but since his horse was still in full gallop, his aim was poor and the bullet hit the yucca instead of the Indian. The latter could now have taken a shot at the White, but he must have been shaking from excitement and anger. His life now hung on the precision of his shot. That's why he did not shoot, dropped as if hit, but held on to his rifle. In the process he marked the sand with the butt of his firearm. He now waited for the White to shoot him at close range. The White jumped from the saddle and first ran to the injured Indian who played dead. He then walked across to the other, who jumped up suddenly, tossed the White to the ground, and shot him through the heart. He had his muzzle so close to the White's chest, so that the wool of his shirt was singed and the bullet exited from his back to become flattened on a rock. This shot caused the White's horse to shy and gallop off towards the right as we saw earlier. The Redskin dragged the corpse of his slain enemy over to his injured companion to show that he had avenged him. Then he scalped him. But that's when he also noticed the approach of the other five foes. He had to get away. He lifted his comrade onto their single horse, mounted and took off. When the five arrived and found their dead companion they dismounted to check on him. They must have discussed the situation. Being bandits they must have figured that someone, maybe from Helmers Home, would recognize the dead man. Found and identified he would have given away their presence which, I'm sure, they wanted to keep secret. This must have given them the thought to mutilate his face to make recognition impossible. And you saw, gentlemen, they executed this in a most dastardly fashion. They did not linger, but resumed the pursuit of the Indians who, by now, had gained a good lead. Before they left, they took all the dead man's possessions. Since the Indian had been an important warrior they even took the saddle and reins from his horse as valuable booty. Then they followed the Reds' tracks, paralleling them, as we saw. We must expect that, despite their horses' slowness, they will catch up with the Indians, since its doubled load slows the Indians' horse down. When you arrived here, Mister Gibson, a vulture was already feeding on the horse's carcass. You drove it away with your shot, which we heard and attracted us. That's how I picture the events, which took place here. I do not think that my assumptions are much different from what really happened, and it would please me to hear your confirmation."

"Well. Since you delight in it so much, I do not wish to take anything away," Gibson retorted. "It seems that you have explained the events that took place here in proper order. I suppose your eyes are as sharp as your mind."

"What concerns my head, I must be content with what I've got, since I can't trade it in," Jim responded. "I hope you realize now, that it was pure nonsense wanting to arrest us. Let me ask you now what you intend to do about this case?"

"Nothing at all. It isn't our concern. It's only Indians we are dealing with here."

"Only Indians!" Jim answered. "Only! Are Indians not human beings then?"

"I don't dispute them to be human beings, but so much lower than us, that it would be insulting to make any comparison."

Jim made a disparaging move with a hand. Tim's big nose twitched up and down, then to the left and right, almost like an independent creature angered by something. He stroked it softly with an index finger as if trying to calm it, then said with forced friendliness, "If that's the case, Mister, then you won't be insulted if we don't compare them with you. These two Redskins acted like heroes, at least the one we think to be the younger of them. It's utterly impossible to compare greenhorns like you with those two. They rank high, much higher than you do. In God's name, don't think yourself better people than them. The Whites came to this country to dispossess the actual owners, the Indians. Rivers of blood and brandy were spilled to commit this murder of nations. Violence, cunning, fraud, and breach of word have worked continuously to decimate the inhabitants of the prairies. They were chased from place to place, from station to station, from territory to territory. No sooner had they been assigned a new territory where they were to live in peace, than another reason was found to chase them away again. They were sold barite as flour, coal dust as powder, and children's rifles as bear killers. When they objected, they were called renegades and gunned down en masse. These poor souls had but two choices and that was to accept their oppression, or to fight their oppressors' destructive avarice onto their last breath. If they resign themselves to their fate, you call them dull-witted and indolent. If they defend themselves, you call them robbers and murderers, to be exterminated without mercy and charity. This is the same as with wild animals. One eats the other and the stronger says: 'I am right!' But I tell you, gentlemen, that I have found men among these persecuted and disdained, worth ten times more than all six of you and even a hundred dozen of your kind. You yourself have made the Redskins into what they are today; everything you object to in them is on your very own conscience. Don't you argue against them, or my anger may explode against you!"

He had talked himself into a holy wrath and with his last words had aimed his rifle at Gibson as if wanting to shoot him. The latter quickly jumped aside and shouted in fear, "Stop, Sir! Do you want to murder me?"

"No, not yet. But if you again say that Indians are to be despised, it's very likely that my rifle will discharge on its own without having first requested my permission. Should you keep up with such insolent talk you can count on anything but my friendship."

"Concerning that, I haven't asked for it yet," Gibson replied defiantly. "We don't need you. We are free men who know very well what is good for us."

"It doesn't look like that to me. You say, for instance, that it isn't necessary to trouble yourselves any further with what happened here. If you think so, it could very well be, that you'll bite a blade of grass before you die."

"Ah, do you think we need to be afraid of other people?"

"Yes. That's what I mean. You are yet much too green for the West."

"Listen, we need not suffer such insults. We came here from New Orleans without trouble and shall also go further without finding any."

"From New Orleans to here," Jim laughed. "Is that to be a significant accomplishment? Any twelve-year old boy can do that. But I'm telling you that from here on it becomes dangerous. We are here at the border where all kinds of people do as they please, people who care very much about the property of others but nothing about their lives. And beyond the Llano lie the hunting grounds of the Comanche and Apache, which you need to be even more concerned about, since they are continuously feuding with each other and just recently dug up their tomahawks for the warpath. Whoever ventures recklessly between such millstones is easily crushed. Here, at this location White bandits and Red warriors did meet. This must concern us. Disregarding the Whites for a moment, we must ask ourselves what the Indians wanted here. If two Redskins venture this far from of their territory one can say, that in nine out of ten cases, they are scouts whose task is to reconnoiter the land for a raid. I'm not quite as much at ease as you are. I neither know the purpose nor the destination of your ride, but we intend to cross the Llano which requires one to keep his eyes open. Otherwise it may happen, that he who closes his eyes in the evening wakes up a sad corpse in the morning."

"Well, concerning our destination, we also want to cross the Llano."

"And where to?"

"We are headed for Arizona."

"In any case, you've never been there before?"

"No."

"Listen. Don't take it crosswise. But this is such carelessness, as I've not experienced before. You seem to see the Llano as a most beautiful area one can just venture across."

"Oh, no! We're not that stupid! We know its dangers very well."

"How so?"

"We heard and read about it."

"So. Hmm. Heard and read about it. That's just as if someone heard and read that arsenic is poisonous and then thinks he can swallow a whole pound of it without killing himself. Didn't you at least think to hire a guide who's experienced with the Llano and its dangers?"

Jim meant well with the six, nevertheless, Gibson shouted angrily, "Don't lecture us like schoolboys. We are men. Understood! And we do have a guide."

"Oh, really? Where is he?"

"He rode ahead."

"That's a peculiar way to guide someone. Where's this man waiting for you?"

"At Helmers Home."

"Well. If that's the case it may be all right. You'll find Helmers Home easily. And if you care you can come along with us, since we also want to get there. May we ask who your guide is?"

"He is a famous frontiersman we were told and he's crossed the Llano several times already. He didn't give us his actual name, but he's usually called Juggle-Fred."

"Good fortune! Juggle-Fred!" Jim called out. "Is it true, Sir?"

"Certainly. Do you know him?"

"Not personally, but we've heard much of him and often."

"What kind of man is he?"

"He's a very able fellow, whose guidance you can trust. I'm looking forward to finally meeting him face to face. In any case, that means we'll ride together, since we too want to get to Arizona."

"You too? What for?"

"It's a private matter," Jim answered cautiously.

"Is that private matter by chance related to diamonds that have been found there?"

"Maybe."

"Then we aren't a match."

"Why not?"

"Because we are traveling over there for the same purpose, which makes you competitors."

"Then you don't want anything to do with us?"

"Right on!"

He said this with such determination, all the while looking with a certain hostility at the brothers, that Jim laughed aloud and said, "That's funny! You are jealous of us. That's just more proof of how green you are out west here. Do you expect diamonds to lie around on the ground in Arizona such that there's nothing to do but to bend down to pick'm up? Even gold prospectors must join forces to be successful, and the diamond chaps need to do that even more so. An individual will go under."

"We are six and have enough money on us not to come to ruin."

"Listen. Don't tell that to anyone. We are honest people you need not fear. Some others, though, would take care that you'd not have to carry all that money much further. But should you feel it to be the most pleasant experience to return with empty pockets, in Gods name, just go on and keep telling everybody. It's all right by me. And that you mind our company is fine by me too. We leave it to you, whether you want to accompany us to Helmers Home. You can't reach this place before nightfall anyway and will have to camp in the open tonight. And it's better to do so in the company of people with experience of the West."

"When will you leave here?"

"Immediately, of course."

"Let me ask my companions."

"That's actually an insult, no matter whether from distrust or business jealousy. But hold your secret conference; we will not bother you. Do as you wish."

He walked slowly to his mule and mounted up. Tim did likewise; then both rode off following the tracks leading west.

The others stayed back for a few minutes to discuss their options then followed the two. When they had caught up Jim turned to ask, "Well, what did you decide?"

"We will join you to Helmers Home, but only that far."

"That's very nice of you. It's the height of feeling to ride with such condescending folks."

Jim turned and from now on the brothers acted as if no one was following them. They nudged their mules to a faster pace, and in true frontiersmen style hung loosely in their saddles bent forward as if sleepy and looking like poor riders. Their six followers, though, sat upright in their saddles as if they were riding show horses.

"Look at those two fellows," Gibson said to his companions. "It's obvious they don't know how to ride. And they claim to be frontiersmen. I can't believe it."

"I can't either," another agreed. "Whoever hangs in the saddle like that shouldn't tell me he's experienced in matters of the West. The story they told from their reading of the tracks must have been humbug. Just look at their faces. Those noses! I have never before seen such repulsive physiognomies. And with all that we are to trust them? Not a minute! And then, to take them along to Arizona! We would be stupid. The fellow really straightened up when I mentioned our money. He presented himself so utterly honest, most likely only because we are six and they are but two. Let's be careful while we sleep tonight, so that they don't ride off early with our money, leaving our corpses behind. Their entire appearance screams that they would refrain from nothing."

"It may be better if we don't even ride with them to Helmers Home. Why should we expose ourselves to danger, if we don't need to?"

"That's right. When it gets dark we will fall back. Let's post guards during the night so that we won't be attacked. It was impudent of them to call us 'green'. To maintain our honor we must show them, that we'll have no further dealings with them."

In the meantime the earlier mentioned hills had come closer. The ground became rocky and Jim and Tim leaned forward ever more to follow the now less distinct tracks. Suddenly Jim stopped his horse, pointed forward with his hand and said, "Look, old Tim. What kind of creatures are those standing over there?"

Tim shaded his eyes with a hand, although the sun could no longer blind him since it had sunk below the western horizon. After he had extensively eyed the indicated location for a while he answered, "These are two well-known types of creatures, five horses and one man, the former probably being worth more than the latter."

"Yes, sure. Five horses, to which also five riders belong. And since there's only one visible, I wonder where the other four are hiding."

"I figure they aren't far away. If we ride on a bit, we may get to see them. From here the distance is still too far to clearly make out individual people."

"All right, then let's get on a bit farther," getting his mule to move he added, "that there are five horses is highly suspicious. Don't you think so too?"

"Of course. If my eyes don't deceive me, it's the five villains pursuing the Indians. We are facing the Whites of whom one has been killed. And now it appears to me, as if I see something human crawling around over there. Watch those moving points."

What he had called points, were four men who walked in a straight line at equal intervals in a certain direction.

"These are the other four whose horses stand over there," Jim suggested. "They are on rocky ground looking for the Indians' tracks, which they must have lost. From the lead they had on us, this search must have engaged them for some time already. That's a sure sign, that they are not good trackers. Now they have seen us. Look! They are running back to their horses. I would be happy if the Indians escaped and will be glad to contribute anything possible to that!"

"And how are we going to interact with them?"

"Hmm. They are bandits, that's for sure. For our own safety, we'll have to have a closer look at them. But I don't think it will be wise to inquire too much into their affairs. It will be best if we don't show at all what we think of them. As long as they don't become hostile, we too can put on peaceful faces. Let's continue then. They are waiting for us."

The six 'Diamond Boys' had now also spotted the group ahead, which caused them to catch up with the brothers, an indication that they felt safer in their company. The five strangers now stood by their horses, their rifles at the ready. When the brothers had approached within about sixty paces one of them shouted in an imperious tone, "Stop there, or we'll shoot!"

But Jim and Tim continued nevertheless. The other six 'Diamond Boys' stopped obediently.

"Hold it!" the man repeated. "Another step and you'll get our bullets."

"Nonsense!" Jim laughed. "Are you afraid of two peaceful travelers? Keep your bullets. We too have got some in our barrels."

The five didn't shoot, perhaps because they were truly unconcerned and had only wanted to impress the newcomers, moreover, also because the quiet demeanor of the brothers had impressed them. They let both approach, but didn't lower their rifles. The one who had issued the command was a broad-shouldered stocky fellow. A thick black beard covered his face obscuring his lips. But from his pronunciation one could figure he had a harelip. When the Snuffles now stopped in front of him, he told them angrily, "Don't you know the rule and custom here in the West, that when you are asked to stop, you do so. Understood! You can thank our indulgence that you are still alive."

"Oh, don't brag so much, man!" Jim responded. "Who do you have to thank, that you too are still alive? We also have guns. We know the rules of the West very well. One of them says: 'Shoot anyone who aims a rifle at you.' You raised your firearms against us, but we didn't respond by the rule, since we saw at once, that you are not the kind of people one can expect a sure shot from. Your bullets would have missed us by a mile."

"By the devil, there you are mightily mistaken. We shoot a fly's head off over a hundred paces, let me tell you. What's your business around here?"

"Can't you imagine it? We want to see the next solar eclipse, which is best viewed from here."

57

The bearded one wasn't sure how to take this so earnestly presented statement. With a very doubtful face he asked, "And when is that to be?"

"Past midnight and five minutes, eleven seconds. I tell you, such an eclipse at midnight is the best one can see."

"Fellow, quit fooling around!" the other flew out. "We'll get you to quit this nonsense quickly. We are not here to have our noses tweaked. Yours are much better suited for that. Watch out, that we will not tweak yours, but a bit differently!"

"You just go ahead," Jim laughed. "We don't mind. But let yourself be warned: Our noses are charged. At the least touch they discharge and are feared far and wide for this. Or haven't you heard yet of the two Snuffles, Sir?"

"Snuffles? You are the two Snuffles?" He called. "By the devil! Yes, we've heard much about you. Jim and Tim, Tim and Jim. They are supposed to be a pair of devilishly droll fellows I've always wanted to meet. I'm mighty pleased to see my wish fulfilled. Your noses are said to jump like monkeys. I hope you will entertain us with a comical show. We will make a very attentive audience. We pay well. Five cents from each."

"Not a bad offer. We couldn't expect a better take from this circus here. But we only perform during a solar eclipse. You'll just have to wait till midnight. But if you can't be patient, just go ahead and do some somersaults yourselves. You look like you've got the talent for it, for you look, as if you had only recently escaped from a monkey cage."

"Don't you dare any more, man! We love to have some fun, but won't lend ourselves to it."

Oh, that means you are some of the finer baboons. Too bad I didn't notice that, and I hope you will excuse my mistake. May I inquire what name your honorable parents have bestowed on you?"

These words were spoken with such convincing cordiality, that the bearded one refrained from answering rudely once more.

"My name's Stewart. Let's leave the names of my companions at the moment. You won't be able to remember them anyway, since your heads appear to be in such a sorry state. Where are you coming from?"

"From somewhere behind us."

"And where are you headed?"

"To somewhere ahead of us."

"These are very intelligent answers. I wasn't much mistaken regarding your poor brains. It looks like you are headed for Helmers Home?"

"Right you are. And since it doesn't come to us, we need to ride to it. You care to come along?"

"No, thank you. It would be very incautious of us to ride with you, since stupidity is said to be contagious."

58

"It's only contagious to those who are already disposed towards it which, in your case, I have no doubt whatsoever. We noticed from afar that you examined the ground very closely. What were you looking for? Hundred dollar bills, by chance?"

"Not that. We were looking for asses and have now found two giant ones in you two, because only an ass can ask such a question. Haven't you seen the tracks in front of your noses?"

"Those tracks are of no concern to us. Only people riding towards Helmers Home could have left these tracks. We too will find the place, without the tracks."

"Did you come by the corpse back there?"

"Yes."

"What did you think of it?"

"That it's a dead corpse. And what's dead doesn't matter to us. If others break their necks, let them. It's no concern of ours."

Stewart gave Jim and Tim a long examining look. He didn't quite trust the indifference that was being displayed. The Snuffles were known as smart frontiersmen. Could they really have passed the scene back there without examining the body and becoming suspicious? But when he didn't find the least ill disposition in their open, honest faces, he said, "We too saw the man and his horse. It would have been a sorry loss to let the saddle and the reins rot out there, which is why we took them along. I don't think you would consider that theft?"

"Wouldn't think of it. Had we come earlier, we would have done the same."

"Right. Then we followed the tracks, although they didn't lead in the direction we were headed. We lost the trail here and haven't been able to find it again."

"I'm surprised. Wouldn't a frontiersman find lost tracks again easily?"

"Sure, that's true. If the rocky area were smaller one could ride around it to pick up the track on the other side where there's soil again. But from here the rock extends for hours to the south, north, and west. Checking it would take hours and for that we haven't got the time with nightfall so close. We decided to quit our examination and to return to our original heading."

"And where is that?"

"We are on the way to Fort Chadburne."

"That's at the edge of the Llano. Might you want to cross it?"

"Yes, we are on the way to El Paso and on to Arizona."

"To get diamonds?"

"Oh, no! That fever won't catch us. We are honest and modest farmers and have relatives over there that obtained some good land for us. We will cultivate it. Others may look for diamonds. A farm bears slower, but more assured fruit."

"Each to his own. Since you are just farmers, I'm not surprised that you won't find the tracks any more. A good scout wouldn't take long to find them again."

"Well, you are known as scouts. Have a look. I'm curious, if you can pick them up again."

He had said this with a sneer, but Jim responded quietly, "We can do that easily, although we aren't interested in the matter. We just want to prove to you, that we find what we are looking for."

He dismounted with Tim following. Both now walked the area in a wide circle. A soft whistle called the mules to follow them like dogs. The brothers did not trust this group at all to leave their animals behind. The Diamond Boys too had come closer after the first words had been exchanged and had followed the conversation in silence. After the Snuffles had left, Stewart now asked them, "You arrived with these two noses but don't seem to belong together. You care to give us an explanation?"

"Why not," Gibson responded. "We met with them at the corpse, but their manners did not contribute to becoming friends with them."

"You did right with that. The Snuffles don't have a good name. I just didn't want to tell them that to their face. We have been warned of them. They are supposed to be the feeders for the gangs who attack travelers in the Llano. Only recently four more families have been killed and robbed and that quite close to here. That the Snuffles are hanging about makes it likely that they were involved in the crime and are now looking for new victims. But they aren't going to get us."

"I thought so too and didn't trust them from the very first moment. They tried to entice us to ride with them."

"Where to?"

"First to Helmers Home and then through the Llano all the way to Arizona."

"Don't do it, Sir! You won't make it across. Are you headed to Arizona for diamonds?"

"We want to buy some, but not prospect for them."

Stewart gave his pals a quick meaningful look, then remarked indifferently, "You won't do any big business, Sir. A diamond buyer needs money, big money."

"Obviously, we've got that."

"But the connection between Frisco and Arizona is unreliable. I suppose you will have your moneys sent to you from Frisco? Then it could easily happen, that you wouldn't have it at your disposal when you need it most urgently. We too carry substantial sums to pay for our land, but instead of having it transferred from Frisco, we rather brought it along in cash. That's safer."

"Well. You aren't the only smart ones. We too carry it with us."

60

"That's smart. But one needs to hide it well. You never know what might happen. We have sewn it into our clothing. Show me the Llano man who will find it. As I've said, I don't trust these Snuffles. They know where we are headed and will tell their good companions to lie in wait for us. But we will be smarter than them and not ride to Fort Chadburne, but take a different route. I advise you to do the same and to entrust yourselves to an experienced guide."

"That we have done already. He is expecting us at Helmers Home."

"Who is it?"

"He's called Juggle-Fred."

"Juggle-Fred?" Stewart called with well-played shock. "Are you mad, Sir?"

"Why mad?"

"Because this character is a well-known rascal. His name should tell you this already. He is into all kinds of deceitful tricks and is known far and wide as a rotten gambler. I would even swear that he's in cahoots with the Snuffles."

"But they claim to have never met him."

"And you believe that? Sir, don't take this crosswise, but this is no sign of great prudence. It's obvious that they would deny having met him. But he's waiting at Helmers Home and they, too, are headed there. Isn't it obvious that's where they intend to meet. After that you will ride off with them, then, in the Llano Estacado they'll cut your throats. Your affairs are none of my business, but at least I've done my duty to warn you."

Stewart said this with such a guileless and caring mean, that Gibson let himself be mislead and, shaking his head, said, "That's not pleasant to hear. We are grateful for your warning and don't doubt that it is justified. But that means, that we are now without a guide. Where do we find another trustworthy one?"

"That's certainly bad. And I don't understand why you let yourselves be called to Helmers Home. What kind of person puts his farm so close to the dangerous Llano Estacado. That he's done so, should have given you the thought that he has contact with the bandits who make the Llano unsafe. He has a store and takes in their loot for which they trade everything they need. Isn't that clear? No one would get me to this place, which is called so tenderheartedly and alluringly by the name 'Helmers Home'. Behind this pretty guise hide the faces of a gang of bandits."

"My goodness. We haven't looked at it this way yet. We have no other choice but to return to look for another guide. We no longer want anything to do with this Juggle-Fred. But tell me: Do you have a guide?"

"We don't need one, since two of my companions know the Llano pretty well. We can rely on them."

"Well. Could we perhaps ride with you then?"

"That's possible, but let me make you aware, that this is careless of you, since you don't know us."

"Oh, one can see at a glance that you mean well, even if the Snuffles wanted to make us believe you are bandits."

"Did they really?"

"Yes."

"For what reason?"

"They investigated the place where the corpse lay very closely, and said you were pursuing two Indians. You had supposedly killed one of them. The other should then have killed your companion, whose face you made unrecognizable."

"By the devil. They really said that?" Stewart asked perplexed. "And they told me, that they didn't care a penny about the body. That proves to you that you can't trust these liars. No honest men act with such deceit. We just happened to come by the place. That we took the saddle and fetter, no one can hold against us. It's the right of the prairie. Then you saw us checking the tracks here, which one does for safety reasons. Would we do this, if we were murderers?"

"No, not really. You don't need to defend yourself. We can see that you are honest people and trust you completely. Tell us then, whether we may ride with you?"

"Hmm," Stewart mumbled thoughtfully shrugging his shoulders. "I want to be truthful. We know you just as little as you do us. Here in the West it's never advisable to get acquainted that quickly without checking each other out. While we are glad you trust us, I think it's better, if we travel separately after all. From this you can see too that we are no bandits as the Snuffles called us. Were we truly such rascals, we would welcome you to accompany us to get your money. But your predicament is nevertheless of concern to me. You could easily meet up with some crooks once more. So let me give you some good advice. We met a large group of immigrants who want to cross the Llano to buy land on the other side. They are mostly Germans from Bohemia and Hesse. We parted yesterday, and know that they were going to camp not very far from here. Their guide is to meet them there tomorrow morning. He's the most famous and reliable expert on the Llano. He's also a modest and pious man by the name of Tobias Praisegod Burton. Join this group and you will be in the best of hands. This group is made up of so many well-armed men, that no one will think of attacking them."

"Do you think so? But how do we find these people?"

"Easy. If you ride straight south from here and push your horses a bit, you'll see a single hillock after about half an hour. From this hill runs a small brook to ooze away in the sand of the small plain to the east. You'll find the group camped by this brook. Even if it will be dark by then, you can't miss them because their campfires should be visible from a good distance. If you follow this advice you will be in good hands."

"Thank you, Sir! You free us from a serious predicament. We shall take off right away to join these Germans. Germans are foolish but honest. Let's take off right away."

"What shall I tell the Snuffles when they ask where you left to?"

"Tell them what you wish, whatever comes to your mind."

"But be aware that you need to mislead them about the direction you are heading now. If you don't they will follow you and you'll end up in their hands after all. To deceive them, ride back for a distance until they can't see you any more, only then turn south. If they ask me why you turned back, I'll find some satisfactory answer."

That done, the two parties separated as if they had been friends all along.

The Diamond Boys retraced the path they had arrived on without giving the Snuffles another look. Once they were out of earshot Stewart, laughing scornfully said to his companions, "They really fell for my instructions. That's another good catch. To buy diamonds. That takes at least fifty thousand dollars. A nice little sum for our pockets. And what do you think about these two Snuffles?"

"Rascals," one of them responded.

"Yes. What innocent faces they made. They really tried to convince us, that they couldn't count to three and yet found out everything. That means they are clever fellows. They read the entire event most clearly from the tracks. They even know that we were dealing with two Indians, and that we made the face of our comrade unrecognizable. Their shrewdness is quite dangerous to us. We need to take care of them."

"But how, when and where? There's no time for it. We need to get on to move the stakes to mislead the caravan."

"Hmm. Yes. We don't have much time. If we let them both get away now, we'll have missed the best opportunity. At Helmers Home they will meet this Juggle-Fred and perhaps the always-out-of-reach Bloody-Fox, our greatest enemy. We've worked too hard for that roast. Those four are liable to snatch it from our fire."

"Let's just gun them down."

"That would be the best, but ---," he mumbled thoughtfully.

"But what," the other asked. "In my opinion we couldn't do any better. We are five and they are only two. They will be unable to defend themselves and will fall by our bullets before they have time to aim their poor guns at us."

"You think so? Well, have a look at them and go ahead: Take a shot. I'd like to see you do it."

He pointed to the brothers who still seemed very much engaged looking for the tracks. In no way did they seem to be concerned about the group so potentially dangerous to them. They also appeared not to have paid the least attention to the departure of the Diamond Boys.

"By the devil!" the bandit cursed. "You are right. I see only now how cleverly these characters move so that they can't be hit by us."

"Yes. With every step they keep their animals between them and us so that we would hit only the beasts and not them. That's how they have circled around. And don't you see how they keep their right hands on the triggers of their rifles while their left hands hold the guns at the ready? If one of us were to fire, he would immediately be killed by a shot from them. They are devilishly smart fellows and their mules, too, have a hundred Satans in their bellies. It looks as if the animals know that they have to protect their masters. They keep pace with them and don't let us out of their malicious eyes."

It was exactly as the bandit said. They were unable to shoot. And now that the two Snuffles had finished their circular investigation, they continued to hold their guns ready for a quick shot as they approached slowly. The mules followed them as if they had been trained to do so, which certainly was the case.

"What do I see? The Boys are gone," Jim said in feigned surprise, as if noticing this only now.

"A while ago. You can still see them back there."

"Where to?"

"Back where they came from, as you can see."

"That I do. But didn't they want to come with us to Helmers Home? Why do they turn back?"

"Because they are stupid fellows. Just think of it, they've lost their money. Can you imagine such carelessness?"

"Oh, they carried money?"

"One of them kept the bills in a satchel in his saddle bag. While we waited here he noticed that a seam in the saddlebag had split and the satchel had dropped out. He had quite a scare. They turned back at once without talking with you. When they rode off they asked us to tell you, that they would meet with you again at Helmers Home tomorrow evening or at the latest by noon the day after and then too, they would leave right away with Juggle-Fred."

"That's fine by me. I'm not going to worry my head off about the real reason."

"You think they might have lied to us?"

"Not them to you, but you to us. I'm not inclined to believe in the lost satchel. Our noses are big enough to smell something rotten. I'm convinced they will take a very different direction once they are out of eyesight."

"Mister, you are once more becoming insulting."

"Oh, no. I'm just telling you my thoughts and thoughts in isolation are never insulting. But let me give you some good advice, Mister Stewart: When you again give someone instructions in the future of which others are not to know, don't wave your arms so very much, for such gestures are just as easily understood as words."

"Did I really gesticulate? I'm not aware of it."

"Very much so. You threw your arms around in the air so that a few times, I was afraid they would come off."

"It can't have been that bad. And it was all right for you to observe my gesticulations. What we talked about, anyone could hear. It wasn't a secret. We talked about the tracks we lost. Really!"

"And so you think one could pick them up again south of here."

"South of here? How do you arrive at that conclusion?"

"Because of your wind-milling arms. With your left you pointed south and with your right you made a move like showing the outline of a mountain. Then you moved your left straight away from it as if indicating a plain. After this you pointed east, then south. It was all so obvious, that I'm going to tell you the entire story."

"Well. Go ahead."

"With pleasure. The Boys returned east and now, that I can't see them any longer turn towards noon. Down there is a mountain, to its left a plain towards which the Boys are to ride. Since they don't know their way around here and with darkness falling soon, this plain cannot be far from here. I know of such a small sandy plain down there. A small brook meanders down from the hill to disappear a bit later in the sand. It would take about forty five minutes to get there from here and I think I'll enjoy camping there tonight."

Speaking these words he looked sharply at Stewart, who could not quite control himself. One could see that he became frightened.

"Do as you wish, Mister, but don't tell us any stories," he called out roughly. I don't care where you are going to sleep. You act as if you had eaten wisdom in spoonfuls. Tell us rather, whether you have found the tracks."

"Certainly!"

"Where?"

"Come along. I'll show you. There's still light enough to see them."

"Go ahead then."

"I'll do that. But my brother Tim will follow you."

"Why's that?"

"To make sure that your rifles don't get any wrong ideas. So, watch over your rifles! If one of them would feel like going off, Tim would immediately send its owner a bullet."

"Mister, you are really getting too impertinent!"

"Oh, no. I only mean well by warning you. Come along then."

Jim walked ahead in the direction from which the tracks had originated. Tim followed behind, his rifle at the ready and watching the five sharply. A bit later Jim stopped, pointed to the ground and said, "Mister Stewart, what is this?"

The latter bent down and inspected the spot, then answered, "A pebble lay on the rocky ground and was crushed by a hoof."

"Can a pebble be crushed to flour like this by a shod hoof?"

"No, this horse must not have been shod."

"Then it must have been an Indian's horse. Come along some more."

Walking on they came across more crushed little rocks.

"This is the track, of course," Jim said. "The line between the crushed pebbles points west. That's where the Indians are headed."

"Indians? How can you know they were Indians?" Stewart asked in an impertinent tone.

"Pshaw!" Jim responded. "The silly Diamond Boys have surely told you, that I've seen through you entirely. We need not play games any longer. You are Llano vultures, while we are honest hunters you can neither fool nor hurt. How you got to get the Boys to trust you I'm not going to ask. In any case, you must have told them magnificent lies. What else you intend with them is of no concern to us. We won't ride south to warn them again. To allow themselves to be lured into the Llano only to be killed seems to be their greatest pleasure and we wouldn't want to rob them of that. We've done our duty and must now take care of ourselves. Here, at this spot, our ways are going to part. You will leave before us, that is: Now! – Follow your Indians, but beware not to aim your rifles on us. We know very well how to deal with folks of your kind. Our muzzles are up. Another word from you or a suspicious move and we will shoot. Turn away from us. Hang your rifles to your saddle horns and mount up. Farewell, and take care not to come into our sight again."

He had stepped beside Tim and both readied their rifles.

"Mister Jim," Stewart shouted angrily, "that's not how to get us to leave. We are ---"

"Bandits! That's what you are!" Jim interrupted him strongly. "We've got four bullets and you are five. We will beat the last one down with our butts. And now I too tell you: Whoever says another word, a single one, I'll send a bullet through his head. Get away quickly now. If we see you a minute longer, you are done for!"

This was said in a voice, which left no doubt that the two were ready to shoot. The five realized that they would indeed face their doom if they made only the slightest wrong move. With impotent anger they obeyed the order, turned, hung their rifles on their saddle horns and, without another word, rode off. One of them carried the salvaged saddle and reins behind him. Only after they had gained some distance in a sharp trot did they slow their animals to a walk and turned around.

"Damn it!" Stewart grated. "That has never happened to me before. Must five men who aren't afraid of the devil run away from those two long-nosed apes! But I'll bet my head that these dogs would have fired if we'd uttered another word. Don't you think so too?"

The others all agreed.

66

"It was truly as if they were all-knowing. These two rascals even deduced the correct meaning from the movements of my hands. If we only knew what they intend to do now?"

"That's easy to guess," one of them said.

"What is it then?"

"They will follow the Boys to warn them again."

"I doubt that very much. Their warning was cast to the wind twice, and the Snuffles are not men who offer their help and advice more than twice. Nevertheless, we must make our preparations. We must turn south. As soon as we see the caravan's campfires we stop and mount outposts which only our pious Praisegod Burton is allowed to pass when he comes from Helmers Home. But the immigrants are not to learn of our presence. Should the Snuffles come after all, we will kill them. Unfortunately, we will have to let the Indians get away now, although, for the life of me, I would have loved to get their horse. Even among brothers it was worth three hundred dollars, maybe even more."

"It was actually foolish to pick a quarrel with the two Reds just for their horses. Now one's dead and the other's gone. And for all that, we have the Snuffles on our tail too. They will probably camp nearby and tomorrow morning, at daybreak, they'll follow our tracks. That's when they will meet the caravan and wreck our carefully laid plans."

"No, they won't! The Boys insulted them and they won't care a hoot for them any more. In any case, they will ride to Helmers Home, where they will tell about our meeting. What will then be decided there, we cannot guess. We must get Burton to break camp early in the morning to put in a good day's march, so that the caravan gets away from here quickly. And we must disappear even earlier."

They continued riding west for a while and then turned south. Jim and Tim had not lowered their guns until the horsemen had been out of firing range. Then the former turned to the latter and with a broad smile, asked happily, "Now, old Tim, how did you like that?"

"Just as much as you," answered the other with a like grin.

"Wasn't that the height of fun?"

"It sure was. If characters like that must waddle around a couple of brave hunters like poodles who've fallen into a bucket of milk, it cannot be otherwise. They were truly after our lives."

"Of course. One could clearly see it from their looks and moves. I'm sure you don't believe the story of the Boys having lost their money either?"

"Wouldn't think of it. They went off down south and we needn't care a bit about them any longer. We've warned them and have no obligation any more. They thought themselves to be exceptionally smart. This Gibson has studied law. I don't see why we should literally carry our assistance after them. If, in their wantonness, they run with their heads into a wall, they ought to find out how they get all the way through without our help. I think the poor Indian has a greater need of our assistance and is also far more deserving."

"Agreed. So let's look for them."

"Yes. We know the direction they took, it's there to the right, towards the old silver mine. The joke with the pebbles which we crushed ourselves, served only to mislead the rascals. I've seen the drops of blood very clearly and wouldn't be surprised if we find the Indians over there by the silver mine."

They continued on, each of them leading his mule. They did not mount in order to see the ground more clearly which now, that the day drew to its close, was becoming more difficult. After some distance they saw a small item on the ground. It was the red, carefully carved head of a peace pipe. Jim picked it up, pocketed it, and said contently, "We are on the right track. This head came off the pipe and dropped unnoticed to the ground. Whether it belongs to the old, wounded Indian, or the young one, we'll learn soon enough."

"It belonged to the old one for sure. It's unlikely that the young Brave has already been up to the sacred mines in Minnesota to obtain the clay for a pipe."

"He might have captured the pipe, in which case he may use it. It's only an inherited one that he may not yet use."

"Has an Indian ever inherited a peace pipe? Isn't it usually buried with its owner!"

"There are tribes who, unfortunately, don't handle it that way any more. The blessed influence of the dear, kindhearted palefaces makes itself felt also in this case. By the way: If I interpret the totem cut into the pipe head correctly, its owner seems to be a chief of the Comanche. It is good that we understand the dialect of this nation quite well. When we get close, we can call them. Otherwise we may be greeted by a few bullets."

The rocky ground now began to rise. To their left the two faced a rock wall. To their right was a mass of rocky debris through which a human could barely advance, much less a horse or mule. They rode on the only passable trail, which told them with some certainty, that the Indians must have passed here too. Finally they stood in front of a huge pile of black tailings which had been extracted from the old mine. By now it was too dark to make out the height of this pile. They adjusted the length of the reins and tied them to two heavy rocks. Then they began to slowly climb the tailings pile. They didn't make any effort to climb silently; rather they did the opposite in order to make themselves heard. Yet after every step they stopped to listen. They had to learn, whether someone at the top had to be called before he made use of his rifle. On one of their listening stops they heard the tumble of a pebble coming from the top.

"Listen," Tim whispered. "We were right to assume the Indians are up there. They are on guard. The injured one will, if he's even still alive, lie inside the mine. The young Indian will be watching at the top. Why don't you call him, Tim."

Tim followed the request by calling upward in a clear, but not too loud voice, "*Tuquoil, omi gay nina; tau umi tsah!* (Young warrior, don't shoot. We are friends)"

Then they waited for a reply. It took a while, but then they heard the question, "*Haki bit?* (Who comes?)"

These were only two brief words, but entirely sufficient to tell them who was standing up there. The two words were of an idiom taken up by the roaming Comanche from their former enemies and now allies, the Kiowah.

"*Gia ati masslok akona* (two good white men)," Tim answered.

"*Bite uma yepe!* (come on up!)" It sounded from above after what must have been a moment of consideration.

The two now ascended higher. When they had reached the top they saw, despite the darkness, the outlines of a human figure, with rifle aimed, standing in front of them.

"*Naba, o nu neshuano!* (Stop, or I shoot!)", the Comanche ordered.

From the figure the brothers knew that they truly faced the young Indian as they had expected.

Tim tried to calm him, "My young, red brother need not shoot. We have come to help."

"Are my white brothers alone?"

"Yes."

"Did they follow the tracks of my horse?"

"We came by chance to the place where the fight took place and read from the tracks what happened. We then followed your tracks and those of your enemies to protect you from them. You are brave red warriors, but they are cowardly bandits who had to flee from us, although we are only two and they five."

"My brother tells the truth?"

"I'm not lying. To show you that we have come as friends, we will now put down our weapons in front of you. Then you may decide whether we can take them up again or not."

They put down their knives and rifles while he still kept his rifle aimed at them, but then said, "The palefaces lips drip honey, but they have bile in their hearts. They relinquish their weapons to gain trust, but then their three companions will follow bringing death."

"You believe us to be two of those who pursued you. We are not. You are mistaken."

"Then tell me where these five are now. You followed their tracks and should know."

"We met them when they looked for your spoor on the rocky ground where they had lost it. We were first very friendly to deceive them. They were unable to find your tracks. But we found the drops of blood of your wounded companion immediately. We did not tell them though, but made a fake track leading west, which they then followed. We told them before they left, that we thought them to be bandits and murderers and aimed our guns at them just like you do at us presently. They had to leave disgraced."

"Why did you not kill them?"

"Because they hadn't done anything to us. We only gun down a person when forced to defend our lives."

"You speak the words of a good man. My heart demands to trust you. But another voice tells me to be cautious."

"Don't follow that voice, but that of your heart. We mean well. Ask yourself why we came here. You haven't done anything to us; therefore we have no cause to do you ill. We know that you are being pursued and have seen from the spoor that your companion is injured. This is why we came here to offer our help. If it isn't welcome we shall leave at once, because it's not our way to force ourselves on others."

A moment passed without reply. He seemed to be thinking. Then he said; "I don't need your help. You can go."

"All right, we will leave but wish only that you will not regret it."

They picked up their weapons to descend the pile of tailings. They had not gone far yet, when Tim stopped to ask quietly, "Have you heard nothing, old Jim? I thought I heard a pebble roll down to the right of us."

"I didn't hear anything."

"But it was very clear. Could it be a person sneaking around there? Let's be cautious."

When they arrived at the bottom of the tailings a dark figure suddenly rose in front of them.

"Hold it, fellow," Jim commanded, aiming his rifle. "Not a step or I shoot."

"Why would the paleface shoot if I have come as a friend," it came back.

He recognized the voice as that of the young Indian they had just spoken with.

"So it's you?" he asked. "You descended parallel to us. That's why Tim heard the pebble tumble which you dislodged with your foot. What is it you want?"

"I wanted to see if white man's talk was truthful. Had you been enemies, you would not have left. Since you followed my request without taking any action against me, you passed the test. You are not some of my pursuers and I beg you to once more climb up with me to see *Tevua-schohe*, my father."

"*Tevua-schohe*, Fire-Star, the famous chief of the Comanche is here?" Tim asked in surprise.

"Yes it is him. But he is dead. I am *Shiba-bigk* (Ironheart), his youngest son and shall avenge his blood on his murderers. The palefaces may follow me."

70

He took the lead and the two followed him again up the hill. At the top he walked toward the rock wall and entered an opening the brothers knew from earlier visits. It was the entrance to the old silver-mine. Thin smoke greeted them. When they had walked about thirty paces into the dark passage they saw a small fire, a meager pile of toilsomely collected wood beside it. The flame's only purpose was to illuminate the dead man who had been propped up in a seated position, his back leaning against the wall.

Ironheart put down his rifle and sat down opposite the dead Indian. He put a branch into the fire, pulled his knees up, and rested his chin on them. In this position he wordlessly stared at the body.

The two frontiersmen joined him in like reverence. They were familiar with Indian custom and knew that they would only insult the son's pain with spoken words. The faces of both Indians were not painted. A certain sign that they had not been traveling with any hostile intent. The dead Indian had been a handsome man, just as the Comanche in general distinguish themselves by good physical characteristics from many other Indian tribes. Even in death his face still shone like burnished bronze. His eyes were closed and his lips firmly shut. The bottom part of his Indian hunting shirt had been opened, so that one could see where the hostile bullet had penetrated. His hands lay cramped up on his upper thighs, another sign of the pain he had experienced in his last moments.

Only after some time did Jim and Tim settle to the floor, quietly, very quietly, as if afraid to disturb the dead man's peace. As is common, the presence of a recently departed is like viewing a relic: A devotional shiver seizes the mortal when he senses the breath of eternity. That is when *Shiba-bigk* raised his head, looked at the two and said; "You have heard of Fire-Star, the Chief of the Comanche? Then you know that he was a brave warrior."

"Yes," Jim replied. "We recognized the chief at once, when we saw him here. We got to know him up at the Rio Roxo, where he helped us when we were attacked by a group of Pawnee."

"Then you will know that he will command many warriors in the Eternal Hunting Grounds. But Manitou did not call him away in battle. The Chief of the Comanche was murdered."

"By those who pursued you, of course."

"Yes."

"Where did this happen and what for did you come here?"

"We had come far into the land of the palefaces. The warriors of the Comanche had buried their tomahawks against the Whites and in recent times lived in peace with them. We did not need to hesitate before we entered their cities. Fire-Star and his people hunted at the river you call Rio Pecos. That's where they met white men who were traveling to the city called Austin. Since other red men made the trail to Austin insecure, they asked Fire-Star for an experienced guide. He decided to accompany them himself and to take me along so that I might see the Whites' cities and houses. We arrived safely in Austin, then returned by ourselves. Today, in the early afternoon, we met the murderers. They demanded our horses. When we did not relinquish them, one of them shot Fire-Star in the belly. The Chief's horse shied and took off with him. I had to follow him since he had been wounded and could therefore not fight the palefaces. Since you have seen the tracks, you will know what happened afterwards."

"Yes, you killed one of them and took his scalp."

"So it was. His scalp hangs here on my belt. But I will also get the skins of the others. During the night I shall lament my father's death and sing the death song of chiefs. In the morning I will bury him here in a temporary grave. Later, I will call the warriors of the Comanche to erect a monument to honor the hero in a manner appropriate to his bravery and honor. But as soon as I have hidden the dead from the rays of the new sun I shall pick up the tracks of the murderers. *Shiba-bigk* is not a famous warrior yet, for not many winters have passed since he was born, but he is the son of a famous Chief and woe to the palefaces whose tracks he's going to follow. They are doomed!"

He rose to step across to his father, he put his hand on his head and continued, "The palefaces swear an oath, but a Comanche speaks without oath. So remember my speech: When Fire-Star's gravesite is completed, all six scalps of his murderers will be dangling from its top. Ironheart has said so, and thus it will be."

3. Ghostly Hour

About noon the following day Helmers, Juggle-Fred, and Hobble-Frank once again sat at one of the tables in front of the house. Bob had not joined them. He preferred the company of the farmer's black stable hand.

The three men conversed about yesterday's events, the duel between Bloody-Fox and the stranger as well as the latter's death. Thus it was no wonder that they talked about a variety of things relating to death and eventually about the subject of ghosts.

Helmers and Fred firmly insisted that it was impossible of a deceased's soul to return and have a corporal presence that could speak since it would lack the necessary speech organs. Frank, on the other hand, energetically defended his belief in ghosts and when the other two persisted in their doubt, he angrily called, "You two are just dumb, very dumb! You can't be helped. Only people like me who have the right mind and occupied themselves from their earliest youth with the here-and-now and the beyond can truly comprehend what is simultaneously above and below ground. Since that's not the case with you, I shouldn't really be surprised and angry that your neglected intellect has forgotten all about spirits and ghosts. Were I a deceased, which fortunately isn't the case, I would carry both of you off by midnight. That would teach you the right lesson."

"Come on. Give us proof, a single one," Fred laughed, "then we will believe you."

"Proof? Nonsense! Evidence doesn't prove a thing! If there's proof for something, I don't need to provide evidence to prove it. One must have seen it, seen it with one's own two eyes. That's the so-called Italian oculier proof, against which nothing can be said. About this, we scholars are agreed---"

"Not oculier, but ocular-proof, you must have wanted to say," Fred interrupted his tirade.

"Oh, be quiet, you mangler of Hebrew!" Frank erupted angrily. "You want to teach me the knowledge of language, language I've traversed for thirty years so that it wore off the soles of my shoes. Already as a toddler I cried in Chinese, slumbered in Aramaic and sucked Polynesian milk from a Sanskrit bottle."

And on it went about the differences between 'oculier' and 'ocular' to eventually return to the confirmation of the existence of ghosts.

"Well, how about it? Did you ever see one?"

"Oh, not just one, but more than half a dozen. Plenty of ghosts have run around me, simply because I'm such a spirited fellow. It's self-evident. I can prove the subject philologically. If there's a word for something, then this something must also exist. Since there's a word for ghost, then ghosts must exist. That's as clear as soap water. The Moritzburg school master, to whom I'm most grateful for my ingenious education, also believed in ghosts."

"Really? What's the name of this illustrious man?"

73

"His name was Elias Funkelmeier."

"So, that was his name. *Nomen est omen*!"

"Please, don't you talk Portuguese with me now."

That's when Fred began to laugh so loud that tears ran down his cheeks. Helmers joined in heartily. Their conversation was interrupted by the approach of a horseman wearing the uniform of a United States cavalry officer. Coming in a hard gallop from the south, the man stopped his horse in front of the three men.

"Good morning, gentlemen, am I right here? Is this the farm called Helmers Home?"

"Yes, Sir," Helmers responded. "I'm the owner of the property."

"Mister Helmers himself? I'm pleased to meet you. I'm coming with an inquiry."

"About what?"

"That isn't explained very quickly. Permit me to sit with you for a moment."

He dismounted and took a seat. The three looked the soldier over who acted as if he didn't notice. His build was stocky and he wore a thick, black beard. The lips were hidden, since he had brushed his mustache over them. His eyes had a piercing look.

"I've come to explain something," he said easily. "We are camped up at Fort Sill and want to enter the Llano."

"What for?" Helmers asked.

"The federal government has learned about the number of crimes committed on the plains in recent times. That requires some fast and severe punishment of the perpetrators. It can safely be assumed that the individual crooks are in contact with each other, which leads us to think we are dealing with an organized gang. It is our intention to carry out a decisive and destructive blow. Two squadrons of soldiers have been dispatched to execute the task of clearing the plains and the surrounding area of this rabble. And as I said, these soldiers are presently encamped at Fort Sill, whilst I am sent to scout and gather information as well as establish contact with the honorable citizens near the boundary. Of course, we proceed from the assumption that every honest man will support us in this endeavor."

"That goes without saying, Sir! I'm glad you came by here, and you can rest assured of my full support. John Helmers is known as a man every decent fellow can rely on."

"We've heard that, which is why I came here."

"Fine. But Fort Sill is up north and you came from the south. How does that fit together?"

"I didn't come directly from Fort Sill, but rather rode almost down to the river to then return along the border of the Llano to inspect the area."

"All by yourself? Why didn't your commander assign several people to you?"

"He didn't think it appropriate. Nor do I! A larger group would have been more noticeable, which is precisely what we wanted to avoid."

"But two, three horsemen can pass through as inconspicuously as a single one. Something could easily happen to a single man, and if you then don't return your people are in limbo."

"Well, as to that, the Major knows very well what I can do and that he can rely on me. You must be aware, that only capable people who know the West well, are chosen to reconnoiter."

"Then you must have done this already for some time?"

"For a number of years, of course."

"Hmm. Maybe this is why I have the feeling we've met before. Don't you think so too?"

The officer looked closely and thoughtfully at Helmers and replied, "No Sir."

"Then you haven't been that far south before?"

"Well, I've actually been much farther south already, but not on this side of the Llano. I got down as far as Chihuahua, even farther."

"As a soldier?"

"No. You know it's forbidden to cross the border in uniform."

"That's correct. Then you must have been in Mexico as a private citizen. Well, I've also been down there a number of times and it might be that I saw you briefly without you noticing me. When must you return to your detachment?"

"That depends on what's happening. My orders are to return as soon as I've gathered the necessary information. If I don't acquire anything important, my comrades will proceed to the Llano on their own. In that case, I am to meet them here at Helmers Home within a week where the two detachments are to take a brief rest."

"At my place? That's very, very interesting. And when will this week have passed?"

"The day after tomorrow. On that day or the next, my comrades are to arrive here."

"Does that mean you didn't find anything important and, therefore, do not return to them?"

"Yes. I must confess that my hard ride didn't produce anything of consequence, it's been quite useless in fact. I didn't meet a single person in this lonely area from whom I could have learned anything."

"That certainly is poor luck. The area's residents could surely have told you more than enough. I don't understand that you didn't look them up."

"I didn't think it wise, Sir. It's been said that some of these residents are in cahoots with the robbers. My inquiry with such farmers would only have resulted in the gang learning the proximity of the troops, which would have obviously jeopardized our strike."

"Well, Sir, don't take it wrong, but you made a very big mistake."

"What kind?"

"That you didn't take off your uniform. If no one was to notice the presence of soldiers, you should have ridden in civilian clothes."

"You are right. But I'm a soldier and must follow orders. But, last not least, I hope I shall obtain some information on the doings of the Llano Vultures here."

"That you can. Only two weeks ago four families left here to cross the plains. They were attacked in the Llano and murdered."

"By the devil! Do you know this for sure?"

"Yes. A trader, by the name of Barton, came by yesterday and told me. He saw the bodies and was so shaken by the experience that he needed some rest here."

"Where's the man? Of course, I must talk to him at once."

"That's no longer possible. He left this morning, Sir. It's also not really necessary to talk to him in person. He told us everything and we can convey it to you just as he did to us. By the way, there seems to be something in the works right now. It would be well advised if your detachments arrive soon."

"What leads you to expect another attack?"

"Because two fellows came here last night who could only have had the intention to spy."

"Really? Could they have truly been spies of the Llano Vultures?"

"It's very likely that's what they were, Sir. One of them got away. The other fared the worse. He bit the dust."

"That's important, very important. Go on, Sir, keep talking."

Helmers had come to trust the officer. He first recounted what he had learned from the trader, then continued telling about yesterday's duel and the stranger's death.

The officer followed the account very carefully. While his features did not change, his eyes glittered. Helmers ascribed this to the soldier's interest in the duel. A careful observer might have noticed that the intense flaring of the eyes was nothing but an expression of anger, even hate. His fist gripped his saber's handle. At one time it even sounded as if he grated his teeth quietly. But, otherwise, he remained very quiet and made every effort to show nothing but intense attention, which the story had to bring forth from every listener. When Helmers had finished recounting Barton's report, he elaborated on the general conditions of the area and the dangers of the Llano Estacado. He concluded that he thought it very difficult, if not impossible, for two squadrons of cavalry to cross it due to the lack of fodder and particularly, the lack of water for the animals. If water were to be carried, a great number of pack animals would be required, which in turn would complicate the move since they would consume much of the extra supplies.

"You may be right," the officer suggested. "But it's not my concern but rather my commander's. Tell me, Sir, what is it about this Ghost of Llano Estacado? I've heard lots about this incomprehensible entity but nothing of any consequence."

"Then you are in the same boat as everybody else. Everyone hears about the Ghost but no one knows anything specific. I can tell you what I know in a few words. The Ghost of Llano Estacado is a mysterious horseman whom no living man has ever seen up close. Whoever sees his face pays with death by a bullet through the midst of his forehead. The dead have consistently been criminals who made the Llano unsafe. Therefore, the Ghost appears to be a person who has made it his task to punish the crimes committed on the Llano."

"Then he must be human?"

"Of course!"

"But how does he manage to be everywhere without ever being seen? He must obtain food and water for himself and his animal. Where does he get it?"

"That is precisely what no one understands."

"And how does he manage never to be seen by anyone?"

"Hmm. You really are asking too much here, Sir. He has been seen, but only from a distance. People talk about seeing him hurtle past like a hurricane with sparks flying ahead of him and behind him. I know someone who has seen him in the night. By a thousand oaths, this man insists that the head, the shoulders, the elbows, the rifle barrel of the rider, even his horse's mouth, ears, and tail are sparkling with small flames."

"That's nonsense!"

"One should think so. But my acquaintance is a truth-loving man, from whose mouth I have yet to hear a lie or exaggeration."

Now that the Ghost had been addressed, Hobble-Frank wanted to comment. Since the conversation was conducted in English, his talk was levelheaded and smooth like everyone else's. Only when German was spoken did colorful yarns come alive in his mind.

"There we are!" he called out. "No one is prepared to believe in the naturalness of the unnatural. I claim that the Ghost of Llano Estacado is not a person, but a ghostly entity, a survivor of the Greek Furies, who retired to the solitude of the Llano like an old man into an attic. That he spits flames and sparks I have no difficulty believing. We mortal beings blow tobacco smoke in quantities from our mouths; why should a ghost then not spit fire?"

"But can a ghost shoot a rifle?" the officer demanded, throwing Hobble-Frank a contemptuous look.

"Why not? At a carnival I've seen a hen triggering a small cannon with a rabbit doing the very same. What a hen and a rabbit can do, a ghost should be able to accomplish just as well."

"You're making use of a very peculiar sort of proof, Sir, but give no indication of much intelligence and acumen."

These words had insulted Frank, who responded accordingly.

"This is true, of course. But I've reason not to talk as scholarly as I could, because with your stupid face I must be considerate of your non-comprehension, should I use terms that go beyond the level of a school boy."

"Mister!" the officer roared. "Who are you to insult a captain of the United States cavalry in such manner!"

"Pshaw! Don't get excited. Whether you are a captain or a shoe-shiner doesn't matter to me. You, yourself, started the insults and now must take mine just as well. If not, I'm ready to settle the issue with a good bullet. Your rank doesn't impress a frontiersman."

It was obvious that it took a lot for the officer to control his anger, but he succeeded in responding calmly, "I would regret very much to shoot you down. I know very well how to handle a rifle, but I'm no rowdy and duel only with officers. Then, too, it would be discourteous to Mister Helmers to spill blood on his property. I intend to stay here until my squadrons arrive, which is why I would like to maintain peace."

"I'm grateful for that, Sir," Helmers said. "If you wish to stay I'll assign you a room and your horse shall find a good place in the stable."

"I'd like that. I shall take my horse to the stable right away. Where is it?"

"I'll take you there, then to my wife, who can show you to your room."

Helmers and the officer departed for the stable. A bit later, Helmers returned to tell the two others that the captain had stayed in his room to rest. Helmers was pleased for the presence of this guest and the arrival of the cavalry. But Frank, shaking his head, said in German, "I really don't like this man. There's something about his face that insults my tender feelings of sympathy. His eyes seem to me like two drops of fat swimming on a lean consommé. They look at you maliciously. There's nothing good behind them. I wouldn't want to test him on his honesty."

After this rather astute assessment of the officer, Frank entered into one of his extended tirades and exchanges with Helmers and Fred, which was eventually interrupted when Helmers pointed to the north. There, they saw three horsemen approaching slowly. Hobble-Frank called out joyfully and rose from his seat.

"Do you know those men?" Fred inquired.

"Very well indeed," was the response. "These are ---, hmm, I'd rather not give you their names yet and wait to see how you like them."

One of the three was short and corpulent, the second thin and tall, the third was of medium build and rode a magnificent black horse. Juggle-Fred, shading his eyes to look at them, said, "Frank, you are keeping their names secret to surprise us. But I wouldn't be a frontiersman if I couldn't recognize these three men."

"Well, who are they then?"

"The two, one of them fat, the other lean, the little one on the tall nag, the tall one on the tiny mule, can only be Fat-Jemmy and Long-Davy. And the third is surely Old Shatterhand."

"How did you arrive at this conclusion?"

"Didn't you say yourself that he would come with Jemmy? Does Old Shatterhand not always ride a black stallion, as everyone knows?"

"Hmm. Yes. You are a smart fellow, although you haven't advanced yet in the languages and sciences to the beginner level of the contra bass."

"Then tell me if I'm right."

"Yes. This time you're right. It's them. They are arriving earlier than I thought. I hope you will receive them with the due respect they deserve."

By now the three horsemen had arrived, brought their animals to a halt, and dismounted. They wore the very same weapons and clothes as on their former ride to the national park. Helmers' and Fred's eyes were fixed on Old Shatterhand, the most famous of the hunters. Without asking Frank for the names of his two companions, he offered Helmers his hand and immediately addressed him in German, "I suppose that we have been announced, Mister Helmers. I hope we are welcome."

Helmers shook his hand and answered, "Yes, Hobble-Frank told me that you were coming, Sir, and it gives me great joy. My house is yours. Make yourself comfortable and stay as long as you like."

"Well, we can't stay very long. We must cross the old Llano to meet with someone on the other side who's expecting us."

"Winnetou, by chance?"

"Yes. Did Frank tell you?"

"He did, and I wish I could come with you to meet the Apache Chief. But tell me, Sir, how do you know me? You called me by my name right away."

"Do you think it requires much acumen to recognize you as the owner of Helmers Home? You are dressed like a farmer and are very much like the image I've formed from the description I received of you."

"Then you inquired about me?"

"Of course. In the Far West it is advisable to learn about the people one is going to visit. I learned that you are German and therefore addressed you immediately in your mother tongue. May I ask who the other gentleman is?"

"I'm usually called Juggle-Fred," the former juggler answered. "I'm a simple prairie runner, Sir, and don't expect you to know my name."

"Why not? Someone like me, who has crossed the West so often and for such a long time, ought to have heard of Juggle-Fred. You are a competent tracker and, what's more important, a decent fellow. Here's my hand. Let's be friends, as long as we may be together. All right, Sir?"

Although there are no ranks in the Far West, it is customary to give heroes their due respect. Fred's happy face glowed with pride in being honored in this way by Old Shatterhand. He took the proffered hand, pressed it heartily, and answered, "Your speaking of friendship is an honor, yet I must earn it first. I wish I could be with you as long as possible to learn from you. I, too, need to cross the Estacado. If you permit me to accompany you I would be extremely grateful."

"Why not? One crosses the Llano with as many people as possible, which is why I would appreciate it if you would come along. Provided, of course, that one need not wait for the other. When do you plan to leave?"

"I've been hired to guide a group of Diamond Boys. These people should arrive here today."

"That fits well, since I too want to leave tomorrow. With you talking of Diamond Boys, I assume you will be going on to Arizona?"

"That's correct, Sir."

"Well, then you'll probably see also Winnetou. The place where we will meet is in that direction. But let me first introduce my two companions."

"I do know them already, because their figures are the best telltale. And Frank has told us their names already."

By that time Helmers had welcomed Jemmy and Davy. Sliding-Bob turned up to take the horses into his care. Everybody sat down and Helmers entered the house to ask his wife to prepare a good repast for his guests. He returned right away with drinks. The men then sat together to discuss yesterday's events, which were first and foremost on their minds.

The officer had said that he wanted to rest. But once he had entered his room he certainly did not. He had bolted the door and paced the room thoughtfully. His room faced north, which is how he had noticed the arrival of the newcomers. He stepped to the window to observe the three arrivals carefully.

"Who might these fellows be and where will they go?" he pondered. "Most likely they also intend to cross the Llano. That's critical. One of them has this excellent horse and gives the impression of being an experienced frontiersman. If these people get onto the tracks of the German immigrants, they can easily wreck our plans. One must even be careful of this Juggle-Fred. It's fortunate that the Diamond Boys will not come to Helmers Home. That means he will wait a long time for their arrival and can do us no harm any longer. I must try to get the other three to also stay here until our coup is done. My uniform looks real, and if Helmers didn't suspect anything, then these three newcomers will likewise not catch on that I am the disguised leader of the Llano Vultures."

He waited for a little while to go down and join the men who by now were eating at the tables in front of the house. This disguised officer was no other than

Stewart who had yesterday attacked and pursued the two Comanche and had met the two Snuffles. Today, one could not see the small hare's lip he had covered with his drooping mustache.

When he arrived downstairs, Old Shatterhand had already learned everything about yesterday's events and Helmers had just mentioned that a United States cavalry officer had also arrived. When the host saw the latter he commented, "There's the captain. He can tell you the purpose of his presence himself. Hello, wife, another plate for the officer, please."

His wife had appeared at one of the windows to check on the guests. She brought out a plate and the officer joined the group. When he heard the names of the last arrivals he became quite alarmed but made every effort not to have this noticed. Nothing could be less welcome to him than Old Shatterhand's presence. He examined the latter closely, which did not go unnoticed by the hunter. Old Shatterhand acted as if he was not aware of the other's scrutiny, giving the officer only an impression of casual attention. The soldier repeated his earlier account. What he did not notice was that Old Shatterhand had pulled his hat lower into his face to observe the speaker from below the brim. When the officer had finished the hunter asked innocently, "And where did you say your squadrons are presently stationed, Sir?"

"Up at Fort Sill."

"And you took off from there for your reconnoitering?"

"Yes."

"Then you have been at Fort Sill and know the conditions there quite well?"

"Of course."

"I've been up there several years ago when Colonel Olmers was in command. Who's the present commander?"

"It's Colonel Blaine."

"I don't know the man. Did you meet him and talk with him?"

"That goes without saying."

"And your squadrons will arrive here within a few days? It's too bad they don't arrive today or tomorrow. We could join them on the ride through the Llano which would help with our security."

"Well. Why don't you await their arrival?"

"For that I've neither the time nor the desire."

"Why not miss a day? The loss of time is compensated for by the advantage of greater security."

"A day only? Hmm. Do you really think it will only be a day?"

"Yes. At most two."

"About that, I think, we are of a different opinion."

"How so?"

"Because I'm convinced that your squadrons will never arrive here."

"How did you arrive at this peculiar conclusion?"

"Because I know very well that there are no troops stationed at or near Fort Sill who are scheduled to enter the Llano."

"So. Am I to assume that you are calling me a liar?" the officer demanded with a roar.

"Yes. That's so! You are a liar," Old Shatterhand confirmed as he continued speaking as softly as before.

"By the devil! This is an insult which can only be washed off with blood."

"Yes, I agree. We should actually do battle. Provided you were truly an officer of the United States which is, however, not the case."

"You've got anything more to say?" Stewart called out while rising threateningly. "I give you my word of honor that this is what I am. My uniform, too, should be proof that you are facing a military gentleman. If you still don't believe it, I request you take hold of your weapon."

Smiling, Old Shatterhand told him, "Don't get all fired up, Sir. If you've ever heard my name, you should know that I'm a man who cannot be deceived easily. I also don't duel with a scoundrel, but should you still insist to do battle, I'm prepared to wring your neck with a single twist."

"Man!" Stewart shouted, while pulling out one of his two pistols. "Say one more word and I'll gun you down!"

He had not yet finished speaking his threat when Old Shatterhand stood in front of him, tore the pistol from his hand and, simultaneously, the other from his holster. He then told him in a very different voice, "Not so rash, man! Normally, those who point a weapon at me are doomed. I'll spare you this time since I have only indirect evidence against you. But let me render these pistols harmless first."

He fired both pistols into the air before continuing, "Let me tell you that I'm also coming from Fort Sill and know its commander very well. Yes, the previous one's name was Blaine, but he was replaced three weeks ago by Major Owens, whom you don't seem to know. You claim to have left Fort Sill barely a week ago and should know Major Owens, if what you are telling is the truth. Since that's not the case, you cannot have been there and the story of the two squadrons and their task in the Llano is a lie!"

Stewart was now in a great predicament. He tried to hide it as much as possible and said, "All right. I admit that my troops are not at Fort Sill. But is this enough to declare my account untruthful? I must be cautious and am not supposed to reveal the actual position of my squadrons."

"Don't tell me such nonsense! You needn't be secretive with me. I'd think that every officer would be glad to have Old Shatterhand as a confidante. By the way, it occurs to me, that it's not the first time I've seen you. Weren't you once apprehended in Los Animas for a train holdup? With the help of some rascals you were able to provide an alibi, although you were guilty. You were acquitted, but only your quick escape saved you from being lynched."

"That wasn't me."

"Don't deny it! Your name then was Stuart or Stewart or something like that, just as you call yourself today. I don't care to check your name and to investigate the purpose of your present masquerade. But lift your mustache. I'm convinced a small harelip is hiding underneath."

"On whose authority are you conducting such an interrogation?" Stewart demanded with impotent anger.

"On my own! But I don't need to see your mouth. I know whom I'm dealing with. Here, take your weapons. Get away quickly and consider yourself fortunate to get off so lightly. But don't cross my path again. The next meeting is likely to be much more uncomfortable for you."

He tossed the discharged pistols at Stewart's feet, who picked them up and replied, "Your claims are utterly ridiculous. You are mistaking me for someone else. That's why I forgive you. My papers are up in my room. I'll fetch them and am convinced that you will ask my forgiveness when you see them."

"Don't imagine things. A frontiersman need not see any papers, which are most likely stolen anyway. But if it pleases you, do get them and show them to the others. I need not see them."

Stewart left.

"What a scene!" Helmers said. "Are you really that certain, Sir?"

"Absolutely," Old Shatterhand answered.

"I thought so right away," Hobble-Frank chimed in. "The fellow's face is that of a totally dishonorable sociopath. I gave him my opinion right away, but he extracted himself quite elegantly from that noose."

Frank once more rose to the issue, even presenting some awful rhymes, after which Jemmy exclaimed, "Stop it! Stop it! Leave rhyming to poets. We need to discuss lots of other things as you might have heard."

When Frank readied himself for an angry riposte, Old Shatterhand cut him off.

"Exactly! Our good Hobble-Frank has shown himself again as the excellent scholar of German literature that he is. But as important as these anecdotal treasures are, we cannot draw from them anything of value to aid our present situation."

Thus Old Shatterhand deflected the little man's anger and directed the conversation back to more acute problems. The hunter inquired about the past events in greater detail and seemed to take a heightened interest in Bloody-Fox. He also asked about the Diamond Boys who Juggle-Fred was expecting to guide through the Llano.

The conversation then turned to the terrors of the Llano and would have continued had not Sliding-Bob together with Helmers stable boy appeared to interrupt the talk. The stable boy asked Helmers, "Where am I to put the many horses which are to come?"

"What horses?" Helmers asked.

83

"Soldiers horses, officer is going to get after he left."

"Ah. He rode off."

"Yes, he gone. Before he left, he said to get many horsemen to Helmers home."

"So he left secretly. It proves that he didn't have a clear conscience. What direction did he ride off to?"

The Negro pointed north.

"That's suspicious," Helmers said, still beholden by his previous conviction in the truth of the *officer's* story. "He should be followed. He claimed that they would come for sure, that he was to wait for them here. Now he rides towards them. I'm tempted to follow him and ask why he didn't tell us earlier of his intention to leave."

"Oh, go ahead. Do it!" Old Shatterhand said smilingly. "You'll not get very far north."

"Why not?"

"Because this direction is only a ruse. The man's no officer, even if he wears an officer's uniform. That means he has no good intentions. Knowing that he has been found out, he thought it advisable to disappear and, of course, took a very different direction from the one he will actually head for."

"But where would he ride to? To the west and southwest is the Llano. He's been to the south. That's where he came from. There's nothing for him in the east. That leaves the north only to which he's headed."

"Mister Helmers, don't take it wrong if I insist that you are mistaken. I assume the exact opposite of what this man told you. All right. He came from the south and rode north. I'm convinced that he means to go south. I wager that if we'd follow his tracks, we would soon see them change from their northerly heading into the opposite southward direction. All he told about the military is bogus."

"Well, I must believe this now too. But why did you let him get away?"

"Because I cannot order him about and cannot prove that he's done anything unlawful."

"At least tell me for what purpose he came here?"

"You seem to think me to be all-knowing. I can only make some guesses. I'm sure he came here to find out something or other. What can it be? Your place is the departure point for many groups to the Llano. I suppose he wanted to find out whether there are any people here planning to take this journey. He must have an interest in such people or expect some benefit from them. Now tell me what kind of interest or what benefit this might be."

"Hmm," Helmers murmured. "I know you think this man is one of the Llano Vultures."

"That's correct."

"Then we should not have let him get away but should have arrested him. But without proof we could not have done that. He learned that Juggle-Fred expects the 'Diamond Boys' here. Maybe he left to prepare an attack on them."

"That doesn't sound only probable to me but rather certain. This man is not alone. There are others waiting for him. We couldn't do anything. I couldn't arrest him, although I knew, that he would hurry off surreptitiously. Now, that he's gone, I can at least satisfy myself whether I guessed right or wrong. I'll follow his tracks. When did he leave?"

"Maybe hour and a half ago," the Negro answered, who had been addressed.

"That means I must hurry. Anyone interested in coming along?"

Everyone wanted to join. Old Shatterhand picked Juggle-Fred to get to know him better. There should be an opportunity on such a ride to put him to a small test. Frank was very dissatisfied with this decision. He told the famous hunter, "But my dear Shatterhand, to take along another is no compliment for someone of my merit. Or are you by chance of the opinion that I couldn't make myself useful in the evaluation of the tracks. If I could come along I would consider this a most exceptional gratuity."

"Well?" asked Old Shatterhand smilingly. "And how have you earned such gratuity?"

"First of all and in general by my earthly existence on the whole. Secondly, by the circumstance that I'm no less curious than the others. And thirdly, that I might be able to learn something after all, if you'd have the kindness to take me along."

"You really think you could learn something still? Such modesty must be rewarded. Come along then."

"Good!" Frank nodded. "I'll dedicate to you my most favorable merits, Sir. I've given the others a shining example with my respectable modesty for their patient and worthy imitation. *Quod Eduard demonstratum!*"

With this misquote he stalked off to get his horse from the stable. Helmers offered Old Shatterhand the use of some good, rested horses, which the hunter gratefully accepted. The two Blacks were asked to get two horses from the pasture and to saddle them. Then Old Shatterhand, Fred, and Frank rode off from right behind the stable to follow the make-believe officer's tracks.

For a short distance, the tracks led north, only to turn briefly east, then south, to eventually head in a southwesterly direction. Accordingly, Stewart had ridden almost three-quarters of a circle with a conspicuously small diameter. Bent low in the saddle to follow the tracks closely, Old Shatterhand rode up front. When he had convinced himself that the tracks no longer diverted from the final direction but led straight ahead, he reined in his horse and asked, "Fred, what do you make of these tracks? Can we trust them to keep the present direction?"

85

"I'm certain, Sir," Fred responded, who was well aware that Old Shatterhand was putting him to a test. "From hereon the fellow shows his true colors. He's riding straight for the Llano and ---"

He stopped thoughtfully.

"Well, what ---?"

"It seems he's in a hurry. The circle he rode around Helmers Home is very tight. He didn't take the time for a larger detour. He also rode in a hard gallop. Something must urge him on."

"And what might that be?"

"If I could only tell that, Sir. That's the end of my knowledge. Maybe you can deduce it easier than I."

"I don't want to rely on guessing. It's better we make sure. We do have enough time and can risk a few hours. Let's quickly follow the tracks."

The three horsemen now also assumed a hard gallop, which they could readily do since reading the tracks posed no difficulty now. Soon it became obvious that Helmers' Home lay at the edge of arable land. The land quickly took on a very different character. To the north of the farmstead there had still been woods. To the south of it only individual trees grew, which soon disappeared. Shrubs became spindlier and more rare. Buffalo grass disappeared and in its place some bear grasses grew, indisputable signs that the earth was getting poorer. Soon, mostly bare, dry sand showed up and the previously rolling countryside changed to that of the flat plains.

Finally, there was only sand and more sand with the occasional island of bear grasses, its flower stalks rising above it. Still later, even this grass disappeared to be replaced by cholla and creeping, snakelike prickly-pear cacti. Stewart had avoided these cacti-overgrown spots since their thorns can be dangerous to horses. Rarely had he given his animal a moment's rest; then it had to gallop again as could be seen from the deeply indented hoof tracks.

Thus it continued on and on. More than two hours had passed since the three had left Helmers Home. At least fifteen miles had been covered, yet it looked as if they could not catch up with their quarry. Helmers' horses were unable to make up Stewart's head start.

Then the three pursuers saw a dark streak in the distance entering the sandy plain from the left. It turned out to be a rise in the land, apparently fertile, but still supporting only scraggly mesquite bushes. The tracks pointed straight to this rise which the three would be able to reach in less than two minutes. Old Shatterhand stopped his horse, pointed ahead and said, "Careful! It would appear that there are people behind those bushes. Didn't you see anything?"

"No," Fred responded.

"But I had the impression as if someone or something moved over there. Let's keep to the left to get the mesquite bushes in between us."

86

They hurried their horses along in an arc to quickly cover the open area where they could be readily seen. When they reached the bushes Old Shatterhand dismounted.

"Stay here and hold my horse!" he told them. "I want to reconnoiter. But keep your weapons at the ready and be prepared. Should I shoot, come quickly."

He lowered himself and disappeared as he crawled into the bushes. Barely three minutes passed until he returned. A satisfied smile played on his lips.

"It's not the officer," he reported, "and neither are his pals beyond the bushes. I think we are going to meet some interesting people. Fred, have you heard about the two Snuffles?"

"Have I heard about them? Not just heard of them, no, I've met them."

"Really? Well, then dismount and come along. I've never met them, but by the kind of noses these two have, it must be them."

"How are they dressed?"

"They wear woolen pants and shirts, laced shoes and beaver hats, belts made from rattlesnake skin, and wear their blankets like coats."

"That's them. Did you see their horses?"

"They have no horses, but mules."

"Then there's no doubt. It's Jim and Tim with Polly and Molly. Great! What a surprise this will be. I have ---"

"Quiet, quiet!" Old Shatterhand warned. "They aren't alone. A young Indian is with them."

"That doesn't matter, Sir. Whoever is with the Snuffles doesn't pose a danger. For several months I was up in the Black Mountains with those two to trap beaver. We had arranged for a signal to recognize ourselves already from afar. I'll sound it now. Let's see how they react. What are they presently doing?"

"They sit resting in the shade of some bushes."

"And their mules?"

"They nibble on the leaves of some bushes."

"Are they tied up?"

"No."

"Now you'll learn that Polly and Molly are just as smart as their masters, Jim and Tim. I bet the two mules will join me here as quickly as their owners. Watch out, Sir."

Fred put two fingers to his mouth and produced a long warbling whistle. There was no reaction.

"They must be too surprised. I'll try again."

He repeated the whistle and had barely finished, when the two animals fell into loud braying. Crushing bushes and everything else in their way the two mules hurried towards Fred. Behind them a loud voice rose, "Hello. What's going on here? Whistling in the wilds of the Llano? Could that be Fred, Juggle-Fred?"

"Yes, it's the Juggler, and none other," a different voice confirmed. "Hurry up, I'm coming too. It's him. The beasts recognized him and hurried over there."

Once more it sounded as if bushes were being crushed. Then they parted, pushed aside by the mules with the two brothers following close behind. When they saw Fred, they rushed to him and not paying any attention to the others hugged him, one from the front, the other from the back.

"Stop it you guys! Don't kill me with your squeezing!" the former Juggler warded them off. "I love to be hugged, but one after the other, please, not simultaneously by two such bears like you."

"Not to worry. We aren't going to kill you," Jim told him. "Really! Juggle-Fred here! What a surprise! But how did you get the idea to whistle? Did you know us to be behind the bushes there?"

"Yes. What kind of frontiersmen are you that you allow yourselves to be spied upon without noticing anything? I hope it's a real surprise to you to find me here in the Llano?"

"Not quite, old Fred. Although we are surprised to meet you here, we knew you to be close by."

"How so? From whom?"

"Ah, that surprises you. Don't you know six men, whose leader's named Gibson and is an attorney?"

"Yes. I'm expecting them at Helmers Home to guide them through the Llano. Did you meet them by chance?"

"That's it. They mentioned your name. We didn't think it necessary to tell them that we know you well, but only claimed to have heard of you."

"So you disowned me, you rascals. Where are these fellows? And what are you doing in these bushes?"

"Of that, later. Firstly we want to know who these two gentlemen are."

"That you will learn right away. The one over there, with the Amazon hat, is the famous Hobble-Frank, and ---"

"Not the great German scholar who traveled to Yellowstone Park with Winnetou and Old Shatterhand?" Tim interrupted. "Is this *the* Hobble-Frank?"

'The great German scholar', Tim had meant in jest. But Frank took it seriously and responded to it himself, "Yes, I'm Hobble-Frank, Sir. How do you know me?"

"Up at the Blackbird River we learned of your experiences, Sir, and admired your actions. But who's the other gentleman, Fred?"

An inquiring look was directed at Old Shatterhand.

"This gentleman?" Fred responded. "Have a good look at him. Who might he be?"

There was no need for them to guess; they were soon told. Ironheart, the young Comanche, had joined them. He just stepped from the bushes, when he saw Old Shatterhand and heard Fred's words, causing him to speak out, "*Nina-*

nonton, the shattering hand! *Shiba-bigk*, the son of the Comanche, is too young to face such a famous warrior directly."

Following Indian custom he averted his face. But Old Shatterhand stepped quickly over to him, put his hand on his shoulder and said, "I recognize you, although several winters have passed and you have grown taller since I saw you last. You are the son of my friend *Tevua-schohe*, the Chief of the Comanche, with whom I've smoked the peace pipe. He is a brave warrior and a friend of the Whites. Where are his teepees now?"

"His spirit is on the way to the Eternal Hunting Grounds, he can enter only after I have taken his murderers' scalps."

"He's dead? Fire-Star dead! Murdered?" Old Shatterhand cried. "Tell me who did this."

"*Shiba-bigk* does not speak of it. Ask my two white friends, who have seen his body and helped me bury him this morning."

Thereafter, Ironheart disappeared once more into the bushes.

When Old Shatterhand turned to the others, he saw the Snuffles' looking at him admiringly. He shook their hands and asked them, "It appears you have some interesting things to tell us. Fire-Star was one of my red friends. I must learn who murdered him. But here, the sun burns too hot to sit. Let's seek some shade, where you can tell me what happened."

Jim and Tim took a direct route through the bushes. The three others led their horses around. At the Snuffles' resting place the young Comanche had already sat down again. The Whites did the same and Jim began the account of yesterday's events. They spoke English. Had they conversed in German, he would have found himself interrupted here and there by Hobble-Frank's famous elaboration and it would have taken the story teller much longer to get to the end of his narrative. Then Jim arrived at the point of their meeting with the young Comanche.

"At dawn today we dug an improvised grave for the dead chief where he is to rest until his warriors can prepare a dignified memorial for him. After that we took off on our pursuit of the murderers."

"I thought you wanted to get to Helmers Home?" Old Shatterhand remarked.

"Yes, that was our original intention. But there was no urgency for it. We have become friends with Ironheart, this young brave warrior, and made his task our own. He was most eager to follow the murderers' tracks, which is why we gave up riding to Helmers Home and joined him."

"I can only commend you for this. Did you succeed in following the tracks?"

"Yes, although it was difficult. The gang had moved southward to a point where they separated, apparently to form a guard line for the purpose of keeping watch on a camp there."

"Who's camping there?"

"We can't tell exactly. Most likely immigrants. We saw the tracks of ox carts and those of many horses. We estimate the number of people who spent the night there to be about fifty."

"They were no longer there? In what direction did they leave?"

"Southwest."

"That means to the Llano. With ox-drawn wagons! By the devil! They either have competent guides, or there's the intention to lure them into a terrible trap. What's your opinion, Jim?"

"The latter."

"Why so?"

"Because the five murderers of Fire-Star have got their fingers in it. The 'Diamond Boys' also joined this caravan. From the condition of the tracks I judge them to have broken camp shortly after midnight. That's conspicuous. It appears, they wanted to get the people away from Helmers Home as quickly as possible."

"I hope you followed the caravan."

"No, Sir. We only had an issue with the chief's murderers. But as we saw from the tracks, they had not joined the caravan but rode straight west. Of course, we followed their tracks. By the way, we found also the tracks of a single horseman, who must have joined the caravan coming from the direction of Helmers Home last evening."

"So. Last evening already. That must have been the honorable Mormon missionary, Tobias Praisegod Burton. The pieces of this puzzle seem to fall into place. Go on, Jim, what happened to the tracks you were following?"

"The fellows rode very fast, which made the tracks well visible. But then we encountered some difficulty, because one of the five separated from the group. His tracks led straight north. We had to follow them for a bit to be sure of that."

"Hmm, these were most likely those of the officer."

"Officer?" asked Jim. "There was no officer among them!"

"I know, I know. But the scoundrels seem to have had access to an officer's uniform. We shall soon clarify this. You spoke with these people. Was there one among them of a stocky build, his face framed by a full, dark beard?"

"That description fits their leader."

"He had brushed his mustache down as if he wanted to cover his lips. By chance, did you make a remark about his mouth?"

"I did. He had a slight hare's lip. I saw it clearly."

"All right. Then we've got that fellow. It's him. He rode to Helmers Home to find out if any danger might be coming from there. Go on."

"I'd rather not continue. To admit to one's own stupidity, isn't the height of pleasure. Why don't you go on, old Tim."

90

"Thanks a lot," Tim responded. "Whoever ate the good meat ought to also chew on the bones. Why am I to continue from where the stupidity occurred?"

"Because you've got such a fine way to make even the deficient appear excellent."

"Yeah, I know! I'm always the one, who's to suffer for the sins of others. But since you are my brother I'll be kind and try to present this stupid story in as good a light as possible. You must know, gentlemen, it's a funny thing, but we later lost the tracks and despite our best efforts were unable to pick them up again."

"Impossible!" Old Shatterhand exclaimed.

"But I tell you, Sir. It's true."

"The two Snuffles lost the trail? If someone else would tell me this I would call him a liar."

"I thank you, Sir. But since Tim Snuffle tells you this himself, you must believe it."

"Sure. But how did this happen?"

"Easy as pie. Over there, where the mesquite ends, rocky ground begins stretching for miles to the east and south. You must see this ground to understand why we lost the tracks."

"I do know it. The Mexicans, to whom this rocky stretch of land once belonged, called it *el plano del diablo*, the devil's plain."

"That's right. You know it? Have you been there before?"

"Twice."

"That eases my conscience, for then you will not think us greenhorns. I must admit that it looked as if the tracks had been blown away."

"But four riders cannot have been blown away."

"No. But if the horses leave no tracks on this iron-hard, smooth rock, then no tracks can be seen, Sir. Despite his youth, our Comanche here is a very competent tracker, but I tell you: even he was at the end of his wisdom."

"I would like to now know whether I would have fared as you did."

"Yes, you! You are a different chap from a Snuffle like me! You and Winnetou would spy the tracks even if the fellows had galloped away through the air. I almost believe they did. I tell you, not the smallest crushed pebble, not the poorest scratch of a horseshoe could be seen on those rocks. Of course, we did what every competent frontiersman would have done. We rode along the edge of the rocky ground to find the spot where these rascals came off the rock and hit sandy soil again. This went so slowly that we're not quite finished yet. We are now already to the north of the point where the single horseman left the other four, to ride to Helmers Home as you said. By the way, when we came from over there we saw a single horseman on the horizon who galloped south. When we reached this bush island we noticed that this man had stopped here."

91

This tweaked Old Shatterhand's ears. He seemed to ponder this information for a while. Then he rose, checked the various hoof prints at the edge of the mesquite bushes, in the process leaving the others a short distance behind. Suddenly, they heard his call.

"Tim, or you Jim, have you also been here where I'm standing?"

"No, Sir," Jim replied.

"Then, all of you come over here."

They followed his request. When they arrived, Old Shatterhand pointed to the bushes, telling them, "Here you can see very clearly that someone entered the bushes. A twig's broken there, its fracture point is not yet dried up. It cannot have happened too long ago. Come with me, gentlemen."

Checking every twig and every inch of the ground, he penetrated the dense shrubbery until he arrived at a sandy spot. The area, about several paces long and wide, was totally bare of any growth. Not the tiniest blade of grass or any other plant could be seen. He knelt down, and it seemed as if he was going to investigate every single grain of sand individually. Finally he rose with a smile only to also look at the bushes bordering the open area. He pointed to a spot and said, "Someone entered this hiding place. I bet that this person dismounted outside the bushes on the rocky ground. Now, tell me two things, Tim: Was it south of here where the one split from the others?"

"Southeast, Sir."

"All right. Did the man you saw leaving here wear a uniform?"

"No."

"Now I'm sure of the following sequence. The leader of the five rode here after he left the others to get the uniform and dress up as an officer for his ride to Helmers Home. After he left there surreptitiously, he returned here to take off the uniform and put on his regular garb."

"Are you saying, Sir, this place is a wardrobe?"

"Yes. At least a hide, a cache. Take your knives and start digging. One can see that the sand has been carefully smoothed over recently."

The two Snuffles looked at him in surprise. But Hobble-Frank bent down and started digging in the sand. He did so with his bare hands as if he were out for Golkonda's Treasures. This induced the others to come to his assistance. Sand flew in all directions. Frank had barely penetrated ten inches when he called in German, "I've got it, Mister Shatterhand! My fingers hit something hard."

"Go on, go on!" Jim urged, also in German. "This hard object could also be rock."

"What!" Frank exclaimed. "You also speak German? Were you too born between the Mont Blanc and Vegesack?"

"My name's Hofmann. That's enough for now. Keep digging."

"I'm digging like a mole and werewolf. It's not rock, but wood. There it is, a lot of thin rods."

"These are cactus ribs," Old Shatterhand explained, "which have been tied together to form the cache's lid."

His opinion proved to be correct. The straight ribs had been woven together to form a square lid which covered the deep hole. The cache was about three feet long and three feet wide and filled to the top with a variety of items. The first things coming to light was a saber and a uniform upon which lay an old, torn newspaper.

"Ah, the officer's get-up and the robber-knight's blade," said Frank, pulling the saber from its scabbard, slashing the air. "If the rascal were here, I would give him a smack on the head."

"Dear Frank, the paper, please," Old Shatterhand interrupted.

"Okay, okay. Right away."

He handed the newspaper page to Old Shatterhand, who unfolded it. It contained a note onto which were written the words the hunter read to the others: *"Venid pronto en nuestro escondite! Precaution! Old Shatterhand está en casa de Helmers!"*

"What does it mean?" asked Fred. "How about it, Frank, you know languages?"

"Yes," the linguist responded. "There's talk of Old Shatterhand and Helmers. But this Chinese is so infected by Indian pre- and suffixes and eaten up by Indo-germanic trichinae that the first word already wrenches my heart in its chest. I rather claim innocence and dedicate myself to checking the uniform."

He began to check the uniform's pockets thoroughly.

Old Shatterhand translated the Spanish lines, "Come quickly to our hiding place! Watch out! Old Shatterhand is at Helmers."

For the time being no one was interested to explore the meaning of these words. Everyone wanted to know the content of the cache first. It held a number of used, but useable clothing of various kinds, sizes and colors, in addition to rifles, pistols, knives, lead, tins of percussion caps and even a small barrel half-filled with powder. The pockets of all coats found in the cache were empty.

"We will burn the clothes," Old Shatterhand suggested. "The other stuff is good booty. Everybody may take what he likes. What's left we shall take to Helmers Home. I'm convinced the Llano Runners have more of these caches to store some of their plunder. The uniform probably belonged to an officer they murdered. Of these finds only this note is of value to me. What are you making of its content, Jim?"

"Two things. First, that the chap has enormous respect for you. He would most likely have stayed longer at Helmers Home had he not met you there. While I don't know all that happened there, it's only my opinion."

"And secondly?"

"Secondly, there are several more fellow-rascals about he's trying to warn with this note. They too intend to enter the Estacado. They too are expected to

93

come here to open the cache. He asks them to meet at a gathering place, he calls a hiding place."

"That's also my opinion. From all this you can see that you need not find the lost tracks again. This man will surely meet with the other four members. To find them, you follow his tracks which, from hereon, will be very obvious. They lead to the hiding place he names in his note. Can you figure why he's asking his people to come there?"

"Of course, Sir. He's after the immigrants."

"I believe so too. And soon, I think, as is apparent from his hurry. He's afraid of me. He's aware with what suspicion I treated him. He's concerned, that we catch on to his tricks and will frustrate them. This is why he will speed up the execution of his plans."

"Then we too must hurry as well, Sir. Am I right in assuming that you will help us?"

"Certainly! First of all, I must have a word with these people concerning the chief's murder. Then we must prevent another evil deed. How do we achieve this? What is your advice?" asked Old Shatterhand.

"Me suggest anything to you? Hmm. Jim Snuffle is to offer a suggestion to Old Shatterhand. That's truly a compliment! No, we are going to follow whatever you suggest. Right, old Tim?"

"Yes," his brother responded. "Old Shatterhand is firmly in the midst of things, while we are still meandering about the periphery. Or can you suggest anything, Fred?"

"No, not I. For that I'm not the best choice. But I can voice an opinion. Wouldn't it be the smartest thing to follow the fellow right away? He's the leader of the gang, of the entire operation. Should we catch him, the deed will not take place."

"Unlikely," Old Shatterhand opined. "While he seems to be the spokesman of the five, we do not know whether he is the true leader of the Llano Vultures. If we catch the latter, we will most likely destroy the Vultures' entire enterprise. I also don't think we can soon catch up with him. Our horses are not the best and the sun is setting soon. It would be night before we could collar him. No, let him go for today. His tracks will still be here tomorrow. All of you stay at this place to apprehend those to whom the note is addressed – should they arrive. I alone will ride back to Helmers Home with the three horses to get Jemmy, Davy, and Bob. By daybreak we will leave from here. I think our ride will not be in vain. There will be nine of us, and I'm convinced we can deal with a gang of about twenty or thirty Vultures, which I think them to be."

His proposal found general acceptance. Each of the others selected whatever he could use from the discovered weapons and ammunition. The clothing was carried into open terrain and there burned with the aid of dried mesquite branches. This pyre was still smoking when Old Shatterhand mounted his horse.

He promised to bring back provisions, including water and on leaving pointed west saying, "It looks to me as if a storm, or whatever, is developing there. Unfortunately, it never brings water to the Llano."

Then he rode off to the north, the three other horses in tow. Made aware of it, the others examined the westerly sky where a small cloud stood above the sun. Golden reflexes played inside its reddish-gray arc. It didn't look dangerous at all and Old Shatterhand's words were taken as just a remark lacking further significance. Only the Comanche kept looking thoughtfully at the small cloud formation and mumbled to himself, "*Temb metan*, the mouth of lightning!"

The men sat down again and the Snuffles were told what else had happened at Helmers Home. This was done with the greatest elaboration and time passed very quickly. The men had no longer paid any attention to the sky which, by now, had taken on a very different coloration. Only the Comanche, sitting silently aside from them, kept observing the change. The small cloud arc, open to the ground, took on the form of a horseshoe, its sides lengthened noticeably until they formed two long narrow arms almost touching the dark horizon. Between them the clear sky was still visible. Then the nearer of the two arms descended whilst the southern sky turned a dusty orange-red. It looked as if a storm was raging there that carried the fine sand into the sky above.

It turned dark in the east as if heavy clouds gathered there, yet none were seen. Suddenly, the Comanche leaped up and shouted, pointing to the black wall rising in the east, forgetting the highest virtue of his race, namely self-control, "*Maho-timb-yuavah* - The Ghost of the Llano."

Startled, the others jumped up too. Only now did they become aware of the sky's dramatic change. Terror froze their look when they followed the direction Ironheart indicated. Above the horizon, at the approximate height of three men, a horseman appeared to gallop along. The black wall as background, the figure was highlighted by a bright halo of light, which followed the rider at the same speed, causing the figure to appear as a silhouette framed by light. The rider's figure, as well as that of his horse, was enormously magnified. His limbs were quite clearly recognizable. With his right hand he held the reins, with his left the brim of his hat. The rifle, slung over his back, bounced up and down. The mane and tail of his horse streamed backwards from the speed of his ride. The ghostly animal flew along as if pursued by hellfire. This all happened while it was still day, a full hour before sunset. It made an indescribably terrifying impression on the watchers. None of them uttered a word or made a sound.

Towards the south the black wall broke off almost vertically. To this spot the horseman was headed. Closer and closer he came. Ten more leaps of the horse, five more, then three, now only one more – and the animal shot into the void, disappearing together with its rider. The bright halo had disappeared with them.

95

The men stood there, speechless. Their gaze wandered among themselves and between the point where the phenomenon had disappeared and were it had first been noticed. Then Jim shook himself as though he was cold and said, "By the heavens, if that wasn't the Ghost of Llano Estacado, I'll never be called Snuffle again. I always thought it to be nonsense, but after this experience one would be crazy to doubt it. I feel totally unreal. How are you doing, old Tim?"

"Just like a worn money bag, which doesn't hold a single red cent any more. I'm empty, totally empty, only skin and air. And see how quickly the sky's changing. I've never seen anything like this."

The upper edge of the black wall had turned blood red with lightning sparking up and down. Then the other arm of the still high up horseshoe-like cloud descended, and the lower it came the broader and darker it turned. To the south appeared what looked like a whirlwind of dust and smoke, coming closer and closer. A threatening dark curtain obscured the sun, the former growing darker and wider by the second. Then the dark cloud seemed to literally fall from the sky. Suddenly, the terrified men were enveloped by an unusual cold. A shrill howl sounded from afar.

"By God, let's get the animals!" Juggle-Fred shouted over the din. "Quickly! Or they'll bolt. Pull them down. They must lie down. Hold them fast, but you too must lie flat on the ground."

All five ran towards the three remaining animals, which snorted anxiously and didn't resist being pulled down. They lay close to the shrubbery and tugged their heads into them. And barely had the men lain down too, when all hell broke loose. There commenced an indescribable whistling, moaning, howling, rushing, roaring, and thundering. The men had the impression as if a heavy blanket had been tossed over them. They were pushed to the ground with such force, that they could not have risen of their own accord, even if they had wanted to. Their limbs felt ice-cold. Their orifices, eyes, mouth and ears were blocked by frozen water. They were unable to breathe and came close to suffocating. Then, just as suddenly, glowing hot air wafted over them and the howling voices of the Llano Estacado died away in the distance.

The animals jumped up neighing loudly. The sudden appearance of dark and numbing night was followed by bright sunshine and life-giving warmth. One could open one's mouth and could again breathe. The five people began to move and freed their eyes from the cloying sand to look around.

They found themselves covered by a foot-high layer of sand, the 'blanket' the tornado had dropped on them. Yes, it had been a tornado, one of these cyclones of the American heartland, which generate such force as cannot be found anywhere else. The destruction such tornadoes wreak are of a most terrible, almost unbelievable kind. They attain a speed of more than a hundred miles an hour and are often accompanied by electrical discharges, which may linger on after the storm has passed. Even the Samum of the African desert does not pack such force, only the terrible sand and snowstorms of the wild Gobi develop such elementary power that is comparable with that of a tornado. The five men rose to shake the sand from their clothing. The shrubbery had formed a barrier for the sand, which had piled up two feet high in front of it.

"God be thanked, that it passed us so mercifully," Jim proclaimed. "Woe to those who found themselves in open country when it hit. They would be lost."

"Not necessarily," Fred disagreed. "Fortunately, these terrible winds have often only a breadth of half a mile, but the greater is their violence. This devastating air turbulence touched us only at its fringe. Had we been in its midst we, together with our animals, would have been picked up like toys and carried through the air to who knows how far and then tossed somewhere to our death."

"That's correct!" Jim confirmed. "I know it. I once saw the destruction a tornado had wrought at the Rio Conchos. It had entered a forest and cut a straight pass through it. Giant trees, some of them probably seven feet in diameter, had been uprooted and lay tossed about like matchsticks. This passage, totally impassable, not a single tree standing inside its perimeter, displayed such a sharp border where, at its left and right, trees still standing were only slightly damaged."

"Ours here was terrible enough," Hobble-Frank added. "My breath had totally left me, so that my clarinet sounded its last chime. I recall that at times we also had storms in Saxony, but they've never been as wild and uncivilized as here. A good Saxon storm is like child's play compared to such an American tornado, a mere May breeze, just sufficient to cool a cup of hot coffee. To top it off, your jackasses almost kicked me to death. Towards the end, they didn't want to stay put any longer and must have thought my noble figure to be ---"

"Mules, you intended to say, Mister Frank," Jim interrupted.

"No, jackasses I'm saying. If they trample me in such a way they're the greatest asses there can be. They squashed the entire artistic design of my Ostrogoth stature. I should actually sue you for damages. But being such a uniquely irreplaceable person and of such pleasant nature, I will cease and desist this time around. But I won't suffer such jackassry again."

At that he threw his rifle over his shoulder and stalked away. The others nodded smilingly at each other and said no word to reconcile him. Fred knew that the little Saxon would soon show up again. The sun, completely hidden earlier, now once more beamed down its beneficent warmth. But its light was of a peculiar coloration, one could have almost called it a saffron-yellow. The horizon became blurred by this color and the earth seemed to be rising above it. This gave the impression as if the five men stood at the lowest point of a huge depression.

The three mounts were still not calmed. They wanted to take off and needed to be tied up. Something was in the air; the lungs resisted inhaling. These were not microscopically small dust particles impregnating the air but something indefinably weird. The Comanche had spread his blanket on the ground and had lain down. Even now, after such a powerful natural event, he still maintained his silent reserve so characteristic of Indians. The three Whites sat next to him and Jim asked him, "Did my young red brother experience such a storm before?"

"Several," the Indian responded. "Ironheart was once tossed far by the *nina-yandan*, the murderous wind, to then be buried in sand. But the warriors of the Comanche found him. He has seen uprooted trees whose trunk could barely be girded by six men."

"But you didn't see the Ghost of Llano Estacado before?"

"Him too, Ironheart saw him three winters ago, when he crossed the Llano with his father. They heard a shot. When they arrived at the spot from where the shot had sounded, they saw the Ghost gallop off on a black horse. At the place lay a paleface with a hole in the midst of his forehead. The Chief of the Comanche knew the dead as a feared murderer."

"What did the Ghost look like?"

"He had the head and the body of a white buffalo, his neck covered by a shaggy mane. He was terrible to look at. Yet he is a good ghost or he would not assume the image of this revered animal. The Comanche know well, that he kills only evil men, while all good people are under his protection. Ironheart knows two Comanche who got lost in the Llano and were close to dying. The Ghost came to them in the night and gave them water and meat, then directed them on the right way."

"Did he also speak to them?"

"He talked with them in the Comanche language. A good ghost speaks all languages, which the Great Spirit has taught him. Howgh!"

He turned away. His last-spoken word conveyed the message, that he had spoken enough and intended to be silent now.

Frank stood some distance away, but when he noticed the two conversing, he had glanced longingly over. He was unable to pout at a distance while others happily talked with each other. He resolved to join the group again, walked over, and said to Fred, "I gave you some time to figuratively slap your chest and to make amends. I hope you realize how severely you sinned against my superlative method of interpretation. Do you honestly admit to it?"

"Yes," Frank told him with a serious face. "We gladly admit, that you are far superior to us."

"Then keep yourself in check next time and don't let yourself be carried away by your global temperament. I forgive you this time, for after an experience like we just survived, we ought all to be willing to reconcile ourselves. To see a living ghost in bright daylight threatens the living daylight out of me. My goose bumps became almost as big as balloons."

He sat next to Fred, who told him smilingly, "You needn't be so terrified. The apparition we saw can be explained by natural means. Just think of the Ghost of the Brocken in the Harz Mountains, whose origin the Brocken Innkeeper Nehse explained so convincingly."

"Nehse? I know him too. His son is a famous civil engineer and lives in Blasewitz. I had the honor to meet him at a country party in Moritzburg where he gave me an elaborate report on the Brocken Ghost. He explained it as being a sap-vapor-enriched air, half ozone and half oxygen, which fog dissolves into glowing hail. But here in the Llano we are dealing with a real ghost. We saw him riding in the sky. It wasn't air, it wasn't fog, but the tangible form of a real supernatural being. This cannot have been an optical illusion!"

"Hmm. As a juggler in times past as I have conjured up artificial ghosts."

"You better be quiet about that, because to produce artificial ghosts is pure swindle. How did you do it though?"

"Either by means of a slanted pane of glass or a camera."

"I can do that too. I once build such a camera obscuriosa myself. The construction went quite well, except that I had forgotten to create the hole where one pours in the ocular lentils. But I also couldn't get the right kind of lentils from any greengrocer. So, I finally put the whole project aside."

This remark caused Frank and the two Snuffles to erupt into such uproarious laughter that even the usually serious Comanche turned around to look at them in surprise. Frank, however, who didn't understand the reason for such hilarity, but realized that it was in connection with his previous remark, entered a state of anger like never before and once again stalked away. The Snuffles and Fred fell silent.

"I didn't figure he would take it so hard. We must appease him by being extraordinarily polite after this. He's a soul of a guy and his grand sophistry is only fun and doesn't harm anyone."

He told the Snuffles what he knew about Hobble-Frank and disposed the two well towards the odd little fellow. Then, of course, the conversation returned to the tornado and the preceding appearance of the Ghost of the Llano. Not that the three were uneducated men. Particularly Fred possessed greater than usual knowledge of the natural sciences. Still, they were unable to explain the apparition scientifically. Some time passed over this until night descended. It became so dark that one couldn't see farther than five paces. That's when Frank ambled in again. He didn't care to be alone at such a place and in such darkness. But his anger had yet to subside fully. Not speaking a word, he didn't settle in beside them, but lay down a little distance away. Nevertheless, he listened attentively to what they were talking about. From his movements they could deduce that he almost rose from time to time to raise an objection when something had been said, which he thought he knew better about. Every time, though, he lay down again. His desire to pout was greater than his propensity to brag with his conceited knowledge.

By now the air had cleared and could again be breathed without effort. A light breeze had risen coming from the southwest, most pleasant after the day's heat. Stars speckling the sky told the men the passing of the night's time. They had stopped talking and made an effort to fall asleep. It was unlikely that any hostile being would surprise them and Old Shatterhand could not be expected to return yet. The Whites readily fell asleep, but the Comanche kept gazing at the sky, although he had not slept the previous night for even a minute. His father's death, or rather his murder, occupied his young, vengeance seeking soul.

Time passed. Suddenly the sleepers were awakened by a shout from the Indian. Startled, they rose to a sitting position.

"*Mava tuhschta* - look over there!" he said, pointing south.

Even in the darkness they could discern his stretched out arm to follow the direction it was pointing. There, where sky met horizon, a brightening, stretched-out semicircle had appeared. While it did not look much out of the ordinary it, nevertheless, attracted the men's full attention.

"Hmm," Jim mumbled, "if this were in the east, I would think we slept that long and it would be daybreak."

"No," his brother Tim objected. "Daybreak is totally different. The borders of this bright spot are much too defined."

"Because it is night! Isn't it?"

"Precisely because it is night, it cannot be sunrise yet. Day and night fade into each other, but the spot over there has well-defined contours."

"Could it be a fire?"

"A fire in the Llano where there's no wood? What should burn here? That would be something new."

"That's true. My goodness, if the sand starts burning, that would be the ultimate. We would have to mount quickly and hurry off. But how else would you explain the phenomenon?"

"I don't know that either. By the way, the bright spot is increasing. The wind is turning too and now comes from the southwest. Presently, it comes from the west and becomes stronger and colder. What is its meaning?"

"It cannot be the aurora borealis," Fred asserted. "And the southern lights cannot be seen here, nor has anyone ever heard of that."

Until now Frank had remained silent but could no longer restrain himself.

"This bright spot at the horizon has a meaning," he said. "For sure, it's connected with the Avenging Ghost. Earlier he rode south. Maybe he has his wigwam there and sits by the camp fire."

The Snuffles almost broke into laughter again but kept their hilarity under control. Fred commented, "You really think a ghost would start a camp fire?"

"Why not? With the wind as cold as it's blowing right now."

Yes, the air had turned sharply harsher. More and more did it turn north.

And down south the brightness rose higher and higher. It looked as if the disk of a mighty big star was rising. It now formed a semicircle, a blood-red core at its center, which became brighter and brighter around its arc, around which dark cloud masses and spitting fire balls seemed to roil. The whole presented a horribly gorgeous sight. The five men stood silently. They dared not speak much.

Now the wind came directly from the north. In the brief time span of a quarter of an hour it had turned around half the horizon but without any whistling and bluster. No, in what rather seemed malicious silence, it traveled towards the grandly illuminated area in the sky. At that it was so cold, that one could have used a fur coat.

"Old Shatterhand should see this!" Juggle-Fred said. "Unfortunately, he can't be back yet, since it must be just past midnight."

"Midnight!" Hobble-Frank exclaimed. "That's the Ghostly Hour. It's certain that over there, where it is burning, something terrible is going to happen."

"What, besides a fire, is there to happen?"

"Don't ask so silly! At midnight, Orkus, the ruler of the Underworld opens its doors and the ghost come wandering. For an entire hour they cause malice and havoc. I know it, because my eyes are open even in the night. And every land and every people have their characteristic ghosts. In Saxony we have the most benign ghosts, but elsewhere they wring people's necks. Who knows the local ghosts' passions. They could be the most dangerous and ugly ones. Let's be careful and --- Oh my God! Wasn't I right? Look over there. There he comes again!"

His last words were spoken in utter terror. And what now happened could truly bring the greatest horror to even the most fearless person. The Ghost of Llano Estacado appeared once more. As mentioned before, the strange light now formed a semicircle in the sky above the southern horizon. Where the left arm of the arc touched the ground there suddenly appeared the image of a giant horseman. The horse was black with the rider being white, the latter having the figure of a buffalo. One could clearly make out the head with its horns, the neck with its shaggy mane streaming backwards, and the body which, towards the back, merged with that of the horse. Sparkling lines of light framed the contours of this image. The horse was in a tearing gallop. It did not move in a straight line, rather it galloped along the arc yet never seemed to lose contact with the ground. Thus it rose along the arc to its highest point from which it descended to the right of the glowing semicircle where it touched the horizon. From there it disappeared as quickly as it had appeared.

Despite the cold air wafting about the spectators had turned hot. Could that have been a delusion? No, it was the indisputable truth! They were mum, could not give expression to their feelings. Even the deliberate Comanche could not restrain himself and uttered one 'Uff' after another. What had caused the Whites to fall speechless had opened his mouth. They all stood there waiting if the apparition might reappear – but in vain. For a while the semicircle kept blazing at the same strength. Then the arc lost its distinct outline and began to fade.

Suddenly, soft hoof beats sounded on the sand behind them. Several horsemen arrived and dismounted. The first was Old Shatterhand.

"God be thanked! You are still alive!" he exclaimed. "I thought you might have been killed and expected to have to dig your bodies from the sand."

"The tornado wasn't that bad," Fred answered. "We were only grazed by it, Sir. You must have truly made haste to be here already. We didn't expect you until much later."

"Yes, we kept up a real par force ride thinking we needed to rescue you. This is why Mister Helmers joined us with his farmhands. We were very much concerned for you. The tornado passed very close to Helmers Home. We saw the damage it caused and from its direction were certain that it must have hit you. Fortunately, it was merciful."

The others, Jemmy, Davy, Bob, and Helmers people in Old Shatterhand's company also expressed their joy of seeing the 'survivors'. Jemmy and Davy had been told that the Snuffles had shown up. While they were glad to meet them, they wasted few words, for more important issues needed to be discussed.

Fred reported briefly about the dual appearance of the Ghost. Jemmy and Davy silently shook their heads. They didn't want to insult the storyteller with doubtful remarks. Helmers commented, "What you are telling us here, Sir, must be the truth, because ten eyes have seen it, but I can neither comprehend nor explain it. There's probably no human being who can irrevocably prove whether we are dealing with a phantom or an actual being."

"Oh, yes, there's such a human being, this being myself," Hobble-Frank piped up. "It cannot have been an illusion, since the figures were seen by us in utter perfection. The Ghost is a supernatural being, which can ride through the air. At the time we were smack in the midst of the ghostly hour. This fact explains the entire apparition and is the best proof that we are dealing with a deceased soul from the heavens. I don't expect anyone to contradict me."

He was mistaken. Old Shatterhand patted his shoulder and told him amicably, "What is one to expect if one dares to contradict you, dear Frank?"

"Hmm, that would depend on who it comes from. I would literally smash anyone with my proofs so that his scientific existence would be destroyed once and for all. But should you risk a small, modest question, I'd make an exception and supply the desired information amicably."

"I don't need information from you. That the second apparition came during the midnight hour is no proof of its supernatural origin. Remember that it first appeared during the day. If you gave me an extensive description of the entire event, I'm convinced I could explain it in detail."

"I dispute that. But since it is you, I'll describe the events, you being the only one of all those present who can impress me."

The little Saxon gave an excellent and very detailed description of the dual ghostly appearances. Old Shatterhand broke in twice with a question. In the meantime the light-show in the south had sunk lower and lower to become fainter and fainter, as if it were in the process of disappearing entirely. For a few minutes it was only a pale glimmer at the horizon, but suddenly it became brighter again. At first it did not rise to its previous height, rather did it glitter like the sparks of a slow-match ever farther to the west. There it stopped, but then, with immense speed grew into a sea of flames illuminating the sky.

"By the devil!" Frank exclaimed. "The story's starting once more. Such a ghostly hour I've never experienced before. This fire is of a supernatural origin, because ---"

"Nonsense!" Old Shatterhand broke in. "This is readily explainable. The fire over there is entirely natural."

"What is there to burn?"

"Dried cacti. As you know, the Llano has huge tracts that are overgrown by cacti no horseman can penetrate. Once the plants are desiccated, a single careless spark suffices to generate a firestorm in the blink of an eye."

"That's correct," Helmers seconded, "and I know for certain that there are broad expanses of cacti to the south and west."

"Well, then we have an explanation for the fire and the two apparent ghosts we will also catch by their scruffs yet."

"Not so fast!" Hobble-Frank dissented. "Apparent ghosts? These were real. And how do you arrive at the idea these were two ghosts?"

"This can be assumed from the kind of figures represented. The first ghost, who appeared during the day, was the make-believe officer. Whoever the second one was I'm unable to say. I don't know anyone wearing a white buffalo hide."

"Give me some peace now, Mister Shatterhand. Although I said that you are the only one who could impress me, it means only somewhat. No human being can ride along the sky, but that is what's happened as us five saw very clearly with our own eyes."

"Yes, the images moved up there in the sky, but their originals rode down here on earth."

"The images? Gee, that's too much now. In all my life I haven't heard of images being able to ride, in addition to it happening in the atmosphere. How do you propose these pictures were generated?"

"By warm air currents like those caused by the fire over there."

"So! You say air currents create pictures. That's something new to me. Until now I thought they could be produced only with the aid of pencils, photography, and other such means."

"By a mirror too."

"Yes, I forgot that one."

"Well then. Under certain conditions air can act like a mirror."

103

"If you say so. Yes, I can see this, because I'm a master in the sciences of air mirror images."

"All right! Will you then admit, that your ghosts were just mirages like ---"

He halted in mid-speech. His attention had been drawn to the fire, dark red on the horizon, now with a roiling cover of clouds above it. Above them, but beyond the flames, suspended in the air, there evolved the inverted image of a flat landscape glowing red as the one below. At the left, where it began, a horseman appeared from darkness, clad in a buffalo skin, the same the men had seen earlier. Now, though, he rode upside down, his head towards the ground.

"--- that one over there," Old Shatterhand continued, pointing to the mirage.

He had not finished yet when a second horseman appeared, chasing the first.

"Oh my goodness," cried Hobble-Frank, "isn't this the one who appeared in the afternoon just before the tornado?"

"Is it him?" Old Shatterhand asked. "Will you agree now, that we are dealing with two very different images? And look, there are more coming."

Following the last horsemen in a gallop were five or six more, also inverted, their figures upside down.

"That's just too much," Hobble-Frank said. "If I were alone, I would become very frightened. This ghostly hour is really getting to be too much. I've heard of ghosts riding through the night with their head under the arm, but for them now all riding upside down, is just too much for me."

"This is nothing horrific. The previous images were refracted several times, the current one only once. And, by the way, we will soon get to know these ghosts. Quickly! Mount your horses, gentlemen! I'm sure the first horseman is the so-called Ghost of Llano Estacado. The others pursue him. And since he's a good fellow, let's see if we can give him a hand."

"Are you out of your mind?" Frank shouted. "That's sinning against the spiritual world!"

Frank continued by quoting Goethe, that humans ought not to test the Gods, but the others would not listen to him and rather followed Old Shatterhand's urging. Their trust in the man gave them confidence, he would not ask of them anything that was dangerous or of a ridiculous nature.

"Shall we also take the pack horses?" Helmers asked.

"Yes. It's unlikely we will return here. But you were to accompany us only to here, Mister Helmers. But given the current circumstances, I'm sure you would want to accompany us a little further."

"Of course! I'd love to trade a few words with the Avenging Ghost."

The two packhorses Helmers had brought along were led by the farm hands. Frank, too, mounted his steed. It wasn't fear that had caused his resistance, but rather his pervasive spirit of contradiction. The group began to move and quickly fell into a full gallop. As soon as the riders had left their previous location the mirage disappeared. Only the flaring fire remained. Old Shatterhand rode ahead followed by the Snuffles, whose mules pursued the hunter's black horse with demoniacal obsession. He did not head directly for the fire, but somewhat to the north of it. He could not see the destination he was aiming for, but had to calculate it. This was quite difficult, since the mirage - now gone from sight – had not provided clear guidance, and the horsemen he wanted to meet, were traveling at high speed.

The small group flew in a wild chase across the countryside. Old Shatterhand had to slow his horse so that the others could follow. They must have covered three miles in ten minutes, yet one could not discern if they had come any closer to the fire, except that its brightness seemed to have increased. Ten more minutes passed. Then Old Shatterhand yelled, raised his arm, and diverged slightly to the right from their previous heading. From there two dots approached, ahead a brighter one followed by one that was darker. Farther back, a number of other dark dots could be made out, eager to catch up with the first two. These were all horsemen. The fire's light shone sideways onto the riders and made the foremost shaggy figure recognizable from afar. Old Shatterhand reined in his horse to dismount.

"Get off too," he called to the others. "Since we come out of the dark, we haven't been seen yet, while we can distinguish them clearly against the light. Have the horses lie down. But as soon as I mount up again, do the same."

They followed his request.

Old Shatterhand had purposely chosen a depression to dismount. Once the horses lay down and the riders had squatted down beside them, it was virtually impossible for someone coming from the firelight and riding into darkness, to make out what lay before him, until he was practically on top of it. The frontiersmen, though, could readily observe the land ahead of them. The first horseman was perhaps still six-hundred paces away, followed by the second at half this span, with the other six at the same distance again.

"What are we going to do about them, Sir? Shall we shoot them?" Helmers inquired.

"No. They haven't done anything to us, and I don't care to spill human blood, except if I have a good reason to do so. I only want to have a word with the first pursuer. Let me do my own thing first. You needn't do anything else. Just chase the other six away."

He unfastened his lasso from his hips and attached its end to the pommel of the saddle of his horse, which lay quietly in the sand. Then he readied the primary loop to surround the torso of a person. The remaining length of the fivefold braided and about twenty foot long rope he wound from between thumb and index finger to his elbow into great loops, which he then took into his left hand. He then kept the very first loop in his right, so that he held this ring firmly between thumb and index finger.

This had been done rapidly so that he was finished with his preparations before the first horseman had even come close. Now the chase approached the depression. The hoof beats of the first horse could be heard now. It was a tall black horse. Its rider carried a white buffalo's head on top of his, its shaggy mane hanging far below his horse's crupper. His face was buried so deeply in the skull, that it was unrecognizable. When he was still ten paces from the depression, Old Shatterhand rose. The rider saw him immediately, but was unable to stop his horse quickly enough, so that he came to a halt only when he stood in front of Old Shatterhand.

"Stop! Who are you?" the hunter asked.

"The Ghost of the Llano," it sounded hollowly from beneath the buffalo skull. "And you?"

"I am Old Shatterhand. You may dismount safely. We shall protect you."

"The Avenging Ghost needs no protection. I do thank you though!"

With these words he again urged his horse on. The exchange had taken only a few seconds. Nevertheless, the other horseman had now come closer. Old Shatterhand positioned himself above the body of his prone horse, straddling the saddle. A slight click of his tongue and the well-trained horse was up. It seemed as if horse and rider had risen from the earth. The sudden appearance also blocked the way of the startled pursuer. He was unable to halt his horse as quickly as he would have liked. His command over his horse was obviously much inferior to that of the Ghost's. He came to a stop only close to Old Shatterhand.

"Hold it!" the latter commanded. "Who are you?"

"By the devil! Old Shatterhand!" the man hissed. "The devil should get you!"

He gave his horse the spurs to hurry on.

"I'm telling you to stay," the hunter commanded.

"Later, when it suits me better."

With these words he was off. But Old Shatterhand was right behind him.

When the rider had mockingly spoken his words, the young Comanche had leaped from the ground.

"Uff!" he shouted. "I know this voice. Ironheart too must speak with this man."

He raised his rifle and aimed, but quickly lowered it again saying, "Old Shatterhand has him already."

The fugitive had barely advanced the length of about ten horses, when Old Shatterhand, right on his heels, swinging the lasso four, five times above his head, slung it after the rider. The rope readily ran off the loops that Old Shatterhand held loosely in his left hand. Its front loop, though, fell over the escapee's shoulders. Immediately, Old Shatterhand halted his horse. The lasso, attached to the saddle, ran off quickly. Then the loop tightened around the rider and pulled him from the saddle. Old Shatterhand jumped off his horse and ran to the man on the ground, who could not free himself quickly since both his arms had been firmly pinned to his body.

In the meantime another event evolved behind the two. The other six horsemen had approached and Old Shatterhand's companions had quickly mounted their now standing horses. The six were very much startled to suddenly see such a superior number of riders facing them. They turned sideways to pass them. That's when they noticed that their leader had been lassoed. They must have felt lost without him and too weak to help him, for they immediately scattered in all directions. This maneuver also served the purpose to make pursuit difficult, but no one intended to do this anyway, since Old Shatterhand had urged them not to. And that they fled, instead of stopping, was the best indication that they did not have a clear conscience. They were allowed to go and everyone gathered around the prone leader. Old Shatterhand had disarmed him and now told him, "You would have been wiser to follow my command. Whoever I command to halt must follow this request, whether of his own accord or by force. Tell me who you are?"

The captive remained silent.

"So you don't care to give me this pleasure either. You don't seem to feel very secure. Then, let me have a look at your face."

He lifted him up to face the shine of the distant fire.

"Wouldn't you believe it!" Helmers exclaimed. "It's our grand officer. I'm pleased to see you again so soon. Your wardrobe back in the bushes has been found and cleaned out. You had hid it poorly. Your uniform, too, was found in there. What do you think is going to happen to you?"

"There's nothing you can do," the man answered angrily. "Who of you can say that I committed anything against him?"

"Yes. That is what you rely on. You haven't done anything directly against us yet. But the plans you have are terrible indeed. Consequently we could apply the laws of the prairie against you. But we are no executioners and will let you go."

"You must, because you have no claim against me."

"Not so. We could prove a few things, but that's not really necessary. We Whites will let you go, but there's still a red man, who has to settle an account with you. Have a good look at him."

The Comanche stepped forward. The man looked at him and said, "I don't know this fellow."

"Don't lie, you crook!" Tim shouted at him. "You probably claim not to know me and my brother either? Didn't you attack the two innocent Comanche, killed one and pursued the other, until we succeeded in getting you off their tracks? That's when we took up pursuit of you. It's very nice of you to cross our

107

path here and save us the effort of having to catch you. Don't imagine you can talk yourself out of your troubles by lying. Cut it short and admit your guilt."

"I am not guilty of anything!" the captive grated.

That's when Old Shatterhand placed his hand heavily on his shoulder and told him, "You are aware of your situation here. I suppose you've learned that I'm a man you can't fool with. What are you planning for the immigrants, your pious Tobias Praisegod Burton is to lead through the Llano? Where are these people presently and why did you burn the cacti? If you answer my questions truthfully you can expect lenient treatment."

But the man was so obdurate to persist in his lies.

"I don't know what you want. I don't know this Indian, also not these two fellows with their terrible noses and least of all a man by the name of Tobias Praisegod Burton. And I've no knowledge of any immigrants."

"Why did you pursue the Ghost of Llano Estacado?"

"Ghost? Ridiculous! The man's a rascal who earlier killed one of our men in our midst with a shot through his forehead."

"You have nothing else to tell us?"

"Not a word."

"Then I'm done with you. We shall take the immigrants in our protection and wreck the plans you have for them. You keep lying to your own detriment. Now my young red brother may say what he accuses this man of."

"This paleface shot the Chief of the Comanche, my father, in the belly, from which he died. Howgh!"

"I believe you," Old Shatterhand said. "From this moment, therefore, the murderer belongs to you. Do with him as you please."

"By the devil!" the captive exclaimed. "That's not very heroic of you. The lasso incapacitates me! It will be easy for the damn Indian to do me in."

The Comanche raised his arm disdainfully and said, "Ironheart does not take scalps as gifts. He will execute the murderer, but only in the ways of a brave warrior. Will my brothers wait for a moment?"

He hurried away into the dark of the night to soon return with Stewart's horse. It had come to a stop soon after its rider had been torn from the saddle. The Indian's acute senses had told him where to find it. Ironheart now dropped all his weapons except for the knife. Then he mounted his horse and told the men, "My brothers may untie this man and hand him also his knife. Then he may mount his horse and ride off to wherever he likes. Ironheart will follow him and fight him. We have the same weapons. Knife against knife. Life for life. If Ironheart does not return within an hour, he will lie dead in the sands of the Llano Estacado."

It was the brave youngster's will and it had to be respected. Stewart received his knife, was untied, and immediately jumped into the saddle of his horse. He chased off shouting, "Your stupidity never ceases. You can't do anything against my plans now. We'll see each other again, and woe to you then."

Ironheart shouted the shrill battle scream of the Comanche and, like an arrow, followed Stewart's horse.

The others stood silent. Once they sat down, a few remarks were made, but the situation was such, that everyone felt low in spirit.

A quarter of an hour passed, then another. The distant fire's strength diminished. Then the men heard the hoof beats of two horses. The Comanche returned leading his enemy's horse. On his belt hung a fresh scalp. He himself was unhurt.

"One of the murderers of Ironheart's father has been sent on the path to follow him," he said, when he joined the men. "The others will soon do likewise. Howgh!"

Thus was the bloody conclusion of the Ghostly Hour.

Karl May – translated by Herbert Windolf

4. In the Yuavh-Kai

The junction of the southeastern corner of New Mexico and Texas is one of the most dangerous places in the Far West. It is here that the ranges of the Comanche and Apache touch, a circumstance, which naturally contributes to the continuing insecurity of the area.

For as long as these two tribes may exist, there can never be a sincere and lasting peace. Their mutual hate is rooted too deeply for that, even when the tomahawk of war is buried, the ruinous fire of hate continues to smolder under the ashes and, with the least provocation, may once again erupt in bloody red flame.

Naturally, the often briefly suspended enmity claims most of its victims where the two tribal areas meet, or rather intermingle. The border is neither a straight line nor is it demarcated in any way. This causes all too frequent reciprocal accusations of border transgressions after which fighting breaks out again.

'The Shears', as the frontiersman calls this dangerous area, is an all too appropriate term. The border is fluid, it moves, its lines open and close like the blades of scissors. Whoever gets caught between them can consider himself lucky if he escapes with his skin intact. The White, who lets himself be seen there, is either a very daring or incautious man. No matter what his persuasion, the vulture of death constantly circles above his head.

Where the Togah River, coming from the Devil's Mountains, debauches into the Rio Pecos, the latter constitutes the border between the Comanche and the Apache at the time of events. To its west the terrain rises to the Sierra Guadeloupe, the Sierra Pilaros and the Sierra del Diablo, while to its east lies the Staked Plain, the ill-famed Llano Estacado.

However, the Llano does not begin immediately at the riverbank, but is separated from the river by a low mountain chain, which sometimes branches into several ranges to the southeast. These ranges enclose long, poorly vegetated valleys, some of which are cut by narrow canyons and valleys, opening towards the Llano.

Within the river's proximity, where the soil is rich enough, one even finds some luxuriant vegetation. For this country, the term 'desert', like for the Gobi or Sahara, should not be used too literally. Where the western edge of the Llano Estacado rises to the afore mentioned mountains, several small seasonal creeks tumble down. Most of them dry up or disappear in the sand but, on their way, spread enough moisture to soak the adjacent ground, so that bushes, even trees can grow near their banks. These lengths of green extend like peninsulas into the ocean of the Llano's sand. Between them, they form broader or narrower stretches where grasses and weeds find sustenance.

There's even the myth of a powerful spring of delicious potable water in the middle of the Llano, rising from deep within the earth and forming a small lake whose banks are seamed with shade-giving trees and bushes. Old hunters talk about it, however, never saw the lake themselves. Learned people, who have heard about it, do not exclude the existence of water as being hydrologically impossible in the midst of the Llano.

Four men, whose appearance did not look very trustworthy, sat at the banks of the Togah River. Their disheveled, straggly head and beard hair looked as if it hadn't seen much care for some time. Their dress displayed a condition every tailor would have declared as beyond restoration or improvement. Their brown hands and weather-beaten faces seemed not to have seen a drop of water for months. But the better they were armed. Each of them had a breech-loading rifle lying beside him and a knife besides the two revolvers stuck in the belt.

Three of them were certainly Yankees. Their tall, lanky figures and their forward-bent, narrow-chested upper torsos, as well as their sharply cut facial features were ample proof of this. But the nationality of the fourth was difficult to determine.

This man was of stocky, broad-shouldered build. He had exceptionally big hands and a face just as wide with big ears sticking from his head. Someone giving him only a brief glance could have mistaken him for a negro. His face was black, or rather a grainy blue-black, but only up to just below his eyes. His habit was to pull his hat low into his face, but as soon as he pushed it back into his neck, one could see that his skin was white down to the root of his nose. Exploding gunpowder had burned the man.

Despite the disfiguration caused by this accident his features were not really repelling. Anyone giving him a good look would surely arrive at the conclusion that he was facing a decent fellow.

It was the same with the other three. Anyone seeing them in their current condition in a civilized area would certainly avoid them. But had he made the effort to get to know them, he would have changed his opinion.

Their four horses were enjoying the grass growing abundantly between the green bushes. One could see that they had been through some hard times. The saddle and headgear was old and had been only poorly repaired.

Their owners had eaten. One could surmise from the bones, which were strewn about, that they had roasted a raccoon on the small fire that now barely smoldered. While they talked, they did not forget to keep a sharp eye on their surroundings. They were in 'The Shears' here, where great caution was advised.

"It's time we decide," said the one who appeared to be the oldest of the three Yankees. "If we ride through the Llano, we will arrive sooner at our destination but may encounter more dangers. And this old coon here is likely the last meat we will have eaten for a while. Should we follow the Rio Pecos down we won't suffer for food and drink but make a detour of almost a week. What's your opinion, Blount?"

Blount, sitting next to him, thoughtfully stroked his beard before finally answering, "Weighing everything, I would say, we ride through the Llano. I think you will agree, Porter?"

"Then let's hear your reasons."

"A week's a long time I'd hate to lose. Along the Rio Pecos we might have to fear the Comanche and Apache, in the plains the Llano Vultures. That's a balance. But then, we need not traverse the entire width of the Llano. If we keep to the southeast towards the Rio Concho, we will get to the caravan route leading from Fort Mason to Fort Leaton and need not be concerned about hunger or thirst. That's my opinion. What's yours, Falser?"

"I agree with you," answered Falser, the third of the Yankees. "I'm actually of the opinion the Estacado is half as dangerous as it is made out to be. Whoever has crossed it brags about its dangers as if they were hell personified. I'm looking forward with pleasure to learn about them."

"Precisely, because you haven't encountered them yet," responded Porter, the first Yankee.

"Did you get to know them yet?"

"No, but I've talked with people whose truthfulness cannot be doubted. They talked about the dangers in a way, which caused goose bumps to travel down my spine. Only now, that we are at the border, do I realize what risk we are taking. None of us knows the Llano. If we get lost, if our water runs out, if ---"

"If, if, and if again!" Blount interrupted. "Whoever deals with too many 'ifs' will never get anywhere. At other times you are such a daring fellow, are you afraid now?"

"Afraid? No! But there's a big difference between caution and fear. And I don't think you've ever seen me anxious. We are four. The majority will decide. It's just that before a decision is made, the issue must be given due consideration. That's what I wanted and there's no reason to ask if I'm afraid. Two have voiced their opinion and decided to cross the Llano. Now, you, Ben New-Moon, tell us whether you'll join them or not?"

This request was directed to the man with the powder-burned face. He put his hand to the brim of his hat, saluting like a soldier to his officer and answered, "At your command, Mister Porter! I'll ride anywhere, even into the devil's kitchen."

"That means nothing. I want a clear answer. Is it down the Rio Pecos or through the Llano?"

"Ah, well, let it be the Llano, if it pleases you. I'd like to get acquainted with this old sand pit."

"Sand pit? Don't be mistaken, you old Moon-face! Do you imagine you can jump in on one side and right away leap out the other? The pit's a bit larger than you seem to imagine. It will take four or five days to get across this sandbox. And precisely because we transect the southern part it's likely that we'll meet Indians."

"Let'm come! I've never done an Indian any harm and therefore need not fear these people. And should they be hostile, well, then we have our weapons. Four good guys who've sniffed as much powder as we have, can take on twenty or more Indians."

"That's very true. But what concerns the smelling of powder, you are ahead of us by a horse's length. An entire barrel of powder must have exploded in your face."

"Nearly so."

"How did it happen? You never told us. Is it a secret?"

"Not at all. But I've no reason to enjoy talking about the event. That's why I usually don't mention it. At the time I was in a bad spot, my life was in danger. The explosion was intended to take my eyesight. Had there not been my old friend Juggle-Fred, I would now be blind or dead."

"What? You know Fred? I've heard much about that man."

"We were good friends and carried out a few coups together, which would have caused other people quite a fright. I'd love to see the old scoundrel again! Who knows in what corner of the prairie his bones may be bleaching? I'm most grateful to him for what he did back then, when he prevented Stealing-Fox's plans."

"Stealing-Fox?" Porter asked in surprise. "Then you too made the acquaintance of this notorious rogue?"

"Unfortunately, yes. I even got to know him closer than I liked. The chap's name was Henry Fox, at least, that's what he called himself. Whether this was his real name, I don't know. It can be assumed that he used different names through time. Where he appeared, no one's horse, beaver traps, or any property for that matter, was safe. And never did people succeed in putting a stop to his practices, for he had developed an uncanny expertise. He always disappeared as quickly as he appeared. Should he cross my path again, I would give him short shrift. He would be sure of a bullet, because I have --- listen!"

He broke off, rose halfway and listened towards the upstream side. The horses too pointed their ears. Hoof beats could be heard approaching. The four men jumped up and readied their rifles.

"Could these be Reds?" Blount whispered.

"No, they are Whites. Only two," answered Ben New-Moon, who peeked from behind the bush that was hiding him from the strangers. "They are dressed like Mexicans. Now they stopped to investigate our tracks, they must have followed here."

Porter stepped over to him to also see the two. They had halted their horses and were bent low to view the tracks in the grass. And, yes, their clothing was of the Mexican style, that is wide slotted pants, colorful vests, short but wide jackets decorated with silver threads, fluttering red neckties, and sashes of the same kind, from which the grips of knives and pistols protruded. To complete their outfit they wore broad-brimmed sombreros and, last not least, huge spurs on their heels.

Their horses seemed to be in excellent condition, which looked somewhat out of place here.

"There's no need to fear these two," Porter said. "These are Mexican caballeros we can welcome."

He stepped from behind the bush and called to them, "Here are the ones you are looking for, gentlemen. Hopefully you're not following our tracks with evil designs?"

The two Mexicans, obviously startled, being so suddenly addressed and seeing the tall Yankee in front of them, quickly pulled their rifles from the saddles where they had hung.

"Leave them be!" Porter urged. "We are honest people you need not fear."

"How many are you?" one of them asked.

"Four. Your rifles would not be of any use to you if we were hostile. You can come closer."

Whispering, the Mexicans exchanged a few words, then drove their horses closer. Only after they had cautiously looked the other three over and the place they were camping did they decide to dismount.

"You're darn distrustful, gentlemen," Porter told them. "Do we look like robbers?"

"Well," one of the newcomers said laughingly, "you don't look too pretty in your coats. And your horses don't look good enough to perform in a circus. Caramba! You look run down, Señores!"

"Can you expect different in this area? It's a ride of a week to the closest settlement. If one has been under way as long as we have, one is obviously not in a condition for a state visit with the President's wife in Washington. If you care to shake hands with us nevertheless, you are welcome. Meeting honest people is always a pleasure, particularly in this dangerous territory here."

"We'll be glad to comply. Permit us to introduce ourselves. We are brothers. Our name is Cortejo. Call me Carlos and my brother Emilio."

The Yankees gave their names too and shook hands with them. Porter kept up his inquiry. "We come from California and want to get to Austin, Señores. May we ask what business brings you so close to the Llano?"

"We don't just want to get close, we want to cross it. We are the chief herdsmen employed at an estancia near San Diego and have been dispatched by the estanciero to collect some moneys for him at Neu Braunfels in Texas. It's a dangerous task, which is why we ride together."

"It will be dangerous only on the way back when you carry the money. It's always dangerous to carry other people's money across the Llano. What we have accumulated in California and carry on us is ours. We have no responsibility for the property of others and are therefore better off than you. Your courage is admirable. We are four and still wondered whether it wouldn't be wiser to detour around the Llano. You dare to cross the plains with just the two of you. That takes some grit!"

"Not that much, Señor," Carlos responded. "Are you familiar with the Llano?"

"None of us has been there before."

"That's something different then. Whoever doesn't know it had better stay away. The two of us, though, must have crossed it probably more than twenty times and are so familiar with it, that we cant' talk of danger any more."

"That's interesting. Hmm! And you are on the way to Neu Braunfels? That's almost the direction we are headed for. Then we could join you, if you don't object?"

When Porter had incautiously mentioned the money he and his companions were carrying, the two Mexicans had traded a quick glance. Now, Carlos answered almost too quickly, "We don't mind in the least. Just the opposite, your company is most welcome, because the more we are, the better we are prepared for the Llano's dangers."

"Very well then, Señor. We'll ride along. You will not regret having met us here. But how about your ride today?"

"Our plan for today was to get down to the Rio Pecos, maybe even to the *Yuavh-Kai*."

"What is that?"

"It's a word from the Ute and Comanche languages and means something like 'Singing Valley'. There's talk that one can often hear otherworldly and incomprehensible voices in the night. Us two, however, have never heard any although we have crossed the valley many times. It looks, though, as if you intended to camp here for the night?"

"No, that would be an irresponsible waste of time. We too had considered riding to the Pecos River and following it downstream to bypass the Llano. But now, that we've met you, and you are willing to have us accompany you, we shall cross the desert. Do you think we'll come across Indians?"

"Hardly. Where we are we have to fear such a meeting more than on the plains. Since we haven't seen any Reds so far, it's unlikely we will see any later. The fellows aren't swarming at the time since their war tomahawks have been recently buried."

"That's good to hear, but what about the Llano Vultures? Those are said to be much more dangerous than the Indians."

"Pah! Don't believe it. You know how often we've been in the Llano and so far we've never had the opportunity to see one of these Vultures. They only exist in the fantasy of stupid and fearful people."

"And the so-called Ghost of Llano Estacado?"

"That's also a chimera which has no equal. Children's tales! The Llano is a stretch of sand like any other. Sure, there's a lot of sand and no water. The ground's so infertile that even ghosts won't grow in it. And tapping certain kinds of the plentiful cacti for their juices easily takes care of the lack of water. There's really no reason to be afraid of the plains."

"I've been told the opposite. But since you know the place, I must believe you. If you don't care to rest here for a moment, we are prepared to break camp right away."

"It would be best if we continue immediately. Will your horses be up to it?"

"They are in much better shape than they appear. There's no need to delay for their sake."

The appearance of the two Mexican's did not give cause for mistrust. But it was incautious of the Yankees to decide to join the two complete strangers so quickly and without further scrutiny. Only one of them did not seem to be so trusting – Ben New-Moon.

He had acquired this nickname because of the similarity of his round, black face with that of Earth's satellite. Maybe he was more experienced, perhaps even smarter than his three companions. Once they got under way along the riverbank he rode behind the group and kept the Mexicans closely in his sight. He had no obvious reason to mistrust them, but an instinctive feeling told him that caution was called for about the two.

They followed the Toyah's right shore downstream. There was no sense of the Llano's proximity with grass, bushes, and trees being plentiful here. Towards evening the trees grew even more plentiful to form a woods through which the Toyah sent its waters into the Rio Pecos.

The Toyah carried a lot of suspended material, depositing it into the Pecos, which, at the time, had a low water level. This had settled in a sandbank slantwise across the latter. The sandbank was discontinuous at several places allowing the waters to flow through, nevertheless, it provided a ford that was easily crossed with only a few places of deeper water for the horses to swim through.

With afternoon not yet gone, it was decided to ford the river still today and to make camp on the opposite side in the *Yuavh-Kai*. The horses managed the crossing well, the men arriving on the other bank with only their trouser legs wet. From there they rode north to pass near the spot where nowadays the Texas-Pacific Railroad crosses the Rio Pecos. Finally, the little group headed for a hillside whose base was overgrown by green shrubbery while its ridge was bare.

117

There, a narrow canyon opened in which a small brook flowed. The two Mexicans entered it and told the others that this was the Singing Valley, which was to broaden farther in. The valley was cut deeply. It did not rise quickly so that the brook had little drop. Its bottom land was grass-covered, but towards its rocky sides, plants with low water requirement were common, a sure sign that they approached a region hostile to plant growth. A bit later the valley's walls receded farther, its floor was covered by loose rubble, and only near the water some poor grass grew.

"Wouldn't it have been wiser to camp in the Pecos valley," Ben asked. "There we would have had fodder for the animals and dry wood for a fire. Here, in the valley, there seems to be less of everything the farther we enter it."

"Just wait, Señor," answered Carlos Cortejo. "A bit further up there's such an ideal spot for camping, that you will be grateful we took you there. We'll arrive there in a quarter of an hour."

Once this period had passed the valley suddenly broadened to form an almost circular basin with a diameter of about one thousand feet. Vertical cliffs without any visible opening enclosed it. Yet, soon enough, the four newcomers noticed a narrow slot on the basin's opposite side, which most likely provided an exit.

Here in this basin the brook originated. The place where the spring erupted lay below the level of the surrounding area, so a small pond was formed from which the water ran off. Its banks were overgrown by dense shrubbery. Beyond the pond, close to the rock wall, one could see a strange kind of plant. The seven to ten feet tall candelabrum-like growths, some of which seemed even taller on closer inspection, had neither twigs nor leaves. The ends of the central trunk and some of their side arms carried small edible fig-like bulbs. These were saguaro. Emilio Cortejo pointed to them and said, "That's where we'll pick our dinner, and the pond is bordered by enough grass and leafy bushes for our horses. I think you will be satisfied. Come on, Señores!"

He put his horse to a trot to ride for the pond. The others followed him. When they were about six horses' lengths from the bushes surrounding the pond they were challenged by a loud 'Halt'. Of course, they stopped at once.

"Who is it?" Porter asked, looking to the bushes.

The others did too, but from where the shout had risen, no one could be seen.

"White hunters," came back the reply.

"And who are you?"

"Travelers."

"Where do you come from?"

"From California."

"And where are you headed?"

"For Austin in Texas."

"Across the Llano?"

"Yes."

"Some of you have honest faces, but not all. We'll give you a try none-the-less, gentlemen."

The bushes parted. Two rifle barrels appeared, followed by the owners of the same. One was a bearded, broad-shouldered man, the other a blond, beardless youngster, barely twenty years old. They were dressed entirely in leather and wore broad-brimmed beaver hats.

"By the devil!" Porter exclaimed. "How many more troops are hidden there by the water?"

"None, Sir."

"You are alone?"

"Yes."

"And you dare to confront six well-armed men?"

"Pah!" the older one responded. "Our guns have double barrels. We would have tumbled four of you from the saddle and for the remaining two our revolvers would have sufficed. We saw you coming. Some of you appear trustworthy. That's why we allow you to join us. However, if it were up to us, the others ought to turn back."

"Don't you think this is insulting?"

"It's sincere and not intended to insult. By the way, I didn't identify the ones I don't care about. So, keep the peace and come to the water."

The six followed this invitation and dismounted at the pond's bank. The horses of the two strangers were already grazing there. At a gray spot of ash, where a fire must have burned, the two sat down. The two looked so similar, that one had to think them to be father and son.

They did not give the impression of being novices of the Far West. The father looked like an experienced, courageous hunter. His youthful son's face displayed such a composed, deliberate gravity that one could surmise he had already graduated from good frontiersman schooling, despite his young age.

The others eyed them half curiously, half suspiciously. Then they took their places beside them and pulled out their provisions consisting of dried meat, a supply of which must always be carried, in case no fresh game is to be had.

"Would you mind telling us, Sir, how long you've been here already," Porter asked who had assumed the position of speaker for his group.

"Since last night," the older hunter answered.

"Already! That looks as if you plan to stay here for a while?"

"That's the case."

"But, Sir, this is a dangerous area. It isn't well suited for settling in."

"It suits us fine, Mister. We have a meeting coming up in the mountains back there. Others, we expect, will come across the Llano through this valley.

Since we arrived early and had nothing better to do, we rode ahead to meet our friends here."

"When will they arrive?"

"In two or three days."

"If you wait that long you may easily get to know some Apache or Comanche."

"Not to worry. We live in peace with them."

"Us too. But one can never trust the Reds. They usually show up in bands and if there's only two, like you, such an encounter can be fatal."

"Maybe, but it doesn't worry us. There's someone else accompanying us who makes up for an entire band of Indians."

"Then you are not alone, but three of you. Where is this man?"

"He rode off to reconnoiter but will soon be back."

"He equates an entire Indian party, you say? Then he must be a very exceptional hunter, maybe like Old Shatterhand. Do you know that man?"

"Yes, but it's not him."

"Who then?"

"You'll see when he returns. He might as well introduce himself personally. My name's Baumann and this young frontiersman here is my son, Martin."

"Thanks for telling us your names, Sir. And since you gave us your names, let me tell you ours. My name's Porter, those two are Blount and Falser, and the dusky moon face here is Ben New-Moon. The other two gents we met at noon today. They come from an estancia near San Diego and Cobledo and want to cross the Llano to collect some funds for their master. They are his chief vaqueros. Their names are Carlos and Emilio Cortejo."

Whenever he gave a name he pointed at its owner whom Baumann then examined closely. The hunter's longest scrutiny focused on the two Mexicans. While doing this, his eyebrows narrowed and his beard twitched slightly. Carlos noticed it and asked annoyed, "Now that you know our names, Señor Baumann, I'd like to ask you who of us carry the faces you like so little?"

"I needn't say this, since those concerned will find out soon enough. So, then your estancia lies somewhere near San Diego and Cobledo? May I ask what its name is?"

"It's the Estancia del Cuchillo."

"And its owner?"

"His name is Señor --- Señor Montano."

Before giving the name he hesitated as if he had to remember it. This was odd. An employee must know the name of his employer. Baumann continued his inquiry without yet voicing his mistrust, "And you are the chief vaqueros of Señor Montano?"

"Yes."

"Are there other such chief vaqueros?"

"No, we are the only ones."

"All right," the hunter said now, "then I will answer your earlier question in telling you in all sincerity, that it's you two, whose faces I don't like."

At once the two Mexicans reached for their knives.

"Señor, that is a serious insult. Earlier it was indirect and we could overlook it and remain silent."

"You will need to bear it now too. I'm used to tell anyone what I think of him, and I wouldn't dream of making an exception for you two."

"Well. What do you think of us?"

Baumann pulled his revolver from his belt as if he intended to play with it, while his son pulled his at the same time.

"I think you are liars, at least liars, if not worse."

That's when the two Mexicans leaped up brandishing their knives.

"Retract this at once, Señor, or we make you do it." Carlos demanded.

Baumann kept sitting quietly but aimed his small, but nevertheless deadly weapon at the speaker and told him, "Don't come a step closer, Mister Cortejo. My bullet would get you and that of my son's your brother. If you reach for your pistols or make any suspicious move you will be expedited from this world without fanfare. My name's Baumann, a name, which doesn't seem to mean anything to you. The Sioux call me *Mato-poka*, the Comanche *Vila-yalo*, the Apache *Schosch-insisk*, the Spanish-speaking hunters El Cazador del Oso, and English folks make it the Bear Hunter, all meaning the same. Maybe now you recall having heard of me."

"What! You are the Bear Hunter, Sir?" exclaimed Ben New-Moon. "I mean, the German who had a store up near the Black Mountains and, on the side, made life difficult for grizzlies."

"Yes. That's me, Sir."

"Then I have heard lots about you. Hadn't you been captured by the Sioux and dragged up to the national park?"

"Actually, that happened to me. But Old Shatterhand and Winnetou got me out. My son here was with them."

"I was told that. This was supposedly one of Old Shatterhand's major accomplishments. If you are this man, I'm extraordinarily delighted to meet you. I hope the minor differences between you and the two Señores can be sorted out amicably. Maybe you will take your word back?"

"The word 'liars'? No!"

"But do you have any proof?"

"Yes. I never claim anything I cannot prove. An estanciero doesn't send his two chief vaqueros through the Llano, you can rest assured of that. He always needs one on his estancia. If the other is truly to collects any moneys, he will send several vaqueros along. And then, the two of us just spent two months in the area between Albuquerque, El Paso, San Diego and Cobledo, and did visit just

121

about any and all estancias along the way. But never did we hear about the Estancia del Cuchillo, nor of an Estanciero Montano."

"You simply missed our estancia," Emilio declared.

"I don't think so. Even if it were the case, I would have heard of it and its owner. Put your knives away and sit down again. I won't be threatened by the likes of you. I don't want to drive you away from my camp, since you arrived with men I consider honest folks. You will be treated the way you act. One cannot be cautious enough at the edge of the Llano, and everybody knows that one ought to fear Whites more than Reds."

"Do you think us to be Llano Vultures?"

"I shall answer this question when we part. By that time I will know, while presently my judgment is only based on conjecture. Should you truly be good people, which I'd wish, we shall surely part as friends."

The two Mexicans looked at each other questioningly. To further their secret intentions it was advisable to appear conciliatory, which is why Carlos said, "Your last words compensate for your earlier ones. Being honest people, we can rest assured that you will soon realize that you've judged us wrongly."

He sat down again, his brother doing the same. Baumann sent his son, the well-known 'Son of the Bear Hunter', to the saguaro cacti to pick some of their fruit to be enjoyed for dessert. While the men ate their meal night fell and a fire was lit for which enough material was found close by.

In addition to nightfall another change took place. The high cliffs enclosing the valley basin kept it apart from the air currents of the plains above, which could develop their full might only there. Down here the air's access was closed on three sides. Air could only enter the basin from the side the Yankees and Mexicans had come, but only if the wind came exactly from that direction and was strong enough to reach the terminus of the valley.

Now, after nightfall, such an air current made itself felt, coming from the described direction. Caught in the basin, it rose up the cliff face with only a minor part escaping through the cleft the newcomers had noticed earlier which, indeed, led to the Llano. This wind did not come in gusts, but came rather steadily. It was definitely noticeable, yet did not affect the fire's flames. It made no sound, not at all like the whistle and howl of a storm, and yet the ear took notice. And whether the lungs breathed easier or more labored, one could not say. The saguaro fruit had all been eaten and Martin Baumann left to get a new supply. He had barely left the bushes behind when he was heard calling, "What is this? Come here, gentlemen! I've never seen anything like it."

They quickly followed his urging. When they had come out of the bushes, away from the pond, they faced a surprising sight. The basin lay in darkness. The light of the small fire, covered where they stood by the bushes, did not reach here. But where the cacti stood they saw numerous small flaming tufts, flickering in an oddly pale colorless light. Such a tuft, producing a wonderful, ghostly image topped each of the saguaro arms.

"What may this be?" Porter asked.

"I've never seen anything like it," Falser added. "It's almost fearsome."

That's when a clear, sonorous voice sounded from behind them past the bushes, near the fire by the bank of the pond, were they had just come from, and where no other human being could be expected to be.

"These are *Ho-haerstesele-yato*, the Flames of the Great Spirit, which he lights when he wants to warn his children."

"Chispita! Who's behind us?" Emilio Cortejo cried in a quavering voice. "Is this an ambush?"

"No," the Bear Hunter told him. "It is my companion I told you about. He returned in his customary way, that is, not letting us know he did."

They turned, and sure enough, there stood a horseman beside the fire topping the bushes. He had crossed the shrubbery and, even on horseback, had made not the least noise. He rode a splendid black stallion saddled and harnessed in the Indian way. His clothing too was Indian, he himself was Indian, his face not showing the least of a beard. Instead an abundance of long black hair hung down his back. In one of his hands he held a double-barreled rifle whose shaft was studded with silver nails. The Yankees and Mexicans expressed their surprise and admiration with loud exclamations.

"Who's this?" Porter asked. "An Indian! Are there more around?"

"No, he's by himself," Baumann answered. "This is Winnetou, the Chief of the Apache."

"Winnetou, Winnetou," it rose from many mouths.

He dismounted, not paying attention to the admiring looks, stepped from the bushes, pointed to the dancing flames, and said, "Because the palefaces camp in this enclosed valley, they are not aware of what has been going on outside. For them to know: Manitou is sending them this fiery message. Winnetou does not know if they can read it."

"What's happening?" Blount asked.

"The *'ntch-kha-n'gul*, a destructive tornado has crossed the Llano. Winnetou saw its black body to the north of here. Woe to those who were surprised by it; they surely have met death."

"A tornado?" the Bear Hunter asked. "Did my red brother observe its path closely?"

"Winnetou estimates the walk of a beetle's he notices. How could he forget to mind the direction of the great storm."

"What was its direction?"

"To the east of here the Llano itself seemed to rise into the sky so that it became dark as in the midst of night. The sun embraced the darkness with beams of blood red. The night quickly advanced towards northeast where Winnetou saw it disappear."

"So the tornado traveled exactly from south to north?"

"My brother says so."

"God bless my soul! I hope it didn't hit our friends!"

"Our friends are wise and experienced. Old Shatterhand knows the meaning of every air current. But the *'ntch-kha-n'gul* arrives suddenly and sends no messengers ahead announcing itself. No horse is fast enough to escape it. Old Shatterhand must have reached the Llano today, and his horse's hooves must have touched the sands of the Llano exactly in the area to which the vulture of a wind flew. He and his companions may lie buried under piles of sand."

"That would be terrible! We must leave. We must get there – now! Let's get to the horses."

Winnetou made a dismissive move with his hand.

"My brother need not hurry. If Old Shatterhand was in the midst of the storm, he is dead, and our help is too late. If he was at the fringe of its path, he remains unhurt and is only in danger of losing his way, since the storm changes the face of the Llano. Yes, we must ride to him, but not now, not during the night, when the Llano looks at us also with different eyes. Daylight must be our guide. Whoever intends to find someone lost, must first take care not to get lost himself. Therefore, my brothers may sit by the fire again. The first light of the day will see our departure."

He lay down by the fire with the others joining him. Involuntarily, they left a distance between themselves and him, an expression of respect for the famous chief, a reason also for a period of silence after they had settled down.

Finally, Ben New-Moon could no longer restrain his desire to learn more about the expected comrades of the Apache. He turned to Baumann to ask him, "I understand you will meet with Old Shatterhand, Sir?"

"Yes, with him, but he's not alone. Others were to join him too."

"Who are these others?"

"Fat-Jemmy and Long-Davy, whose names you might have heard."

"Of course I know these two famous frontiersmen, although only from the stories of others. Is it only them accompanying Old Shatterhand?"

"No. There will be two more you may also have heard about, since you've learned about Old Shatterhand's travels to the national park. They are Hobble-Frank and Sliding-Bob. Frank didn't want to travel with us, but rather with Old Shatterhand to learn more from him, and Bob tagged along. That's the only reason the two aren't here. It can be expected that others will take the opportunity to join the travel though the Llano under the guidance of the famous hunter. He may lead a sizeable company, which is a comfort to me. The larger the group the better they can assist each other when danger arises such as that of the tornado."

"It's a pity, a real pity, that we six must continue on our way tomorrow morning. I would have loved to meet these friends of yours."

"That's not quite possible, since you want to get over to Austin. But then, we too, will depart early in the morning. Tell me, Sir, if you don't mind, how did you get your black face and thus your name."

"For both I have to thank one of the biggest crooks who's made the Far West unsafe and may still do so, Stealing-Fox."

"Oh, that one! I haven't heard anything of the fellow for some time, but would love to meet him."

"Did you also have any dealings with him?"

"He with me. He stole my money chest and got all my savings with it. He called himself Weller then. But from some information I gained later I concluded that it was the notorious Stealing-Fox. I could never pick up his tracks, but heard recently, in New Mexico, that he's supposed to be still alive. He now calls himself Tobias Praisegod Burton and, under the mask of a pious Mormon missionary, tried to lure a company of travelers into the Llano. But one of them recognized him and when he became aware of it, he disappeared quickly."

"Death to him! Had I been there, he wouldn't have got away. I would have fired a railroad-size tunnel through his head. I'm almost tempted to remain here a bit longer, since he's supposed to be in the region. I'd really like to settle my account with him."

"Had he designs on your life?"

"On my life and property. That was up at Timpa Fork in Colorado. I had come from Arizona, where I had made a good strike as a gold prospector and carried a nice bundle of money, which I had traded the gold dust and nuggets for. On the way a trapper joined me, who also wanted to get to Fort Abrey on the Arkansas. The man's appearance and manners seemed trustworthy, and since one dislikes traveling alone in the Wild West, his company was welcome."

"You probably told him that you carried money?"

"I sure didn't! But he must have guessed it, because I caught him one night when he went very quietly through my pockets. Fortunately, I awoke. He gave the excuse that I had moaned so badly in my sleep, that it was his intention to open my coat, so that I could breathe easier. Of course, I didn't believe him and from thereon was very much on guard. You can imagine what that meant."

"Very well. One is alone in the wilderness with a crook. One must sleep and yet keep an eye on the other at all times so as not to come to harm. That's a difficult task. A knife stab, a bullet, and life and property are gone."

"Concerning that, I could rest easy. I had seen through the fellow soon enough. He was basically a coward. To steal and defraud, yes, but he did not have the guts to spill blood. We camped at Timpa Fork. It was a hot day, but the wind blew strongly to make the heat bearable. I love to smoke and had stuffed my pipe anew, you know, a short pipe with a veined head, good for a quarter bag of tobacco. I had chosen such a large head so that I had less need for frequent stuffing. Just when I intended to light my pipe the man said, that he had heard a turkey in the bushes. I put the pipe away, took my rifle and headed out to get us a meal. I found not a trace of the bird, but came across an opossum, which I shot. When I returned about half an hour must have passed. Right away the fellow began to skin and gut the animal. I reached for my pipe to light the tobacco. I had some difficulty because of the wind, which is why I lay down flat with my face to the ground. I pulled my hat down against the wind and struck fire. It worked this time. I took a few draws. There was a hiss and a bang and fire struck my face. At the same time the crook grabbed me by the neck, pressed my head into the dirt, and with the other hand went through my pockets. I was so terrified that he succeeded in grabbing my wallet. But I got him by an arm and held fast. I was stronger than he was but momentarily blinded. He held onto the billfold. I got a hold of it too and we pulled back and forth. It came apart, with him jumping up. We separated. He had one half and I had the other. I leaped up and pulled my knife. Fortunately, I had my eyes closed at the very moment of the explosion, otherwise I would have been blinded. But my lids were seared. I could open them only a bit, just sufficiently to see the man, and jumped him with my knife. This gave him enough courage to pick up his rifle and aim it at me. A piercing pain closed my eyes. I felt I had lost. The shot rang out, or rather a shot, but to my surprise I wasn't hit. I wiped my eyes and opened them with great effort. I didn't see the fellow, but from across the creek an imperious voice threatened, 'Hold it, murderer!' Then I heard quickly disappearing hoof beats. The crook had jumped on his horse and escaped. He did this with half my billfold which, it turned out, held half my fortune."

"Peculiar," Baumann said. "So he had been disturbed?"

"Yes. A very well known frontiersman by the name of Juggle-Fred was close by and had heard my shot with which I killed the opossum. He had followed the sound on the other side of the creek and had seen us the moment the crook aimed at me. He fired at him, hitting him in the arm. This is why the rascal dropped his rifle and ran for his horse to gallop away. Juggle-Fred got his horse and crossed the creek. His timely arrival saved my life. Pursuit of the thief was impossible. I was unable to do it and Fred couldn't leave me, since my face had to be cooled with water day and night. We camped at Timpa Fork for more than a week, where I suffered from severe pain. I had lost a large sum of my savings, but was glad my eyesight had been saved."

"What did the thief call himself?"

"Weller. But when we finally got to Fort Abrey and described him, I learned that this was a false name. It had been Stealing-Fox."

"So he stuffed the pipe's head with powder during your absence?"

"Yes. Only at the top did he pack a bit of tobacco to deceive me. To gain the time required for his deed, he invented the turkey's call. He knew I would take off right away to shoot it, since I was a better hunter than he. He was a tall, lean fellow with facial features I shall never forget. I know I will recognize him the moment I see him again."

The two Mexicans had followed the conversation with great interest. They often glanced meaningfully at each other, unnoticed, they thought. But another person observed them closely in turn – Winnetou.

His gaze, seemingly averted, nevertheless kept close watch on them. Seeing the exchange of glances he, with his great sagaciousness, discerned that the two must have some relationship with the thief.

Baumann, the Bear Hunter, observed Winnetou, in turn. He knew his red friend who, with his horse, had so suddenly and unexpectedly appeared by the fire. How he had done it, Baumann could easily explain to himself. The Apache had returned from his reconnoitering, and, following his habit, had left his horse a distance behind to creep up on the campsite. He might very well have seen from their tracks, that strangers had arrived, and decided to have a good look at them before letting himself be seen. Once he had seen enough to get an impression of their character, he had silently withdrawn to return on horseback and act as if he didn't know about them. While they had all walked past the other bank of the pond to look at the flames and were noisy enough not to hear the hoof beats of his horse, he had approached the camp from the opposite side.

He now sat there; his eyes seemed to gaze idly at the pond's shimmering surface. But Baumann saw clearly, that from below his long, dense eyelashes a sharp glance was directed at the two Mexicans from time to time.

The Apache did not trust them. That was sure. The son of the Bear Hunter had earlier been on his way to pick more cactus fruit, but the surprise over the marvelous flames and Winnetou's return had prevented him from completing his task. This suited the Mexicans well, who were eager to exchange a few words surreptitiously. This was only possible if they left the fire. Hence, Emilio Cortejo got up and said, "Earlier we wanted to get some more cactus fruit, but were distracted by the flames. Are you coming along, Carlos? Let's see that we get some."

Baumann wanted to object. He guessed, that the two's intention was to talk secretly about something and wanted to prevent it. The words already on his lips, he became aware of a peremptory gesture of the Apache's, commanding him to remain silent.

The brothers left. They had barely gone past the bushes when Winnetou said in a low voice, "These white men do not have honest eyes, and their thoughts are evil. But Winnetou will find out what they are after."

He scurried to the other side and through the bushes there.

"Does he not trust them either," Porter asked. "I wager they are decent people."

"It's likely you'd lose this bet," Ben New-Moon answered. "I didn't like them from the very first moment."

"I don't go by that. One ought to mistrust a person only once one has proof for it."

"These two men deserve it," the Bear Hunter declared. "No estanciero sends both his chief vaqueros away at the same time. And look at their horses, Sir. Do they look as if they've had a ride from San Diego to here behind them? If I estimate correctly the ride must be at least three hundred miles. Horses, who have covered such a distance, such a wild area, look very different. I figure these animals have a permanent place nearby and I wager a thousand dollars that these two fellows are nothing else but feeders for the Vultures of Llano Estacado."

"Thunder and lightning!" Porter exclaimed. "You really mean that?"

"Yes, I do!"

"Then we would have got into some wonderful company. These fellows were to lead us through the Llano."

"In God's name, don't do it. It would surely be your end. Believe me. I'm an old bear and have learned to read people's faces."

"Well, I'm no greenhorn either. I must be of the same age you are and have lived on the prairie since my early youth. Isn't it possible that these men deserve our trust after all?"

That's when Martin Baumann made his voice heard. He had remained silent so far because of his youth, "They truly do not deserve your trust, Mister Porter. I'm willing to say this to their faces."

"So? What reason do you have to think badly of them, young man?"

"Didn't you notice the looks they exchanged when the story of Stealing-Fox was told?"

"No. I listened to the story, and didn't observe these people."

"In the West one ought not only listen, but also see, because ---"

"For goodness sake! To you want to lecture an old fox?"

"No, Sir! I only intended to convey that I not only kept my ears open while the story was told, but also my eyes. Since my father didn't trust them, I too observed them closely. I could do this easily and unnoticed, since they didn't pay any attention to such a young, inexperienced fellow like me. I saw the looks they traded, from which one can conclude that they do know this Stealing-Fox."

"That's what you think? Hmm! This Fox is supposed to be around here to lure people into the Llano, and these fellows may know him. That would be quite a connection, and not a nice one. It seems to me, there are developments in the air, which could be fatal for us. The ghostly flames on the cacti over there don't make me feel any easier. I'm not superstitious, but such apparitions don't come by chance. They always mean something."

"Of course, they signify something," the Bear Hunter said smilingly.

"Yes, but what?"

"Electric tension in the atmosphere."

"Electricity? Tension? I don't understand. That's too sophisticated for me. Although I know that it is possible to electrify a person, but fire and flames, and these on cacti? You really want to attribute this to electricity?"

"Indeed, Mister Porter. Is lightning not also a fiery phenomenon!"

"Obviously! And what a one."

"Well then. At the root of lightning is electricity, which I don't think I need to explain. And what concerns the little flames we saw earlier, sailors often see these on the masts and yards of sailing ships. They can be seen on church towers, the tops of trees, and the tips of lightning rods. These tufts of light are called St. Elmo's fire. Escaping electricity generates them. Have you heard about the Ghost of Llano Estacado?"

"More than I like!"

"Have you also been told that the figure of this mysterious entity is often bathed in fiery flames when seen in the night?"

"Yes, but I don't believe it."

"You can be confident of it. One time, up in Montana, I happened to be on an open plain during the night. There was sheet lightning all around, but no real thunderstorm developed. Suddenly, small flames played on the ear tips of my horse. I raised my hands into the air, and lo and behold, small flames also appeared on my fingertips, causing a peculiar sensation. It's the same with the Avenging Ghost. When he rides across the Llano, his body presents the highest point on the plain. When it is night and there's strong electrical tension St. Elmo's fire plays over his body."

"You really believe in the existence of this Ghost of the Estacado?"

"Yes."

"And think him to be a human being?"

"What else?"

"Hmm! I've heard lots about him, but never took the time to give it much thought. But since I'm facing the Llano now, I obviously want to know what to think of it. It's even possible he will appear to us on the ride. What's then to do?"

"If I would encounter him, I would shake his hand and tell him what a marvelous guy he is. It is ---"

He was interrupted by Winnetou's return. He came in a hurry, but silently like a snake slithering through the grass. He sat down at his place again, put on an unaffected mien, and acted as if he had never left the place. Earlier, while the Mexicans walked slowly towards the cacti, he had crawled on hands and feet a small distance away from them, then had risen to run for the cacti grouping. Due to his moccasins' softness and his great experience, his steps had been inaudible. He arrived at his goal before the Mexicans and hid among the saguaros. It was so dark, that the two gatherers were forced to very carefully collect the fruit by their sense of touch. By now the small flames had disappeared.

Just when he had found cover the brothers arrived. They talked with each other and that in clear American English! It was obvious that they misrepresented themselves as Mexicans. Winnetou understood their every word. They had already spoken on the way and their current talk was the continuation of their previous conversation.

"I'll pay him back the insult, this so-called Bear Hunter," Carlos said. "But it's clear our task is now more difficult then we previously thought. The Apache showing up has turned things the wrong way."

"Unfortunately! He can't be misled by moved stakes."

"Did you have a good look at his horse?"

"Of course! It's the most wonderful horse I ever saw. Only Old Shatterhand is known to have one like it. We must make every effort to get it."

"That's obvious. But how?"

"It's best we let the fellows fall fast asleep. Then we kill them."

"You think this is possible? We are looked at askance, which means, they will be cautious. I don't think they will assign one of us to guard duty."

"There you are right. They will be careful. But let's try nevertheless. We can only work with our knives, silently, with a stab into the heart."

"And if this plan won't work?"

"That would be bad! But think, seven horses, particularly the Apache's, then all the weapons and the money! Just the two of us to share all this loot! That would be a coup. But if the situation will not be right we must call on our comrades. Here, in an open fight, the two of us would surely succumb. Let's give an excuse to split from them. Winnetou, together with the two Bear Hunters, will ride towards Old Shatterhand. The Yankees will join them having lost their guides in us."

"We ride as far as the Killing Bowl, where we will find one of our sentries who can bring our comrades. This makes sure we will get them all, even Old Shatterhand and those accompanying him. But let's not linger any longer or their mistrust will grow. My hat's full of fruit."

"Mine too."

"Then let's go."

They left, but Winnetou whisked away faster ahead of them. Avoiding all noise he returned to the fire in an arc and sat down. Thus the thought of having been overheard could not arise in the brothers. Everyone took some fruit, except Winnetou. Rejecting them, he said, "The Chief of the Apache does not eat what comes from the sumach."

"Sumach?" Emilio Cortejo asked surprised. "Doesn't Winnetou know the cactus fruit?"

"He knows the cacti and their fruit."

"And yet he mistakes the cactus for the poisonous sumach. That's impossible."

"Winnetou makes no mistake. He gives this fruit the name of the sumach, because they are poison."

"Poison? Why should they now be poisonous when they were all right earlier?"

"Because they were touched by hands that bring misfortune and death."

He spoke these very insulting words with such calm, as if conversing about something trivial.

"Ascuas!" Carlos Cortejo shouted. "Are we to put up with this? I demand that you take back these words!"

"Winnetou speaks only words he has previously considered well. He has never regretted a single word he has spoken and shall not take these back either."

"But we have been insulted!"

"Pshaw!"

With this exclamation the Apache had made a disparaging gesture with his hand. This word, together with his hand motion, conveyed such disdain, was such an expression of self-confidence, that the two found it wise to remain silent. Even had the chief been all by himself, they would not have been inclined to enter into an open fight with him. And here were several others who would certainly take the side of the Apache. For this reason Emilio soothingly said to his brother, "Keep quiet! Why quarrel? It's no use weighing an Indian's words."

"You're right. To keep the peace we act as if nothing's happened."

Winnetou did not respond. He stretched out in the grass and closed his eyes to give the impression he was going to sleep. This brief sequence of events, although now seemingly resolved, had left a troubling impression on the others. Winnetou, speaking such words, must surely have overheard some evil the two were planning. What were their plans? He had not said anything, proof that no hostility from the two was imminent. But the smoldering distrust had increased, with the result that no one had any inclination to continue talking. There arose a silence as telling as if the suspicion had been discussed.

The Bear Hunter and his son followed Winnetou's example. They also bedded down with the others following suit. After a while it appeared as if everyone was asleep, although this was not the case. The Cortejos were unable to sleep because of their plans, and the other Whites because of their mistrust.

Half an hour or more passed. Even if the estrangement had not taken place, the men would have been unable to sleep. The atmospheric tension had also increased. Barely audible crackling pervaded the bushes. A soft wind had arisen, and was slowly increasing, it began to move the branches of the bushes so that they touched each other more frequently. It looked as if barely visible sparks were exchanged among the tips of the branches.

Suddenly, everybody rose. A sound had risen, a very peculiar one, as if a bell had rung way up above the men. The sound persisted for about half a minute, came lower, swelling, to descend onto the bushes and fading over the waters of the pond.

"What was that?" Ben asked. "There are no church bells here! If I didn't know that ---"

He stopped. A second tone arose, higher in pitch than the first. It sounded as if coming from a mighty trumpet. It slowly swelled, lessened, and faded away in a diminuendo, even a trumpet virtuoso could not have produced.

"This is *Yalteh yuavh-kai*, the Voice of the Singing Valley," the Chief of the Apache explained.

"So that is it!" the Bear Hunter said. "Listen again."

A faint sigh wafted through the air. This sigh became a tone of utter clarity. It had the sound quality of the principal pipe of an eight-foot organ. For a while it held. Then a second, softer tone above it arose, which kept on going after the first could no longer be heard. These sounds were so peculiar, that one was inclined to shudder, yet simultaneously, so sublime they were touching the soul. It was as if an invisible, giant wind player was testing his instrument, but such an instrument never existed in Orchestrology.

The men listened silently, waiting whether the phenomenon would repeat. And yes, they could feel another current wafting through and over the bushes, bringing a series of tones quickly following each other, harmonizing with each other in their extraordinary clarity. They persisted for varying periods. The deeper ones were of greater length and, with the higher ones fading more quickly, formed a harmonic sequence, always repeating the same tones of the natural scale, yet in various inversions of triad, seventh and ninth chords.

There was nothing one could compare these sounds to. No known instrument could produce sounds of such sublime majesty to which others joined seemingly emanating from the smoothest throat, the softest lips.

At one time it sounded in the deepest maestoso, like from a sixteen or even thirty-two-foot organ pipe, then it rose above, mild and clear, like a vox humana or an Aeolian harp. And between these two alternated in varying height and touching expression the voices of a cornet, a trombone, a viola da gamba and an accordion. Sometimes it sounded open and bright, at other times subdued. And yet, all these artificial descriptions are incapable of conveying a concept of the nature, color, and effect of these sounds that filled the valley. Eventually, as if gathered in a confined zephyr, they escaped above it.

The listeners did not dare speak. Even the two unscrupulous Mexicans were touched. The men stood under the mighty dome of the sky, seemingly supported by the surrounding vertical walls of the valley basin. From an invisible organ chorus emanated sounds, now in thunderous tones, then like angels' voices, here like the deep, growling call of surf, there like voices of the spheres from a better and purer world. Even the coarsest mind was unable to prevent a holy shiver.

In addition to this, another phenomenon made its appearance, not to be perceived by the ears, but by the eyes.

It was as if the sky had risen higher, had become more distant. The few stars visible seemed to have become smaller. In the southwest, where the sky seemed to rest on the cliff face, a bright-yellow dot suddenly appeared. At first its circumference was clearly defined. It seemed to have erupted from the starry background and, while at first it moved slowly across the sky, it then straightened its path and with increasing speed sped towards the valley.

The closer it came, the larger it grew and the better one could discern that it wasn't a disk, but a ball.

Its outline became diffuse. Lightning-like beams sparked from it, and a tail was formed, shining brighter and more vivid than that of a comet.

The ball was no longer simply yellow. It seemed to consist of liquid fire, sparkling in a multitude of colors. It seemed to rotate about its axis; at least that was the impression given by the swirling colors. Its speed increased frighteningly. Then it looked as if it stopped briefly in mid-flight just above the basin's center. A thunderous noise sounded as if several canons had been fired simultaneously. The ball exploded into many fragments, which lost most their luminescence during their fall. The tail remained visible for a few seconds yet. There was a splash in the waters of the small pond, when a heavy, glowing object struck the surface with an enormous hiss. The men were all wet.

Now the firmament was as dark as before. The stars were visible once more, but only as miniscule points of light. Then a full, mighty sound consisting of several octaves one upon the other roared in unison over the frightened men's heads. Only Winnetou had kept his usual calm even now. There was no circumstance, which could rob him of this characteristic.

"*Ku-begay*, the fire ball," he said. "Great Manitou has thrown it from the sky and smashed it onto the Earth."

"A fire ball," asked Blount. "Yes, it looked like a ball. But did you see its tail? It was a dragon, the devil, an evil spirit going about at midnight."

"Pshaw!" the Apache answered, turning from the superstitious individual.

"Yes, it was a dragon!" Porter seconded his companion's opinion. "I've never seen one, but I heard others telling about it. My grandmother saw it dropping into the fireplace of a neighbor's, who had given his soul to the devil, traded it for money."

"Don't make a fool of yourself, Sir," the Bear Hunter said. "We no longer live in the Dark Ages, when people believed in dragons and ghosts. Or when the stupid where told to believe in it, so that the smart ones could benefit."

"What existed then also exists now. Or do you claim to be smarter than I?"

"Pah! I don't pride myself in my smarts. In the olden times all unexplainable apparitions were thought to be the work of the devil. Today though, and God be thanked, the sciences have advanced sufficiently to do away with Beelzebub and his famous grandmother."

"So you too are one of these enlightened, so-called scholars?"

"I'm no scholar. But that a fire ball is no devil, I do know."

"Well, what is it then?"

"Nothing but a small burning meteor, intercepted by Earth and drawn upon it."

"A meteor? A falling star?"

"Yes."

"What ignoramus has put that one over you?"

"Someone you wouldn't dare call an ignoramus, namely Old Shatterhand."

"He? Is that true?"

"Absolutely! When spending evenings together, sitting at a campfire, we often discussed such apparently inexplicable phenomena and found for everything a natural explanation. If you think you are smarter than this man, then have it your way. Didn't you notice that something fell into the pond?"

"I heard, saw, and felt it. Didn't we all get wet!"

"Then, if your opinion is correct, the devil fell into the water and since we forgot to pull him out, he must have drowned."

"He wouldn't drown. He would have gone on to hell."

"Great. He can dry himself at the fires down there, after he got wet up here and thus keep himself from getting a cold. If we could drain the pond, we would find a hole at its bottom with a stone, a meteorite buried in it."

"A stone? Hmm! It could have killed us."

"That's true. It was fortunate for us that it fell into the water."

"I don't want to quarrel with you. But did Old Shatterhand, by chance, also explain the sounds we heard earlier?"

"We didn't talk about the *Yuavh-kai*, no, but I recall that he spoke of the well-known Sackbut Pass in the Rattlesnake Mountains. If wind blows through the narrow, deeply cut canyon, sounds arise like those from a trumpet. The defile is the instrument and the wind the musician."

"This explanation sounds windy enough to me, but I don't want to argue about this either. Believe what you want and I think what I care about."

"The Bear Hunter is correct," Winnetou said. "There are many valleys where such sounds are heard. The Chief of the Apache has also seen the stones that Great Manitou has tossed from the heavens. The good Manitou has given each star its pathway, and if the fireball leaves its way, it must shatter. I will try to find the stone's track in the water."

He said this in a peculiarly raised voice and in leaving, walked along the pond's edge to disappear into the night. The others settled down again to wait for his return. No one spoke. Only Martin Baumann whispered to his father, "What

134

is Winnetou up to? He spoke so loudly as if he wanted someone else to hear his words beside us. That he was going to look for the stone was surely just a ruse."

"Of course," the Bear Hunter answered. "I bet, there's someone near who is spying on us. The way I know the Apache, he has noticed this one and left to sneak up on him and seize him. Let's wait and see."

They didn't have to wait long. Within a few minutes' time there was a noise in the bushes behind them as if an animal was crashing through. There was a brief, fearful cry, followed by Winnetou's voice, "The Bear Hunter may come here. A scout spied on us."

Baumann quickly rushed to where the voice had come from. It did not take long for them to reappear with a third man, obviously an Indian from his clothing.

What keen sight it took to discover a hidden spy in the shrubbery in the midst of night. And only a man like Winnetou would be able to sneak up on him and overcome him without much resistance.

Everyone surrounded the three. The captive had been armed with only a knife Winnetou had snatched from him. He was of small, slim build. His face could not clearly be seen due to the darkness.

But Winnetou's eyes were used to the dark and he knew whom he had caught.

"Why did my young red brother not come openly to us? We would have welcomed him cordially."

The captive did not respond, which is why the Apache continued, "It's my brother's own fault that he is a prisoner now. But nothing is going to happen to him. Here, I return his knife. He may return to his people to tell them that they are welcome to us and may rest here."

"Uff!" the captive called in surprise, while accepting his knife. "How do you know that our warriors are close-by?"

"Winnetou would have to be a little boy, if he could not tell."

"Winnetou, the Chief of the Apache?" sounded the young warrior's voice in great surprise. "You returned my knife. Do you think me to be an Apache?"

"No. My young brother does not wear war paint. Nevertheless, I assume him to be a son of the Comanche. Did the Comanche take up the tomahawk against the Apache?"

"No. The tips of the war arrows are buried in the earth, but there is no love between us."

"Winnetou loves all people without asking their names and color. He is willing to light the pipe of peace to smoke with you here at the fire. He does not ask why your brothers have entered the Singing Valley. They know that everyone coming here will camp by these waters. This is why they stopped back there and sent you to scout if someone was here already. Is that not so?"

"Yes," the Comanche confirmed.

"Should you once again lie under bushes to spy on other warriors, keep your eyelids down, for it were your eyes which gave you away. What is the number of your warriors?"

"Two times ten."

"Then go to them and tell them that Winnetou and eight palefaces will receive them as friends. This all without knowing the purpose of your approach. You need not tell them that I caught you. I shall not mention it."

"The Chief's great kindness brings pleasure to my heart. I shall not keep anything secret but tell the truth, so that my brothers will be convinced that you will receive them amicably. To be discovered by Winnetou's eyes is no disgrace, but I will remember the advice he has given me."

The circle of men surrounding him opened and he hurried off.

The Whites and especially the Mexicans voiced their opinion that it would be risky to permit the approach of twenty Comanche so readily. But the Apache declared decisively, "Winnetou always knows what he is doing. If the warriors of the Comanche ride to the Singing Valley, it cannot be for a fight against the Apache. Located beyond this valley is the grave of one of their highest chiefs. They want to visit it to sing the annual death song. We must light a bigger fire so that we can better see their faces. To be safe, we will receive them not here, but outside the bushes."

They stoked the fire and added more wood. While this was done Winnetou led the Bear Hunter and his son beyond the bushes and told them quietly, "The two palefaces are not what they claim to be. They speak the Yankee language and want to kill us here. They are members of the Llano Vultures. Winnetou guesses that the Comanche are headed for the Llano. The two Mexicans are not to learn this. This is why he told them the ruse of the grave site beyond the valley."

He could not continue, since the others came from the bushes. They had stoked up such a large fire, that its shine even penetrated the shrubbery and sufficiently illuminated the area in front. Of course, they carried their weapons and were prepared to use them should the Comanche, contrary to Winnetou's expectation, turn hostile.

Soon the hoof beats of many horses could be heard. The Comanche had arrived, but stopped a short distance away. Their leader dismounted and slowly approached. Winnetou walked towards him and offered his hand.

"The warriors of the Comanche are welcome," he said. "Winnetou does not ask what they want here. He knows they want to visit the grave site of their chief to then peacefully return to their wigwams."

This he had spoken loudly, but silently he quickly added, "My brother may confirm this. I will later talk with him secretly."

The Comanche played along and said, "My hand shakes Winnetou's with pleasure, he is the greatest warrior of the Apache, but is always a chief of peace.

We are prepared to smoke the calumet of peace with him, for we are not on the war path and want only to honor our dead chief."

"Winnetou believes in the assurances of his brother and invites him and his warriors to smoke the peace pipe at our fire."

The two chiefs shook hands. For the time being, this was sufficient proof that the Comanche had no hostile intentions. Winnetou led their leader to the fire, his people following them.

They first spread around the grassy area of the pond, to water and stake their horses. Then they joined the others, in ones and twos, by the fire. It had become crowded there, since the ringed site between the water and the bushes was not very wide. It was necessary to sit shoulder to shoulder to form a circle, within which Winnetou and the leader of the Comanche took their place.

One of the last Comanche to join the circle, after he had finished taking care of his horse, now approached to find a place. Before sitting down he looked around. When he saw the Cortejo brothers, who did not notice his attention, his dark face contorted suddenly and he shouted, "Uff! *Aletehlkua ekkvan mava* - what dogs are sitting there!"

Since everyone was still in the process of settling in, not all heard his shout. But the leader of the Comanche heard it. He rose quickly and asked the man, "*Hang tuhschtaha-nai* - who do you see?"

"*He-ehlbak, enko-ola uah-tuhvua* - them, the Llano Vultures."

"*He-ehlbak hetetscha enuka* - where are they?"

"*Mava he-ehlbak kenklah* - there they sit!"

With these words he pointed at the two make-believe Mexicans. Since these questions and answers were exchanged in a loud tone of anger, they had caught the attention of all present. Hearing the words: *enko-ola uah-tuhvua* – the Vultures of the Llano, every single one of the Comanche had leaped up again. Threateningly, they reached for their knives. Quickly, the setting had changed from a peaceful one to one of hostility.

The Whites had not understood the words, not being familiar with the Tonkawah or Moqui dialects. But seeing the threatening demeanor of the Reds, they rose too and reached for their weapons. Only Winnetou remained sitting peacefully. In a commanding voice he said, "My brothers should not become excited. If the red men see two of their enemies among us, I assure them, that we have nothing to do with them. Because of these two not a single drop of blood must be spilled. What has the warrior of the Comanche to say against them?"

He spoke in the customary jargon of the area, a mixture of Spanish, English, and Indian dialects. The Comanche answered in the same lingo everyone understood.

"I was hunting at the waters of the *Tovi-tschuna*, the Whites call the Fly River. There I saw the tracks of two horsemen, which I followed. I saw them sitting under a tree and sneaked up on them to hear what they were talking about.

137

They spoke of the Llano Estacado, which is to be crossed by a large train of white men in a few days. The Vultures of the Llano are gathering to attack this company. From the men's words I learned, that they are part of the Vultures. I asked the Great Spirit if I should kill them. His wisdom told me to let them live, because only then would it be possible to ---"

He was going to say something Winnetou didn't want the Mexicans to hear, which is why he quickly interrupted the speaker, "I know what my brother is going to say. I have heard enough. Did you recognize the men, that no error is possible?"

"It is them."

"What do the two palefaces say to this accusation?"

"That it's a stupid lie," Carlos Cortejo answered. "We never were at the Fly River."

"It is them!" the leader of the Comanche cried, "because we have ---"

"My brother may let me speak," Winnetou interrupted once more to prevent him from spilling information the Cortejos were not to know. The Comanche, though, became annoyed at the interruptions, which ran very much against the Indian custom of politeness and consideration. He was not smart enough to perceive the reasons and shouted angrily, "Why am I not to speak? Who is in the company of murderers is himself a murderer. Did the Chief of the Apache invite us in to commit a treachery?"

That's when Winnetou put down all his weapons, stood up and said, "Did my brother ever hear of Winnetou being treacherous? The Apache's word is like a rock upon which one rests securely. My brother may follow me and keep his weapons. Howgh!"

He left the circle and walked slowly beyond the bushes into the open.

The Comanche considered what had been said for a moment, then followed him. Before he left, though, he gave his people a sign to watch the Mexicans.

Outside, Winnetou took him by his arm, led him a short distance away, stopped there, and said, "My brother did not understand me. Winnetou was camped here already when the Whites arrived. He observed them and found out that two of the men are Vultures of the Llano. In this he agrees with the warriors of the Comanche. But why should these poisonous snakes learn that they have been found out. Then we would have to kill them. But it is smarter to let them live for a while. May my brother tell me why he followed them?"

The Comanche was embarrassed. He answered, "Fire-Star, the Chief of the Comanche, rode with Ironheart, his son, east to the wigwams of the Whites. They are returning through the Llano and should right now be in it. They will meet the caravan of the Whites and will also be attacked by the Vultures. This is why we left quickly to find and to protect them. We could not know where the Vultures will gather, which is why we let the two palefaces live to follow their tracks to their companions. At the Toyah River their tracks merged with that of four other

Whites we also thought to be Vultures. And now we have met you. What are your intentions?"

"I shall ride with you, because I too expect friends to come through the Llano who do not know about the impending attack of the Vultures. The Vultures' lair is at the Killing Bowl. But since I don't know where this place is, I shall let the two Mexicans escape, so that they will unknowingly become my guides."

"Who are the people you are expecting?"

"Old Shatterhand and several more palefaces."

"Old Shatterhand, the famous white warrior? With your permission, we will accompany you."

"Not only does Winnetou permit it, he asks for it. It appears that the usually dispersed gang of Vultures is gathering this time for a major strike. We must use this opportunity to destroy them in one fell swoop. I think ---"

He stopped, since inside by the pond loud shouting arose. Several shots sounded and hurried hoof beats could be heard beyond the campsite. The two leaped back to the fire. Coming out of the bushes they were faced with a lively scene. The Comanche had hurried to their horses and were ready to ride off. The Mexicans were nowhere to be seen. Ben, Porter, Blount, and Falser stood there, as if not knowing what to do. However, the Bear Hunter with his son had remained sitting quietly at the campfire and now called to Winnetou, "The fellows ran off."

"How did it happen?" the Apache asked.

"They leaped up so suddenly and ran for their horses, that they were past the bushes before anyone could reach for their rifle to shoot them down."

"That is good! Let them go. They ride to their death anyway and that of their companions. The sons of the Comanche may dismount and stay here. But at daybreak they shall leave the Singing Valley to hunt for the human carnivores of the Llano Estacado."

These words were spoken so loudly that everyone could hear them.

However, the Comanche got off their horses only, after the command had been repeated by their leader, who then explained to them why it would be wise to let the two escape for the time being.

5. The Ghost's Home

"My darling, my darling,
My love child so dear,
My joy and my smile,
My pain and my tear."

The dear, old Tennessee lullaby sounded through the still morning air. It seemed as if the branches of the nearby almond and laurel trees dipped in the same measure, while dozens of humming birds flashed around the old Negress like colorful sparks. She sat alone by the water.

The sun had just risen above the horizon and its brilliant beams swept across the clear waters. High up in the sky a king vulture drew circles. Closer by, at the edge of the water, several horses nipped at the juicy grasses like equine gourmets. On top of a cypress a mocking bird, its head tilted, listened to the song of the Negress and, when she had finished, imitated the closing notes with its "Mittir, mittir, mittir".

Above the feathery tops of low-growing palm trees, their images reflected by the water, tall cedars and sycamores spread their proud boughs. Below them large, colorful dragonflies hunted for flies and other small insects. Behind the little cottage, not far from the water, a bunch of small parrots fought for some golden grains of maize.

From the outside it was impossible to identify the material from which the little cottage had been built. Its four sides as well as the roof were totally covered by the dense vines of the white-flowering passion plant whose yellow, sweet, egg-like fruit peeked from the fullness of the leaves. The setting reminded one of the tropics. It was like being in a valley in the south of Mexico or central Bolivia, and yet, this small lake with its passion vine-covered cottage and its southern, luxuriant vegetation lay nowhere else, but – – – in the midst of the feared Llano Estacado. It was that mythical water, talked about by many, yet never seen by anyone.

"My heart leaf, my heart leaf,
My life and my star,
My hope, my delight,
My sorrow, my care!"

The black woman continued.
"Mikkehr, mikkehr," the mocking bird echoed the last two words.
But the songstress paid no attention to it. Her eyes were fastened on an old photograph she held in both hands which, in between the verses, she had lifted to her withered lips to kiss.

141

Many, many tears had dropped onto the faded picture, a Negress with a black baby in her arms. The little one's head had been kissed into oblivion and washed away by tears.

"You my good, dear Bob," she said tenderly. "My little Bob, my small Bob. I'm your mother. Our Missus was good and friendly. She made picture of herself, also of Sanna and little Bob. When Missus died, Massa sold Bob, and Sanna only had picture of Bob. I kept it, when was sold myself. Kept it also when good Massa Bloody-Fox brought me here. I will keep until old Sanna die and never see Bob again. He be strong, big man now and not have forgotten his dear, good mother Sanna. Oh, my darling, my darling, my joy and my ---"

She stopped and raised her head to listen. Her snow-white wooly hair contrasted sharply with the dark complexion of her face. Someone was approaching. She jumped up, put the photograph in a pocket of her calico dress and called, "Jesus, Jesus, Sanna glad! Fox come back finally. Good Bloody-Fox back again. I quickly fix some meat and bake corn bread."

She hurried for the cottage, but had barely reached it when Fox appeared through the trees. He looked pale and exhausted. His horse was sweating profusely and stumbled tiredly. Both must have had a hard ride.

"Welcome, Massa!" the old woman greeted him. "Sanna hurry and bring food right away."

"No, Sanna," he answered, lowering himself out of the saddle. "Fill the water bags, all, all of them! That's what needs to be done right away."

"Why bags? Who for? Why will Massa not eat? He very hungry!"

"That is true, but I will take what I need myself. You have no time for cooking, but must fill the water bags with which I will leave again right away."

"Jesus, Jesus! Off again. Why you leave old Sanna always alone in midst of big, wide Llano Estacado?"

"Because a large caravan of immigrants will otherwise die for lack of water. These people have been misled by the Vultures."

"Why did Massa not guide them better?"

"I could not get close to them since they were surrounded by many Vultures. It would have meant my death had I dared to break through their guard circle."

"They will kill the poor, good immigrants."

"No. Brave, strong hunters are coming from the north whose help I expect. But their help would be in vain, if there's no water. The immigrants would surely die without it, even if they were rescued from the Vultures. Therefore get me the water, Sanna. Water, water, and quickly! I will load all our horses with the water bags, and will leave only my horse here, since he's too worn to continue."

Fox walked to the cottage entering it through the door framed by the passionflowers. A single room formed its inside. Its four walls were built of reeds and fine mud from the small lake. The roof was made of long cane stems. From an earthen fireplace extended a hood also constructed of cane and mud. An iron kettle hung underneath. Each of the other three walls had a small window kept free of the passion vines.

From the rafters hung slabs of smoked meat and on the walls all kinds of weaponry common in the West. Furs covered the floor. The two beds consisted of leather thongs strapped to wooden posts and were covered by bearskins. The finest ornament of the room was the shaggy skin of a white bison with the skull still attached. It hung opposite the entrance and stuck in the wall on both sides were at least twenty knives, into whose horn or wooden handles a variety of symbols had been carved.

A table, two chairs and a ladder reaching to the ceiling, constituted the entire furnishings of the little passion vine cottage.

Bloody-Fox stepped to the bison skin, moved his hand across, and said to himself, "The Ghost's uniform. Beside it, the knives of the murderers, felled by his bullets – – twenty-six already. But when will I meet the one, who has earned death more than any other? Maybe never? Pshaw, I'm still hoping. Again and again, driven by his conscience, the villain will return to the place of his crime. Now I must rest for fifteen minutes."

He dropped onto one of the beds and closed his eyes but not to sleep. What images must pass through the mind of this young man!

After half an hour Sanna entered to tell him that the water bags had all been filled. He jumped from his bed and lifted one of the furs lying on the floor. Below it was a small covered depression from which he removed a little metal covered box. It contained ammunition with which he filled the bag hanging from his belt. Then he climbed up the ladder to provision himself with meat. When this was done, he walked outside to the lake's bank, where eight large leather water bags lay, two each tied together by strong leather straps. Bloody-Fox had already saved many lost travelers from dying of thirst by their content.

Five horses stood at the banks of the small lake. One was now saddled up with the gear from the tired horse Blood-Fox had returned on. The others he loaded with the water bags in such a way, that one bag hung to the right and left of each animal. The horses were lined together with Bloody-Fox on his steed leading the way.

With a knowing hand the Negress had helped in this task, showing that this was not the first time she had done it. Now she said to him, "Massa Fox a bit here and right away go in danger again. What to happen of poor, old Sanna, if Massa Fox shot dead and not come back?"

"I will come back, dear Sanna," he answered. "My life is under a mighty protection. Were this not the case, I would long since be dead."

"But Sanna so very alone. Has no one to talk with. Only horse, parrots, and picture of little Bob."

"Well, maybe this time, when I return I shall bring some company. I will meet men, I am prepared to show my home to, although I have kept it a secret so far. There's also a Negro among them. His name's Bob, just like your darling boy."

"Negro with name Bob? Oh, Jesus, Jesus. Maybe he has mother name of Susanna, but called Sanna?"

"I don't know that."

"Was he sold from Tennessee to Kentucky?"

"I did not ask him."

"Maybe he my little boy!"

"What do you think? A thousand Negroes are called Bob. How can you hope that this one is yours. Don't get carried away. Maybe I will bring him along. Then you can ask him yourself. Farewell, Sanna! Take good care of my black horse."

"Good bye, Massa! Oh, Jesus, Jesus, Sanna now alone again. Bring Negro Bob here, bring him."

He nodded at her with a smile, set his lineup to move, and quickly disappeared through the trees.

The cypresses, cedars, and sycamores by the lake were old trees. The almond and laurel trees Bloody-Fox had planted, also the little grove of chestnuts, almonds, and oranges he was now passing through. A strip of dense, fast-growing bushes, intended to keep the wind and sand from the little oasis followed this. The young man had dug small trenches from the lake to water this shrubbery. Where the moisture ran out, plant growth quickly turned to various types of cacti, followed eventually by the bare, vegetation-free sands of the Llano.

Once he had reached this area he put his train into a gallop, so that they soon disappeared like small black dots on the horizon. About noon of the same day, a half-day's ride to the northwest of the little oasis, a large group of horsemen moved northeast through the Llano Estacado.

In their lead rode Winnetou with the chief of the Comanche, behind him the Bear Hunter with his son Martin, in turn followed, riding side-by-side, by Ben New-Moon, Porter, Blount and Falser. The Comanche warriors formed the rear of the group.

They rode silently, as if every sound might cost the life of one of their group's members. The rearguard's eyes swept the horizon to the left and right. Mostly, though, they kept looking at their two leaders, particularly Winnetou, who hung low to one side of his saddle to keep close watch of the tracks they were following.

These were the tracks of the Cortejo brothers, which they hoped, would lead them to the Killing Bowl. Suddenly, Winnetou halted his horse and jumped from the saddle. Many tracks were noticeable in the light sand. It looked as if several horsemen had ridden a carrousel. Not only were there hoof tracks, but also footsteps to be seen. These riders had dismounted to more closely inspect some tracks.

While the others waited Winnetou scrutinized every imprint of the widely trampled ground. In the process he slowly walked, bent forward, for quite a distance to the right. When he returned he told the chief of the Comanche, but loud enough so that everybody could hear, "Here, the palefaces came across other tracks and dismounted to check these. Five horses lined together in a horse train made these other tracks. Had riders mounted them, they would not have been tied together. It was therefore a train of five animals with only one rider. This man passed here about three hours ago. The two Whites, who called themselves Mexicans, met his tracks about two hours ago and then followed them. My Comanche brother may look at the tracks, whose edges are still fairly sharp yet partly collapsed. He will confirm that the tracks are at least two hours but no more than three hours old."

The Comanche slid from his horse to also investigate the tracks. When he was finished, he agreed with Winnetou entirely. The Bear Hunter also dismounted now to slowly circle the area of disturbance in a bent-low posture. Then he also walked to the right, but farther than Winnetou. There he squatted down to inspect a spot more closely. A moment later he signaled Winnetou. When the Apache had joined him, he said to him, pointing to the sand, "The Chief of the Apache will see, that the rider dismounted here. Why did he?"

Winnetou's eyes followed the tracks farther to the right. Then he answered, "The man is a paleface, as I can see from his foot prints. He is the age of a young man. He lost water, as can be seen beside the tracks of his horses. Thereafter, he no longer lost any. He dismounted here to close the barrel or water bag that was leaking."

"Is my red brother of the opinion, that it was only one barrel or bag?"

"Only one was leaking, but he carried at least eight. There must have been two per horse. Accordingly, four horses carried eight water bags."

"Why so much water? He did not need it all for himself and his horses."

"No. He must have been on the way to a place where many need water. He is either a Vulture, who is on the way to bring water to his fellow-beasts, or he is an honest fellow, who is out to rescue other decent people. He must know of such people. Who could they be?"

"Maybe the caravan of the immigrants that is to be attacked?"

"My brother is probably right. Let us mount our horses again and follow the tracks which have joined here."

They got on their horses and followed the tracks at an increased pace, which now led exactly north, no longer northeast.

There was nothing but sand and more sand in which the tracks were clearly marked. Only here and there did the pursuers encounter bare rock. All in all, the

145

Llano gave the impression as if its ground had once been the bottom of a lake, which dried up hundreds or thousands of years ago.

At times, gray-brown strips became visible to the right or left near the horizon, cacti thickets no one would be eager to pass through.

Thus it continued on and on. The tracks they followed became fresher and fresher, a sure sign that they were catching up with those they followed.

The afternoon almost gone, they reached a spot where the tracks once more spread out. Not because new ones had been added, rather because the riders had stopped here. Winnetou, once more got off his horse to check. He first walked a distance to the north. When he returned, he checked just as far to the east, then told the others upon his return, "The man with the water rode straight north. The two Mexicans contemplated here whether to follow him but decided to ride towards sunrise. Who shall we follow?"

"My brother is best suited to determine this," the leader of the Comanche responded.

"Let me tell you my opinion then. Those, the young man is headed for, are in the north. He is a good person, since his tracks continue differently from those of the Mexicans. We could follow his' to warn him. But since the Mexicans turned so abruptly away from his tracks the Killing Bowl must be close. They rode there to meet the other Vultures and to warn them of the man with the water. They will surely follow his tracks to prevent him from saving their victims. His tracks are so fresh that we could catch up with him before evening. My brothers may choose now what to do. Shall we follow the man with the water to support him, or shall we ride to the Killing Bowl to seize the Vultures there so that they cannot harm him? If we follow the man's tracks, they will not attack him once they see us, but may also escape us. If we catch them at their lair, we can still follow the man's tracks, which will lead us to the party he is going to help."

Winnetou had explained the situation so clearly, that it did not require any lengthy discussion. The Comanche, anyway, kept silent, except for their leader. He quickly consulted with the six Whites, then told the Apache, "We shall ride for the Killing Bowl, that is, follow the tracks of the two Mexicans. Does this suit my red brother?"

Winnetou nodded assent and directed his horse onto the east-leading tracks. He could have urged the horses of his party to a faster pace to quickly catch up with the Mexicans, but this was not his intention. The sooner he would reach the two, the less he could hope to learn of the location of the Killing Bowl.

It was important to get to see this place. Hence, he maintained a pace commensurate with that of the Cortejo brothers, which he could discern from their tracks.

About a day's ride to the northeast of the oasis a long train of about twenty ox-drawn wagons moved in a long drawn-out line through the Llano. Spaced at regular intervals, they were guarded by armed horsemen. The sturdily-built

146

wagons were each drawn by six or eight oxen, who had their difficulty pulling the heavy loads slowly through the sand. The animals were tired and exhausted. One could also see that the horses carrying their riders were barely able to continue. Their tongues hung out, their flanks pumped, and their legs trembled as they walked.

The drovers of the wagons also stumbled weakly alongside the oxen. The men's heads hanging low, they barely seemed to have any strength left to crack their giant whips to drive the draft animals to one more effort. Men and beasts of this caravan gave the impression of being on their last leg.

Only the horse of their guide up front looked fresh and agile showing no sign of fatigue. Its rider, however, sat just as bent-down in his saddle as all the others did, as if he too were suffering from terrible thirst. Yet when one of the women or children in the wagons sounded a cry of lament, he involuntarily sat up straighter and a devilish smile of satisfaction played on his lipless mouth. He was none other than Tobias Praisegod Burton, the pious Mormon missionary, whose task it was to lead the party entrusted to him to their certain demise.

Now, one of the horsemen at the head of the train gave his horse the spurs, which brought him with a great effort to Burton's side.

"Sir," he said, "we cannot continue much longer like this! We haven't had a drop of water since we gave our last to our animals. And that was yesterday morning, when we discovered that the last two barrels had, incomprehensibly, leaked out completely."

"That's due to the heat," Burton explained. "The staves no longer closed because of the heat."

"No, Sir! I inspected the barrels. As long as there's water in the barrel the staves will stay closed. Someone drilled holes in them, so that the water could slowly and unnoticeably run out through the night. There's someone among us who intends us harm."

"Impossible! Whoever drains water secretly would also die of thirst."

"I thought so myself, but that's how it is, nevertheless. I kept all this to myself, said not a word to the others, so as not to increase the already poor spirit of the people. I secretly watched everyone I could think of having committed the deed, but could not see anything from which I could conclude who the culprit might be. The animals are suffering, the women lament, and the children cry for water, all in vain. There's not a single drop to be had any more. Look up there! The vultures are circling as if they knew we'd soon fall victim to them. Are you sure we are on the right track?"

It had been Burton himself who had drilled into the barrels during the night. At the time he had drunk and had also watered his horse. He had also filled the large tin which, carefully wrapped and stowed behind his saddle, would refresh him and his horse secretly during the coming night.

"Of course," he responded pointing to the stakes stuck at large intervals into the sand. "Don't you see our guideposts, which we can rely on?"

"With certainty? We've all heard that these stakes are at times moved by the Llano Vultures, and put into a different direction to lead travelers to their death."

"Yes, that did happen in the past. But it doesn't happen any more, since a stop has been put to the villains' practices. Then, too, I know the area very well and know we are headed in the right direction."

"This morning you said that we are here in the terrible midst of the Llano. Why, precisely were the stakes placed through here? At other places we and the animals could have found some sustenance, some moisture from the fruits of the large cactus fields."

"It would have meant a long detour. Let me assure you, also to calm you, that if we hurry up a bit, we will reach such a large cactus field by evening. Tomorrow, we will then reach a spring, which will put an end to our suffering."

"Hurry up? Don't you see that the animals are unable to increase their speed."

"Then lets stop for them to rest."

"No, no, we cannot do that! If we stop, we'll never get them to move again. Once they lie down, they will refuse to get up. We must keep them stumbling along until we get to the cacti you mentioned."

"As you like, Sir. I don't suffer any less than you. But look, here you see the tracks of a large group of horsemen who has traveled in the same direction just ahead of us. They wouldn't dare to head in this direction if they wouldn't know it to be the right one. We need not fear anything. Tomorrow, by this time, all will be over."

He was very much correct with his words, since the planned attack was to take place before the time he had just given. The horsemen ahead of them were, obviously, his compatriots, who had placed the stakes in the wrong direction. He secretly smiled into his beard when the other seemed calmed by his ambiguous words.

Between Fox's oasis and the Killing Bowl lay a several hour long and almost as wide impenetrable field of cacti. No horse, no human could cross it. This was the reason why Bloody-Fox had never taken this direction and thus had never come to the Killing Bowl. He hurried north at the western border of the field. Had he turned east at its northern perimeter, he would certainly have discovered the depression, which had so often already become the ruin of many. But he knew the ones he wanted to save to be northeast of him, which is why he took this direction once the cactus field lay behind him. The sun burned implacably. Its heat penetrated his suit. His horses sweated, but he did not allow them any rest. Continuously scanning the horizon he drove on. Now, where sky and earth came together, a number of dispersed black dots appeared.

"These are the immigrants," he shouted with delight. "I knew they would come from this direction. I will be there in time."

He urged his horse on with his spurs, his pack animals with loud shouts of encouragement, and the group flew across the plains. Although, he soon noticed that he was facing only horsemen and no wagons, he believed that they formed the advance of the wagon train and headed directly towards them. Only when he had already come quite close, did he become aware of the large number of men, but also of their behavior. They had noticed him too now. Instead of awaiting his approach though, they split into three groups. One group stopped, the other two rode to the left and right towards Blood-Fox, as if to encircle him and make escape impossible. Seeing this, he rose in his saddle to get a better view of the situation.

"Heavens," he called. "These are more than thirty men. That can't be the advance party of the immigrants. They have some pack horses with stakes along. By the devil! These are the Llano Vultures I've run into. Now they're out to get me. It's impossible for me to take on that many. I must escape. He turned to gallop away. However, he could not get enough speed with his tied-together horses, particularly with his animals already being fatigued. The pursuers gained on him. He drove his own horse hard, but this caused the pack animals to resist and kick out. This slowed him down considerably, becoming dangerous."

Some of the pursuers had already approached within rifle range. Suddenly, the lead line of Bloody-Fox's horse broke and the four pack animals broke away.

"I've lost them and the water too," Fox grated. "But I shall collect my pay for this."

He calmed his horse and stopped, aimed his double-barreled rifle --- a shot, a second one, and the first two of his pursuers fell from their mounts.

"Now, let's go! They won't come close again. There's nothing else I can do right now for the suffering people, but to find Old Shatterhand and to get him on their trail."

While he angrily voiced these words, he galloped north. Shouting madly, the Vultures pursued him for a short distance, but when they saw that his horse was superior to theirs, they turned back to the spot where their two companions had been shot.

And, not quite a day's ride farther north from the oasis, there was another troop of riders on their way south. It was not strong in numbers, but rather by the intelligence of its members, that is, Old Shatterhand and his friends.

They were following deeply indented, broad tracks. Leading in the direction of the caravan, they were those of the Vultures, who removed the guideposts ahead of it to re-stake them in the sand in the direction of the Killing Bowl.

As usual, Old Shatterhand rode up front with Ironheart, the young Comanche beside him. Jim and Tim Snuffle were close behind, followed by Hobble-Frank and Fat-Jemmy. The others formed the rear guard.

149

Old Shatterhand was silent. He never left the tracks leading to a point on the horizon out of his eyes. Only their observation seemed to occupy him. The less quiet though were the others, with Frank being the loudest and most wordy of them. The conversation dealt with a subject dear to his heart and about which Jemmy, riding next to him, seemed to have a different opinion, since the little Saxon was just exclaiming angrily, "When it comes to scientific subjects you're always off your rocker. If you hadn't met me, you would still be stuck in deepest ignorance. It's only my intellectual buttermilk, which raised you to and has ever since maintained your mental acuity. And you claim that the fireball we saw came from the firmament. As if the firmament had nothing better to do than to irradiate your dark spirit with glowing balls and rockets!"

"Well, then give me a better explanation," Jemmy challenged him laughingly.

"Don't want to!"

"Why not?"

"Because I would then raise your intellectual level once again by several degrees Fahrenheit, without you ever noticing it."

"Or is it, because you yourself don't know of a better explanation?"

Their dispute was terminated by a shout of Old Shatterhand's, who pointed towards south to say, "There comes a horseman, a single rider. It takes great courage to travel by oneself here, as well as an excellent knowledge of the Llano."

"Who may that be?" Tim asked. "He seems to approach us as quickly as he's able to."

Old Shatterhand stopped his horse, pulled his telescope from the saddlebag, and aimed it at the rider, who approached them in a hard gallop. When he lowered it he said in a tone of pleasure, "It is Bloody-Fox, who disappeared so quickly the other time. Let's wait for him here."

Shortly thereafter Bloody-Fox recognized the individual riders of the group. He already waved from afar and shouted, "What fortune to meet you, gentlemen! Quickly, I need your help."

"For whom?" Old Shatterhand asked.

"For a caravan of German immigrants, who will most likely be attacked tonight by the Vultures."

By the time he had finished these words, he had arrived at the group and shook hands with them.

"Most assuredly they are the same we are looking for," Old Shatterhand nodded. "Where are they?"

"Southeast of here. They seem to be headed for the big cactus field."

"That I do not know."

"It is the largest in the Llano. I counted more than thirty Vultures, but shot two of them. They have pulled the stakes and have reinserted them in the direction of the cactus field. It is impossible to penetrate it. From it I conclude that the immigrants are to be killed there."

"How far is it to reach these people?"

"Three hours in a gallop."

"Well, then let's get going and not lose time. We can still talk on the ride."

The little group now chased across the plain. Bloody-Fox kept to Old Shatterhand's side and told him about his encounter with the Vultures and the loss of his four packhorses. The hunter looked at him sideways and said with a knowing smile, "Five horses you have, Fox? Hmm! And that in the midst of the Llano! Does it also include the one the Avenging Ghost rode when he passed by us?"

"Yes, Sir," Fox nodded.

"I thought so."

"I cannot keep my Ghost haunt secret much longer since I must take you there. I also need not play this game any longer, since we can eliminate the entire gang this time in one fell swoop. I'm missing only one. A particular one!"

"Which one?"

"The gang leader from long ago, when I was the only one who survived of my group. But who knows where his bones are bleaching now."

"Fox, despite of your youth, you are a real hero. You have my respect! Some time later, you may tell me everything in greater detail. But already now, I know what kind of a man you are and what dangers you have dealt with victoriously. And since you own so many horses and seem to be able to come and go as you please, it is certain that you must have a place in the midst of the Llano Estacado where there's water, trees, grass, even fruit."

"That I do. I live by a small lake beyond the cactus field."

"Ah, a lake even. Then the old myth is true after all. Please describe the place to me."

Bloody-Fox did. No one else but Old Shatterhand could hear the account, and he was not going to reveal the secret at this time.

After a while the horses were allowed a slower pace for a distance so as not to stress them too much. But then they were urged into a gallop again.

Just when the sun was setting, the group arrived at the wagon tracks, which they now followed southward. This was not too difficult, since a partial Moon soon rose spending sufficient light for the pursuit. When they had traveled for about an hour Old Shatterhand suddenly halted his horse, pointed ahead and said, "There are the immigrants. You can see their wagon fort. Wait here. I will approach it secretly, then let you know what's going on."

He dismounted and sneaked away. Half an hour later he returned and reported; "Twelve large ox wagons have been moved into a square, with the people sitting inside. They have neither food nor drink, not even material for a fire. Their guide has betrayed them, or they would have these supplies. The oxen lie exhausted and moaning on the ground. They are almost gone and will certainly not rise tomorrow morning. What little water we carry will not be enough for these people. To save the animals we must make some rain."

"Make rain?" Hobble-Frank asked. "You mean to say, you will get it to rain, here in the middle of the Llano?"

"Yes."

"What? How? Really? That's too much for me. You are a very obliging man, Mister Shatterhand, but to make clouds and to milk them as you please, no. What's going to produce the clouds?"

"Electricity. But I have no time now to explain that to you. To make water, I need fire, a very large burning surface. Bloody-Fox spoke of a mighty cactus field nearby to the south of us. Let's hope I can produce a good downpour shortly. But now come along."

He mounted his horse again to ride for the wagon fort. The others followed shaking their heads. Yet, at the same time they were wondering about the promised rain and were curious about the poor people they had come to rescue.

The wagons had been moved so close together that no horseman could enter between them. But the approach of the little group was heard. They dismounted in front of the wagons, hearing a voice inside.

"Listen! Someone is coming. By God, will they bring help or are they Vultures?"

"We are not Vultures. We will bring you some water," Old Shatterhand called in a loud voice. "Come here and let us in."

"The devil!" another displeased voice shouted. "Might this be --- Wait, you others. I will have a look."

The man came closer, leaned over one of the shafts and asked, "Who are you, strangers?"

"I'm called Old Shatterhand, accompanied by my friends, all of them good people."

"Old Shat --- the devil may get you!"

The man who greeted the saviors with this curse was no one else, but Mister Tobias Praisegod Burton.

"Ah, it's you," Old Shatterhand said, who had recognized him even in the dark. "I'm extremely pleased to meet you again."

But Burton had run off already. He knew that every moment counted for him now. He dashed to the opposite side where his horse stood, pulled a wagon shaft away to provide an opening for his escape, jumped in the saddle and galloped off. Behind him rose the joyful calls of the people he had tried to lead to their ruin.

"You just wait!" he grated. "I shall return soon and that will mean the end of also those, who think they have come to your rescue. Old Shatterhand! What a catch we will make."

He did not have to ride long. Only fifteen minutes later he met his companions, who were waiting here to be fetched for the massacre.

They were not at all disappointed that such a famous hunter had joined the immigrants. They were even delighted, figuring that there was now more loot to be had. Never did they consider that their attack might fail. Obviously, they could not now take their victims without a fight and had to wait for sunrise to be able to distinguish friend from foe.

The two supposed Mexicans had also found their compatriots. In the Killing Bowl they had found only a single sentry who had led here. They had told of their experiences in the Singing Valley, with which they caused great joy. It was decided to first overcome the immigrants, then to find Winnetou to ambush his party for more rich booty.

That the Apache could be so close already never occurred to them. But close he was.

He and his group had reached the Killing Bowl, but found it deserted. This murder basin consisted of a rough-lined and rather deep depression, at whose bottom was a muddy pool. It's water may have oozed from the not too distant little lake of the oasis, the Ghost's haunt. Though turbid, it was precious in the midst of the Llano, which is why the Vultures had made it their base. As often as they spread across the plains, they always returned here, where one of them had to keep guard and to relay messages.

Today, this man had left with the two Mexicans, which is why Winnetou found the place deserted. But his sharp eyes soon told him the direction he had to follow. He followed the tracks of the three men and by evening arrived at the place where the Vultures were camped. His companions had to wait. He himself crawled like a snake to the group of villains. He observed Burton's arrival and watched him sitting down with them. With little cover available, he was unable to approach them closely to overhear what they were talking about, but at least he was able to count their numbers. Then he returned to his companions.

"Thirty and five Vultures," he reported. "At this time tomorrow their flesh will be eaten by real vultures."

"What are they planning over there?" Ben New-Moon asked.

"They are out for booty which must be north of here, since the Mexicans rode in this direction. A messenger just arrived from there indicating that the attack could begin. My brothers will now ride north with me, where we are certain to come across the people to be attacked."

He mounted his horse and, riding in a wide arc so that he and his people would not be spotted, the group headed north.

Very soon they saw the wagon fort ahead with guards now posted outside. By now Old Shatterhand had taken this precaution. When they were hailed by these people Winnetou responded, "You white men need not be concerned. Here is Winnetou, the Chief of the Apache, with help, meat and water."

His sonorous voice carried well and barely was he finished, when the delighted voice of Hobble-Frank could be heard from inside the wagon fort, "Winnetou? Grand! But where the Apache is, there must also be the Bear Hunter and his little Martin. Let me out! I must get out to hug them. This is just like Christmas! To run into my best friends here, in the midst of the Sahara and in pitch-darkness too! What a joy!"

Climbing over one of the wagons and jumping down he halted in surprise when he faced the number of Comanche.

"By gosh, what's this?" he asked. "That's a whole battalion of cavalry at our doors! That looks mighty suspicious. Come on out Mister Shatterhand to have a look at all these ghosts wandering the Llano on horseback."

But by then Martin Baumann hung already on Frank's neck with the Bear Hunter grabbing him from behind. A happy meeting took place now. Winnetou also greeted his old friends joyfully to say, "My brother Shatterhand must also be here. Has he not heard my voice?"

"Oh, yes. Here I am!" he called.

With the help of some of his friends he had moved two wagons apart and now came out to hug his red friend to his chest. The others followed, Jemmy, Davy, Juggle-Fred, Jim and Tim, the first to greet their friends, the latter to meet Winnetou as quickly as possible. All this produced an excited air with questions and answers flying about and hands to be shook, but without much noise as the precarious situation demanded.

Only one stood alone, serious and sad, with his fellow-tribesmen, the young Comanche, Ironheart. They were surprised to find him here. Sadly, he told them of the murder of their chief, his father. They listened silently, but inside they swore death to the Vultures.

The welcome finished, everyone became busy inside and outside the wagon fort. It was widened so that the large number of Comanche could also be accommodated. From afar, the Vultures were not to see the large number of opponents they now faced. The horses too were brought inside. The Comanche distributed among the immigrants their meat and water, which they carried in gourds. Old Shatterhand promised that more would be available shortly. However, all the supplies were still not sufficient to entirely still the thirst of the poor people.

Other interesting and unexpected scenes evolved, like when Ben New-Moon recognized Juggle-Fred who had saved him from the murderous hands of Stealing-Fox. But soon, a deep silence descended on the wagon fort. No one slept especially those who had to catch up exchanging the experiences they had since last seeing each other. They spoke only in whispers, so that not a sound was to be heard outside the wagon fort.

Old Shatterhand had taken command. He sat next to Bloody-Fox to hear his life's story, but more so to have him describe, in greater detail, the area they were in. Not a single Vulture was to escape, so that their operation was to be put to an end forever.

What interested him most was that, besides the large cactus field to the south, a second one was located to the east, although much narrower, but also much longer than the first. Fox said, that a rather narrow stretch of sand extended southward between them, which led to his Ghost haunt.

"Very good!" Old Shatterhand said. "Then, not a single one of these villains will escape. Should they become aware too soon of our superior numbers, or if they flee after their first attack, we chase them between these two cactus fields and ignite them. That will also provide water for the draft animals."

"But doesn't that mean the Vultures will find my refuge and escape from there?"

"No, Fox, because you will ride there now with ten Comanche to 'welcome' the fellows we are going to drive towards you. They will arrive there in good time, since I wager, the attack will not take place until morning."

This plan was put into effect immediately. The wagon fort was opened once more to let Fox and ten Comanche out. Then silence resumed.

The guards had been posted a good distance from the wagon fort and had received orders to retreat quickly and silently and to creep underneath the wagons of the fortification upon the enemy's approach. Inside stood the horses, ready for the immediate pursuit of fleeing Vultures. Every man had received specific instructions of what to do.

Thus the night passed. Finally, the sky brightened in the east and the wagons silhouettes as well as other objects and men could be more easily discerned. Not a bit of morning fog had risen. Once the light increased further one could see the Vultures' horses to the south, a little more than five hundred paces away. They thought their time had come and put their horses on the move, arriving in a gallop.

They did not expect that more than a single guard would be on duty at the wagon fort.

The guards had withdrawn and all men stood on the side from which the attack was coming.

"Do not shoot the horses! Aim at the riders!" Old Shatterhand commanded.

Then the Vultures were only fifty, forty, now twenty-five paces away.

"Fire!" Old Shatterhand called.

More then thirty shots rang out. Immediately, the band of attackers broke into a confused mob. The dead and wounded dropped from their horses; rider-less horses ran everywhere. The remaining horsemen, some of them wounded, brought their animals to a hard stop. A few, maybe ten, were left in the saddle.

"Hurray, hurray! Old Shatterhand and Winnetou!" Hobble-Frank shouted.

155

When the Vultures heard these names and became aware of their large loss they quickly turned to gallop away to the south with Mister Tobias Praisegod Burton, the most terrified, in the lead.

"Off you go! Each of you to your place!" Old Shatterhand commanded.

Two wagons were quickly moved so that the hunters could all get out. The immigrants hurried to the dead and wounded Vultures. Everyone else, not needed right here, took on the pursuit of the bandits, yet without great hurry. Only two of them urged their mounts to their maximum speed, Jim and Tim Snuffle.

Ten Comanche rode first east, then turned south to block the path of the fleeing and force them to take the direction between the two cactus fields. All others, with Old Shatterhand and Winnetou in the lead, rode south in a trot following the Vultures, who galloped and thus seemed to get away from them.

The bandits were furious to see their attack come to naught. They chased ahead without talking to each other. Curses escaped their mouths. Only when they had reached the Killing Bowl, did they come to a stop.

"What now," Burton asked, hanging gasping on his horse. "Here, we cannot stay. The dogs are following us."

"Obviously!" Carlos Cortejo agreed who, like his brother, had not been wounded. "Straight through the cactus field we cannot ride, so let's turn to the right. Come on!"

They headed for the given direction but soon saw smoke rising in the distance.

"By the devil!" Emilio shouted. "They beat us to it. They have ignited the cacti. We must turn back."

They galloped back past the Killing Bowl towards the east. After barely ten minutes they saw Old Shatterhand to their left who, with his band, approached them diagonally. A great fright took hold of them. They gave their steeds the spurs to get past them, and it looked as if they might succeed. When they were unsuccessful with this maneuver, they tried to break out to the side but soon noticed that this, too, was impossible, their path blocked by the ten Comanche waiting in the distance.

"It's the devil's game today!" Burton screamed. "I believe this Winnetou is with them. I heard his name called. We must veer left between the two cactus fields."

"Is there an exit from it? Is this not a cul-de-sac?" Carlos asked.

"I don't know. I've never been there in my life. There's nothing else we can do."

"Then let's hurry so that we beat the fire."

They chased to the right, southward, exactly in the direction Old Shatterhand wanted them to go. So, finally, he too let his horse feel the spurs. From the left he was joined by the ten Comanche, from the right by the two Snuffles, who had completed their task, and all of them now followed the

Vultures between the cactus fields towards the distant Ghost haunt, Bloody-Fox's oasis.

Carlos Cortejo had been right to warn of the fire. It came closer, slowly at first, but gained speed.

The dried cactus had been there for centuries, sometime sprouting anew. There was plenty of material to burn. At first the flames licked about slowly. Then they began to run, to jump, finally to reach as high as a tree. Soon the entire broad expanse became an unbroken sea of flames, whose terrible loud crackle sounded like thunder from a distance. The rising heat produced an ever-growing air current, eventually turning into a storm. The more the fire spread, the more it traveled south to finally cover there an area of several square miles, the more its effects became evident, just as Old Shatterhand had expected. The sky lost its blue, at first turned a pale yellow, then gray, darker and darker, and truly, heavy, dark clouds gathered, which were not made of smoke. The strong winds massed them to become a heavy cloud cover, which eventually covered the entire sky.

The air felt glowing hot, the sand seemed to burn. Up in the sky lightning-bolts flashed. Then a few raindrops fell; a few more, more still, until rain began to fall like in a tropical thunderstorm.

The immigrants had meted out quick justice and had shot the wounded bandits. They had gathered the few belongings of the dead and collected their horses. Then they were to wait for the return of their friends, but --- without water. They saw the fires. They noticed the cloud buildup. They felt those first drops of rain and, finally, stood in the refreshing rainfall, a splendid downpour. Hurriedly, they fetched whatever containers they could find to catch the life-giving liquid. The exhausted oxen, too, showed life again. They bellowed, rolled in the mud, and received water to drink. The animals were saved and with them their masters. Without these animals they would have been unable to continue --- all this was the work of Old Shatterhand.

Shortly after daybreak Bloody-Fox and his ten Comanche had arrived at the oasis. The Indians did not frighten Sanna. She enjoyed seeing other people, but right away asked Bloody-Fox about the Negro Bob. Fox put her off until later and went straight for the cottage. When he stepped outside he wore the bison skin.

"*Timb-ua-ungva* - the Ghost of the Llano," Ironheart exclaimed, who had come with this group of Comanche. The others, too, stared at the solution to the so often talked about riddle, but kept quiet. Bloody-Fox mounted his horse again and, together with his troop, left the oasis to ride to the southeastern corner of the cactus field. His eyes kept searching the north. There, a dark cloud now rose against whose underside bright flames erupted.

"The fire will drive the Vultures towards us," he said to Ironheart. "Maybe my red brother will find one of the murderers of his father among them."

157

He readied his rifle; Ironheart did the same. The cloud moved closer with the fire advancing more quickly ahead of it. Minute by minute the air became more oppressive. But the fire could not reach them. The border of the cactus field kept its progress in check.

"Uff!" shouted one of the Indians, pointing north. "They are coming."

Yes, it was them, the Vultures, but there were only three. Their pursuers had already killed the others. Their horses were dripping wet and the riders could barely keep themselves in their saddles. A short distance behind, one could see Old Shatterhand and Winnetou, followed by the others. The wild chase came closer. Yet the pursuers were not rushing their horses. They wanted to keep the last three Vultures for Bloody-Fox and the Comanche.

The first was Burton, way ahead of the other two. He saw the trees, a miracle in the Llano, and headed straight for them. Fox rode towards him. When the Mormon saw him, he screamed in horror and hit his horse to get the last from it, hoping to reach the cover of the trees.

Now the two others arrived and had to get past Ironheart. He recognized them as the participants in his father's murder. He aimed his rifle --- two shots, and they tumbled from their horses. He rode over to them to collect their scalps.

Meanwhile Bloody-Fox hunted the pious Burton, the worst of the Vultures. They headed straight through the trees and for the cottage. In front of it Burton's horse collapsed, tossing him from the saddle. In the blink of an eye Fox was by his side, tore his knife from his belt and bent down for the coup de grace.

But he leaped back, a scream of terror on his lips. With the fall Burton had lost his hat and he could see that the man had worn a wig. It had come off and his natural, short-cut hair could now be seen. His face was swollen and distorted from the exertion of the tough ride and the eyes stared emptily at the young man. He had broken his neck. And now Bloody-Fox recognized him as the murderer of his parents. When the caravan with which his parents traveled had been attacked, he had heard the name called and this name – Fox – was the only thing he had saved in his memory. He had called it again and again, which is why Helmers had given it to him as his own.

Now, the others rode in. All of them, except Old Shatterhand, were very much surprised when they saw Bloody-Fox in his white bison skin.

"The Ghost – the Ghost of Llano Estacado – it is Bloody-Fox – It's him, he's been the one!" the shouts rang out.

Fox did not pay attention to them. Pointing at Burton's body he said,

"There's the murderer. Now I know why he looked so familiar. He's dead now and I will never find out who my parents were."

Ben New-Moon saw the dead and shouted, "This is Stealing Fox! He's finally been eliminated. Too bad he broke his neck. Now I owe him a bullet forever."

"Good that he is dead!" Old Shatterhand said. "With him the last of the Vultures has died and peace has come to the Llano. And should some of them still be around, it should be easy to hunt them down from here. An oasis like this no one could have imagined."

Sliding-Bob was here too, yet he paid no attention to the dead or the now revealed Ghost of the Estacado. His eyes and those of Sanna had met. She hurried towards him and asked, "You maybe Bob?"

And when he nodded she continued, "Your mother name Sanna? You see picture here of Sanna with little smiling Bob?"

She held up the old photograph. He threw a look at it and, with a shout of joy, leaped from his horse. The two of them hugged and, for the longest time, could utter only unintelligible sounds of joy.

Little can now be added. The Vultures had been defeated. The Comanche rode off to guide the immigrants here, so that they could recover from their hardship by the lake, before they were guided through the Llano to their destination. The fire ran out of fuel and the huge cactus field lay in ashes.

It was very busy at the Ghost's haunt. Bloody-Fox was the hero of the day and had to tell his story in every detail. But his report was for the most part gloomy. He expressed his decision to stay here, at the oasis, to keep the Llano free of bandits. Sanna and Bob said that they would not leave him.

Fox's account was of such interest to the frontiersmen, that even the oftentimes so talkative Hobble-Frank remained silent and did not interrupt him a single time. But when the little Saxon walked with Jemmy and the two Snuffles around the small lake, Tim asked him, "Well, Frank, after we have now entered the lair of the Ghost, do you still maintain that the Ghost of Llano Estacado is a real ghost?"

"Oh, be quiet!" Frank answered. "If I've erred once, there are higher regions of existence, and what cannot be comprehended by the none-comprehending, every Saxon can see the moment it happens."

"Yes, the Saxons, and especially Moritzburg. That is the ultimate pleasure," Jim laughed.

"Keep off with your pleasures, you old Snuffle. You don't know me yet by far. But since we will be together for a few months to come, you will yet get to know and admire me. Eventually, my personality is giving everybody cause for esteem. Isn't it so, Jemmy?"

"Right on," Jemmy nodded, a slight ironic smile playing over his lips.

"There you hear it, both of you. And don't you actually have to thank me, because had I not met Bloody-Fox up there at Helmers Home, we would never have found out about the Ghost of the Llano. I should demand this recognition right now. It's then up to later generations to cast me in iron or chisel me in marble, so that my name shines in golden letters as it does up at the national park, where I hope the world will soon gawk at my monument."

ABOUT THE AUTHOR

Karl May (1842 - 1912) is today hailed a German literary genius. His unequaled imagination gave birth to a whole collection of characters that lived through exiting and realistic adventure tales that captivated generations of German readers both young and old. Yet his writings were never available to English readers.

ABOUT THE TRANSLATOR

Herbert Windolf was born in Wiesbaden, Germany, in 1936. In 1964 he emigrated to Canada with his family to provide his German employer with technical services for North America. In 1970 he was transferred to the United States and eventually became Managing Director of the US affiliate. He has translated several literary works from German into English, among which is Karl May's, "The Oil Prince", published by Washington State University Press and "The Treasure of Silver Lake", published recently by Nemsi Books. In addition he has taught a number of science courses at a local adult education center, and has written several science essays and travelogues.